THE FACADE

EDEN FALLS ACADEMY

CHERRY BLOSSOM
ROMANCE

the Facade

JUDY CORRY

Cover Design by Judy Corry

Couple Illustration by Wastoki

Developmental edit by Cara Seger

Edited by Precy Larkins

www.judycorry.com

For James, Janelle, Jonah and Jade.
I love you!

PLAYLIST

Girls Like Us by Zoe Wees
Unstable by Justin Bieber (feat. The Kid LaROI)
Safest Place to Hide by Backstreet Boys
Bucket List by Mitchell Tenpenny
Ruin My Life (Clean) by Zara Larsson
The Most Beautiful Things by Tenille Townes
Hard Sometimes by Ruel
Invisible by Zara Larsson
Imagine by Ben Platt
Flicker by The Piano Guys
Believe by Justin Bieber
Replace You by Kayden
Ghost by Justin Bieber
When I Look at You by Dylan Brady
Who Am I by NEEDTOBREATHE

1

CAMBRIELLE

"HAVE you guys decided what you're dressing up as for the Halloween dance?" my friend Scarlett, a senior with auburn hair and high cheekbones, asked Elyse and me when we joined her and her best friend Hunter at the table in the great hall for lunch.

"I'm not sure," Elyse said with a shrug. "Usually, Ava and I plan our costumes together, but since she and Carter are coordinating this year, I'm not sure what I'm doing."

Ava and Elyse were identical twins who had just come to Eden Falls Academy at the beginning of the school year. They had caused quite the stir when they first arrived, catching most of the guys' attention at our private school since they were new and gorgeous. But things had settled down a bit now that we were almost two months into the school year and Ava had paired off with my older brother Carter.

"Any ideas what you'd like to dress up as? A character

from a movie, or something else?" I asked Elyse, hoping to be helpful.

"I was thinking about going as Elizabeth Swan from *Pirates of the Caribbean* or maybe even Cher from *Clueless.*"

"You would make the perfect Elizabeth Swan." Scarlett's eyes widened with excitement. "You have the perfect bone structure to pull off the Keira Knightley look."

"You think so?" Elyse asked, her cheeks coloring slightly as Scarlett and I looked at her.

"You would look so good," I agreed with Scarlett. "Were you thinking of wearing one of the fancy gowns? Or the pirate clothes?"

"One of the gowns," Elyse said. "My mom has a dress she designed that would be perfect for it." Elyse and Ava's mom was a famous fashion designer, and so of course she would have the hookups for something like that.

"Dang, you're going to look so good. All the guys will be asking you to dance all night," Scarlett said, her tone envious. "Don't you think so, Hunter?" She glanced at Hunter who was, as usual, reading something on his phone.

When he didn't respond, Scarlett nudged him with her elbow.

"Uh, what did you say?" Hunter asked, finally looking up from his phone.

Scarlett eyed Hunter somewhat impatiently and said, "I was saying that Elyse dressing up like Elizabeth Swan is like every guy's fantasy."

"Oh..." Hunter narrowed his green eyes and seemed to take in Elyse's long, brown hair and olive-complected skin for a moment, as if picturing her in eighteenth-century clothes. With a shrug, he said, "I guess I can see it."

And then, he immediately went back to reading whatever he had up on his phone screen.

Scarlett cast our aloof friend a wary glance, like she wasn't sure what to think about how distracted he'd been all year. But then she shrugged and turned her brown-eyed gaze to me. "What about you, Cambrielle? Have you picked your costume yet?"

"I just got the last piece of it yesterday," I said, unable to keep a smile from lifting my lips as I thought about the costume I'd been working on for weeks. Dressing up was one of my favorite things to do, so of course Halloween was one of my favorite holidays.

"And what are you going to be?" Elyse asked.

My smile turned mischievous. "It's a secret."

"It's a secret?" Scarlett asked, her eyes brimming with intrigue just as I'd hoped. "And why is that?"

I shrugged. "I just want to surprise everyone."

Which was true. I did want to keep the Kelana costume my mom and I had been pulling pieces together for over the past few weeks a secret. Kelana being the main character from my favorite romantic fantasy movie.

Though, what would have been even more true was to say that I wanted to surprise a *specific* person with my costume. That person being the super-hot and amazing Ben Barnett.

Ben was in the grade above me—a senior like most of my friends—and I'd had a crush on him ever since last spring when he led the boys' soccer team to the state championships.

There was just something about a guy who could handle

a ball and lead his team to victory that was super attractive to me.

But since I was painfully awkward around guys I liked, I'd never dared do anything about my crush—in fact, I hadn't even said a single word to him since the school year started. I didn't go up to high school gods like Ben.

But I had a plan. I was going to channel my inner Kelana at the Halloween dance and under the disguise of my glittery, pink masquerade mask, faerie-queen makeup, and beautiful one-of-a-kind dress, I was going to finally ask him to dance.

And if the dance went well, I was going to ask him out.

Sure, asking Ben out before I revealed my true identity probably wasn't the greatest plan, but it was all about baby steps at this point. I mean, he would be graduating at the end of the year, and since we were already in the last week of October, there wasn't a whole lot of time left for me to get up the nerve to make something happen.

And if my plan totally bombed and I completely humiliated myself in front of Ben, no one would be the wiser because no one would know it was me.

"Will you give us any hints about your costume?" Elyse asked, searching my face with her golden-brown eyes. "Is it a real person, or maybe a character from a movie?"

I shook my head. "Sorry, but this secret is going to remain locked down tight until we're at the party. I'm not even letting Carter or Nash know."

Carter and Nash were my older brothers who also attended our school.

"Well, aren't you mysterious," Scarlett said.

I shrugged. "I guess so."

Elyse seemed to realize that I wasn't going to give any hints because she turned to Scarlett and asked her what she was planning to dress up as.

Scarlett poked at her salad with her fork. "I'm trying to convince Hunter here to dress up like an astronaut so I can be the pretty alien he finds on Mars." She bumped her shoulder against his. "But so far he's pretty set on not dressing up."

Hunter glanced over at his best friend with a smirk on his lips and said, "When I'm already dressed as the coolest person in the room, why would I dress up like anything else?"

"Why indeed?" Scarlett shook her head, a slight smile lifting her lips at Hunter's cocky statement. But when Hunter went back to looking at his phone, she glanced at Elyse and me and said, "I'll keep working on him."

The rest of our friends joined us at the table with their lunch trays, so we made room for them. My older brother Carter and his girlfriend, Ava—who was Elyse's identical twin—sat on the side where Scarlett and Hunter were.

Carter's best friend Mack, who was also our next-door neighbor, slipped into the spot on my left. And Elyse scooted closer to me to make room for my other brother Nash.

That's right, my brothers and I actually chose to sit at the same table during lunch because we got along, strangely enough.

Now how did I come to have *two* brothers who were both seniors but not twins, despite the fact that they shared the same dirty-blond hair and aqua-blue eyes?

Well, that's a long story, but basically, we all had the same dad—the famous billionaire businessman Joel Hastings

—but while Nash and I were full-blooded siblings born a year apart, my dad got Carter's mom pregnant a few months before he married my mom, so Carter was only seven months older than Nash.

Yep, my dad wasn't just good at making money in his early twenties. He was also accomplished at producing heirs as well.

So my dad had three kids all born within a year and a half of each other in addition to being the stepfather to my oldest brother, Ian, who came from my mom's first marriage.

Things were crazy when we were younger, and my parents had to hire a full-time nanny to help with all the chaos my brothers and I created. But we were all best friends now, and I knew that when Nash and Carter graduated at the end of the year, leaving me all alone for my senior year, I was going to miss them.

I was going to miss all my friends actually, since yep, you guessed it, they were all seniors and I was the only junior among us.

"So I was just asking Cambrielle and Elyse what they were going to wear to the Halloween dance," Scarlett said once everyone had gotten themselves situated around the table. "What are the rest of you planning to dress up like?"

"I was thinking that I'd probably just go as myself," Mack's deep voice sounded from beside me. "I mean, why dress up when I could just go as the coolest person I know?"

"Hey, that's what I said," Hunter said with a smile, slipping his phone into his pocket now that the rest of the crew had joined us.

"Great minds." Mack held out a hand to give Hunter a fist bump across the table.

Hunter bumped his fist against Mack's knuckles. Bemused, I just shook my head, because while I loved my brothers' best friends, they did have a certain arrogance to them.

Though, I guess I couldn't really blame them. They were all basically the princes of Eden Falls Academy—popular, confident, and belonged to the nation's wealthiest families. And while I was definitely not attracted to my brothers— because *ew*—I'd be lying if I didn't admit that Hunter and Mack were super cute.

So cute that when we were all in middle school, I'd totally had a huge crush on Mack.

I'd gotten over that crush eventually, and moved on to liking other guys like Ben, of course. But yeah, Mack, Hunter, and my brothers did have most of the female population at our school crushing on them.

And yes, they knew it, too.

It must be nice knowing so many people wanted you.

Nash cleared his throat, bringing me back to the present as he answered Scarlett's question. "I was planning to go as the Phantom."

"Really?" Elyse turned to my brother with a smile on her glossy pink lips. "*The Phantom of the Opera?*"

Nash nodded. "I figured I might as well start getting into character early since I'll be playing him soon."

Nash and Elyse were both big into the theater program at our school, and while the auditions for the winter musical weren't for several weeks, Nash was basically a shoo-in for the male lead. He'd already played bigger roles in last year's musicals—not the lead yet since the drama teacher Miss Crawley liked to fill those with seniors when possible. But only something crazy would keep Nash from winning the part of the Phantom. And I was pretty sure Elyse had a good shot at getting the part of Christine.

As for me, I was still trying to decide if I wanted to audition to be one of the dancers. So far, I'd only worked as a crew member because unlike my brother who was a spotlight hog, I preferred to keep attention away from myself. But I did miss dancing, and since there would be other dancers on the stage with me, I figured it might be time for me to pull out my ballet shoes again.

"Did you already say what you're going as, Cambrielle?" Mack asked from beside me, breaking me from my thoughts.

"Oh, um." I licked my lips. "It's a secret."

"Really?" Mack raised a dark eyebrow, his brown eyes filling with intrigue the same way Scarlett's had earlier. "And why's that?"

Because I need anonymity in order to put myself out there.

"Just for fun," I said instead. "I figure I'd keep everyone on their toes. Not all of us can go as ourselves like you apparently are."

"And you're sure you can't tell me?" He cocked his head to the side. "You already know I'm great at keeping secrets."

And when he winked, my cheeks burned because I knew exactly which secret he was referring to.

He must have noticed my blush because a wicked grin slipped onto his lips. In a low voice next to my ear, he whispered, "Which reminds me. Have you gotten your room all ready for me to stay in tonight?"

My eyes widened and I almost gasped out loud before I

caught myself. "What?" I glanced around the table to make sure no one heard what he said.

Thankfully, everyone was looking at Carter and Ava as Ava told them all about the costumes they were considering.

"I'm kidding." Mack chuckled, apparently loving my reaction. "I already know I'm staying in Ian's room. Your dad obviously doesn't know that I already spent a few nights in your room last month."

"And we're going to keep it that way." I gave him a warning look before making sure our friends—and most importantly, my brothers—were still paying us no attention.

"Should I be offended that you want to keep me your dirty little secret?" Mack whispered in my ear, making chills race from my neck and down my whole body.

I shivered uncontrollably and whispered back, "Since my dad and brothers would kill you if they ever caught wind of that, then yes, I'm pretty sure I'll be taking that secret to the grave."

Mack pouted. "That's no fun."

I raised an eyebrow. "Well, since I'd like to see you graduate instead of have you come to an untimely death because my family found out, I think it's fine to not be fun."

Not that anything scandalous had happened those few nights he'd slept in my room. Sadly for me, the only times I'd ever been kissed had happened during a game of Spin the Bottle.

What had actually happened was that Mack started sleepwalking again when his parents went to New York for the first round of special treatments for his mom's brain tumor. I had found him asleep on the bank of my family's pond one morning when I'd taken my horse out for a sunrise ride.

When I'd gone up to him to ask why he was sleeping there, he had tried to play it off—pretend like he'd just gone on an early morning swim with the fish but got tired afterwards. But I had overheard Mrs. Aarden telling my mom about Mack's sleepwalking episodes since her diagnosis, so I knew better than to believe him.

And when I heard footsteps on the path outside my open balcony window the next night, I hurried down to help him before he could end up in the pond again.

When it happened a third night and he still wouldn't ask my brothers or anyone else for help, I decided to sneak him up into my bedroom so that if he had another episode, I could catch him when he first got up instead of having to chase him through the woods between our houses.

He came to my room the rest of that week, climbing up the tree by my balcony just after my parents and brothers had gone to bed for the night. And starting out in my room had apparently done the trick because he ended up not sleepwalking any of the nights he stayed on the trundle bed beside me—maybe his subconscious knew he had help close by and he was safe.

And so even though my family probably would have freaked out if they'd known I had a seventeen-year-old guy— one I'd had a major crush on at one point—sleeping just a few feet away from me at night, I was glad that he'd at least trusted me to help him when he wouldn't tell my brothers.

"What time are you coming over, anyway?" I asked Mack as he wolfed down some of his teriyaki chicken.

He swallowed his bite of food and wiped his mouth with

a napkin before saying, "They're heading out after my dad gets off work, so I'll probably be there before dinner."

There was a hint of anxiety in his eyes at the mention of his parents leaving. And I hated seeing it because I hated that his family was even dealing with this. Dealing with the possibility of his mom not being here to watch him graduate.

Whenever I saw the fear in Mack's eyes, I wanted to give him a hug and tell him that everything would be okay. But since he didn't seem to ever want to bring attention to what was going on in his personal life—always preferring to make everyone laugh instead of talking about his family's crisis—I just gave him what I hoped was an understanding smile and said, "Well, my mom and Marie planned to have your favorite pork burritos for dinner, so we'll keep you well fed while your parents are in New York."

2

MACK

"YOU BE good for the Hastings, okay?" My mom pulled me into her frail arms for one last hug. She and my dad were about to leave for the hospital in New York where my mom would be receiving some experimental treatments for her glioblastoma multiforme brain tumor.

My parents' things were already packed into the Bentley behind us, and in just a few minutes, I'd be rolling my suitcase to my best friends' house where I'd be staying for two weeks.

"I'll try to stay out of trouble," I said, hugging my mom tighter and resting my cheek against her scarf-covered head—her beautiful, long black braids a thing of the past. My mom was tall for a woman at five-foot-ten and had always been a little soft around the middle when I was growing up. But lately, it always caught me a little off guard whenever I hugged her and could feel her ribs.

My mom wasn't supposed to feel frail.

Mom pulled away from the embrace so my dad could

hug me next. At six-foot-seven, he was two inches taller than me. Even though my dad was white and I had more of a light-bronze skin tone since my mom was black, most people didn't seem too surprised that we were related because we were giants compared to most people we met.

My dad had been on his way to the NBA before my mom's first brain tumor took him from that path right after college and had led him toward becoming one of the best neurosurgeons in the country instead.

Yes, my dad was a neurosurgeon but his wife was dying of the kind of brain tumor that was, so far, considered incurable—the white shark of brain tumors as they called it.

I'd probably say it was ironic that one of the best neurosurgeons in the world couldn't heal his own wife, if it didn't piss me off so much.

My dad patted me on the back. "Have a good two weeks, son. Hopefully, we'll be back with better news soon."

I nodded as we pulled away from the hug. Even though I knew my parents needed to get on the road so my mom could get a full night's rest before her treatments tomorrow, I didn't want to say goodbye quite yet.

So before my mom could walk to the car with assistance from my dad, I gave her one more hug and said, "Get feeling better, Mom."

"I'll do my best, Macky," she said, using the nickname she'd given me when I was a toddler. "And while I'm doing that, please try not to tease Cambrielle too much while you're living over there. She already has three brothers; she doesn't need another."

"But Mom," I whined. "That's what I'm supposed to do,

isn't it? I'm supposed to treat them like we're really family, right?"

Mom gave me a warning look, the look I'd seen hundreds of times when I was trying her patience. "Joel and Dawn have enough to handle with three teenagers of their own. If I hear that you caused any trouble while I'm away..." She held up a bony finger. "I'll kick your butt when I get home."

"I'm counting on it." I shot her a mischievous grin.

Of course I knew she'd never kick my butt in reality, since she barely spanked me more than a handful of times as a kid—and only after I'd *really* earned it. But if she came back with the energy to kick my butt after spending two weeks at the hospital, then it would mean that the treatment was doing something.

And with Thanksgiving coming up in just a few weeks— which was when the doctors had initially predicted would be a day she'd be lucky to survive past—I was desperate for this new treatment to buy her more time.

I knew saying goodbye to my mother was inevitable, because so far, my dad and his colleagues hadn't figured out how to use voodoo magic to treat patients. But having months or even years versus weeks and days would at least make it so I could breathe again.

I hadn't felt like I'd really drawn in a full breath since her diagnosis last year.

My dad and I helped my mom into the car, and when she struggled to buckle herself in—a sign of the paralysis slowly taking over her left side—my heart squeezed in my chest.

This new treatment needed to work.

My dad walked around to the driver's side of the silver

car, and when he noticed my mom still struggling with the seatbelt, he reached over and helped her.

My parents waved goodbye to me one last time. After I watched them drive down the driveway, I swung the garment bag with my school uniforms over my shoulder and gripped the handle of my gray suitcase and wheeled it down the paved sidewalk we had put in years ago that served as a shortcut between our house and the Hastings family's estate.

A minute later, the huge stone country house came into view through the mostly bare trees. Even though I'd gotten used to climbing up the big tree by Cambrielle's balcony and sneaking into her room last month, I made my way to the front door like a normal person, since I was actually invited here by her parents this time.

"Hey roomie," Carter said with a smile after he opened the door. "Come on in." Stepping back, he gestured for me to walk inside the mansion that he and his family called home.

I always joked that my family's modern-style home seemed like a shack compared to the Hastings' estate, which most people found ridiculous since my parents had the second biggest house in our small town of Eden Falls. But this house was just massive with an indoor pool, basketball court, conservatory, ballroom, theater, bowling alley, and basically every amenity a person could ever dream of having.

My dad was a neurosurgeon and my mom had been an interior designer before she got sick again. But their couple million-dollar net worth had nothing on the billions that Carter's family had as the seventh richest family in the United States.

Thankfully though, the Hastings were all pretty down to earth...for the most part.

"Marie said dinner will be ready in about fifteen minutes," Carter said as he led me up the grand staircase with marble floors and an intricately designed handrail. "So that should give you some time to get settled before we eat."

"Sounds good," I said, sniffing the aroma of the sweet pork burritos cooking in the kitchen. Cambrielle had said that their chef, Marie, would be cooking my favorite meal, and so I'd made sure to save lots of room for dinner.

Carter led me down the hall past his and Cambrielle's rooms to the room that was across from Nash's bedroom.

The Hastings family had plenty of guest bedrooms in their mansion, but Carter had told me I'd be staying on the second floor with the rest of the family so I wouldn't be off in the west wing by myself.

My mom and dad had warned Mr. and Mrs. Hastings about the sleepwalking episodes I'd had the last time they'd gone out of town, but it was probably a good idea that I would be sleeping near everyone else.

I just hoped my subconscious would do what it did those nights I'd stayed in Cambrielle's room and realize that I wasn't all alone in their house, so I could just stay asleep in bed.

I really didn't want to wake up soaking wet after sleep-walking to their pond again. It was late October and long past the time when anyone would believe I was just going out for a refreshing midnight swim.

"Here you go." Carter swung the door open to his older brother's room, revealing a very minimalistic interior with only a king-sized bed, a small couch, a bench at the foot of the bed, and a dresser in the large space. "Ian just moved into the pool house over the weekend, so I think most of the drawers in the dresser should be open for you to use if you want."

Ian was the oldest son of Mrs. Hastings, coming from her first marriage. He'd recently graduated from Yale and had just moved back to his family's estate to help Mr. Hastings manage the many investment companies run by Hastings Industries.

"Nice," I said, plopping my suitcase and garment bag onto the navy-blue duvet. I'd only packed enough stuff for a week—I figured I could just run to my house next door if I needed extra clothes. But having a whole dresser would be an upgrade from having my deodorant and toothbrush stuffed in the back of one of Cambrielle's bathroom drawers.

"I'll see you downstairs when you're done, okay?" Carter said. "I'm supposed to help set the table tonight since Dawn and Dad think we need to learn to take care of things like that before we go off to college."

"Ah, so you have to start doing what I've been doing since I was three," I teased, unable to keep a smirk from my lips.

"Yeah, yeah." Carter made a face like he knew how ridiculous most people would find it that he and his siblings were only just now learning to do the household chores the rest of us commoners had been doing our whole lives. "I told her I'd be fine since I helped Señorita Silvia with chores all the time at the orphanage. But Nash and Cambrielle didn't think it was very fair for me to get out of helping, so I have to pitch in, too."

Carter had lived in an orphanage in Guatemala for a few years after his mom disappeared and before his dad found him. He joked about it now, but I knew from the various stories he'd told me through the years that his life there had been hard in ways I could never imagine.

"Well, while you're setting out the dishes, could you make sure to put my plate next to Cambrielle's? I don't want to accidentally play footsie with your mom when I'm trying to flirt with your sister."

Carter's eyes widened for a moment, like he thought I was serious about playing footsie with his little sis. Then he narrowed his eyes again and said, "Yeah, pretty sure I'll be putting you two at opposite ends of the table. The last thing my sister needs is to be one of your weekend flings. She doesn't need to be tempted by you."

"Kind of like how you're seducing Ava?"

"Pretty sure Ava is the one who likes to tempt me." Carter shook his head, a hint of a smile on his lips at the mention of his girlfriend.

"Well, you know she's my sister now, so maybe I should start pulling the 'I'm your girlfriend's older brother' card on you, my friend."

"That's still so weird, isn't it?" Carter leaned against the door frame. "That Ava and Elyse are your half-sisters?"

"Yeah. It's definitely not something I was expecting when they first showed up at school." I unzipped my suitcase, remembering how shocked I'd been when my dad had told my mom and me that he'd gotten the twins' mom pregnant way back in the day and I had two half-sisters that none of us had ever known about.

My mom had her first brain tumor when she was twenty-two. She'd been dating my dad ever since high school, but when she'd gotten the first diagnosis, she'd freaked out and broke up with my dad without any explanation.

Heartbroken and confused, my dad ended up rebounding with Mrs. Cohen at their high school reunion. She'd gotten pregnant and told him about it. But my dad ended up having a mental breakdown from the stress of everything with my mom and the unplanned twins. So when Ava and Elyse's mom realized my dad wouldn't be much help with anything, she had faked a miscarriage and cut all ties with her past.

It was only after the girls showed up at school in September that they started putting the puzzle pieces together. Then just a little over a week ago, the truth all came out and I found out that I'd almost asked my own sister on a date.

So even though things sucked with my mom's tumor right now, my being distracted with everything going on had actually paid off in that regard since it had kept me from making out with one of my sisters.

I shuddered just thinking about how bad the gossip at our school would have been if I'd found out a week or two later.

"Do you think Elyse knows you were planning to ask her out?" Carter asked.

"I hope not," I said, pulling a stack of T-shirts from my suitcase and setting them in the dresser behind me. "I mean, I'm sure it was pretty obvious that I liked her since I flirted with her while you were flirting with Ava during our study sessions. But I just hope everyone interpreted it as me just being nice to the new girls."

"Yeah, not sure that's likely with your reputation." Carter chuckled. "But if anyone says anything, I'll tell them that's all you were doing. Kind of like how you're always just being nice to Cambrielle and don't really have plans to ever take her out."

"Your sister is pretty hot," I said, only because I knew how much Carter hated it every time I mentioned how pretty Cambrielle was. "And she's just down the hall. It would be kind of convenient."

Carter folded his arms across his chest and gave me a challenging look. "Almost as convenient as me living just down the hall from you and being able to tell everyone that the reason you stopped showing up at school is because you caught a cold and not because I dismembered you in the night."

I couldn't help but laugh. "Well, it's a good thing I'm not actually planning on taking advantage of your sister then, isn't it?"

"Yes, it is."

And from the fierce look on his face, it was probably also a very good thing that neither Cambrielle nor I had slipped up and told him that I'd already snuck into her room several times.

I shook my thoughts away before Carter could ask what I was thinking about.

"Anyway," Carter said, pushing himself away from the doorframe and standing to his six-foot-three-inch height. "I'm gonna head down to the kitchen. I'll see you down there."

"Okay," I said, grabbing a handful of the black socks that I wore with my school uniform to stuff into the dresser. "Just remember to put me by Cambrielle."

Carter rolled his eyes. "Not happening."

Once he was gone, I made quick work of hanging my

school uniforms up in Ian's mostly empty closet and shoving my toiletries in one of the bathroom drawers.

I was just on my way downstairs to give Carter some pointers on how to set the table—thanks to my lifetime of experience—when I heard Nash teasing Cambrielle in her room about her crush on Ben Barnett.

"You know that one way to get Ben to notice you would be to actually talk to him, right?" Nash was saying just before I took a detour into Cambrielle's room.

"Yeah, yeah," Cambrielle said. "I'm working on it."

"Remind me how just staring at him when he's studying in the library but never actually walking within ten feet of him is working on it?" Nash teased.

Cambrielle chucked a light-pink pillow to where Nash sat on the chair in the corner beside the gas fireplace.

Nash, used to getting pillows thrown at him by his siblings, just took it in stride. "Thanks, my head was getting tired." And then, he promptly slipped the pillow behind his head.

Cambrielle shook her head at her brother, her back still turned to me as she stood beside her bed. "You're one to talk. I mean, haven't you wanted to ask Elyse out since the beginning of the year and yet all you've done is friendzone yourself?"

"It's completely different," Nash said.

"And how's that?" Cambrielle crossed her arms.

"Well, you see, I actually do talk with Elyse on a regular basis."

"But that's not—" Cambrielle started but Nash held up a finger to continue his thought.

"I'm just taking things slower because I have plans."

"And what are those plans?" Cambrielle asked, unconvinced.

"Well, you see, I had wanted to let my buddy Mack here have a shot at the beauty first." Nash glanced behind his sister to where I stood, a smirk on his lips like he'd just been waiting to say that in front of me.

Cambrielle turned around, her bright blue eyes wide, surprised I had overheard their conversation.

Nash continued, "And now that Fate has intervened and shown me to be the better candidate..." He winked, obviously teasing me about the fact that fate had a twisted sense of humor since Elyse was my half-sister. "I'm now just waiting for Fate to play her next card by placing Elyse and me as the leads in the winter musical. Then once she's playing the Christine to my Phantom, I expect for the chemistry to show itself on stage."

"So you're hoping for the on-stage romance to carry off stage?" I raised my eyebrows.

"I don't usually like to mix my personal life with my art, but if something happens naturally, then who am I to go against Fate?"

"And you think Fate would have plans for two of my best friends to both end up with my half-sisters?" I asked, skeptical about Nash's belief in Fate.

Because if Fate was real, so far I wasn't a fan of her interference in my life. In fact, if I was to meet Fate someday, I was pretty sure I'd punch her in the face and tell her to mess with someone else's life since my family had had enough of her interfering ways.

But Nash must not have known about the beef I had with Fate right now because he just shrugged and said,

"Why not? Makes sense that Ava's twin would be attracted to a similar look as her sister."

And yet, I was pretty sure Elyse had had a crush on me until last week. And I couldn't look more different from my blond-haired, blue-eyed friends.

"I guess we'll just have to see if this play goes the way you hope. Who knows, maybe Fate will interfere, and Miss Crawley will put someone else as the lead."

Nash's jaw dropped, and ever the dramatic, he put a hand to his chest and said, "How dare you speak such blasphemy in my presence."

Yeah, Nash was a weirdo when he got into character.

I shrugged. "I'm just saying it might be a good idea to have a backup plan in case things don't go your way."

I had certainly learned that if anything was sure in life, it was that you could make all sorts of plans for how your life was going to go but you better be prepared to come up with a whole new set of plans at a moment's notice because sometimes all it took, like in my mom's case, was a really bad headache or a seizure to change your life forever.

Feeling my chest tighten as my mind started to think about what was coming for my family in the next months, I drew in a deep breath and tried to bring myself back to the present moment.

Tried to remind myself that as long as my parents were still seeking treatments, it meant there was still a chance of my mom watching my basketball games this year or seeing me graduate in June.

Cambrielle's room was decorated in light pinks and golds. I stepped inside, hoping it would help my overwhelming thoughts disappear. Cambrielle's decorating tastes were definitely a lot more girly and whimsical than my black and white room at home, but I'd always felt a sense of calm in here.

After staying in Cambrielle's room for a few nights and receiving the best night's sleep I'd had in the months before and several weeks since, I came up with the theory that just like how some humans had comfort animals, this place served as my comfort room—a sanctuary of sorts. Every time I stepped into her room, a sense of calm would come over me —like a shelter from the anxiety that usually plagued my mind way more often than I'd like these days.

I was just laying myself along the foot of Cambrielle's bed when Mrs. Hastings' voice sounded over the intercom system. "Dinner will be ready in five minutes. Please come down before it gets cold."

"You don't have to tell me twice," Nash said as he lifted himself out of the cozy, cream-colored chair that I'd enjoyed sitting in on those few nights Cambrielle had let me stay over. "I've been craving Marie's sweet pork burritos all day."

"Me too," I said as I rolled onto my back, about to get up from Cambrielle's queen-sized, four-poster bed.

But once Nash left the room and was out of earshot, I couldn't resist teasing Cambrielle a little. I rolled back onto my side, propped my head on my hand, and looked at Cambrielle with a half-smile on my lips. "Your bed sure is comfortable."

"Yeah?" she asked, her expression wary as if she was worried about where I might be going with this.

"Yeah." I smoothed my palm along the ripples of her white comforter. "I mean, I only lay down on Ian's bed for a minute before coming in here, but I can't help but feel that as your family's special guest, it's only right that I stay in the most comfortable bed in the house."

"And you think that's my bed?" Cambrielle raised an eyebrow.

"Definitely." I moved up so I could lie back against the stack of throw pillows she had at the head of her bed. "I think you should trade me."

"What?" She pulled her head back in surprise.

"I know how much you pride yourself on being a good hostess," I said, placing my hands behind my head as I leaned back even farther. "And we don't even need to make a big fuss about it to the rest of your family. Your room and Ian's room share a balcony, right? We could just use that to do the switcheroo and no one would be the wiser."

"But I like my bed," Cambrielle said. "And my room."

"Me too," I said, glancing around at the feminine decor. "I've actually been considering having my room done the same way."

"You want a pink and gold bedroom with frilly throw pillows and white furniture?"

"It's nice." I shrugged. "And we already know how well I sleep in your room." I winked.

Her cheeks flushed, and I loved the way the slightest mention of those few forbidden nights caused her to get in a tizzy.

She looked toward her open door, as if checking to make sure no one was there, and then in a hushed tone she whispered, "You need to stop saying things like that. Everyone's going to find out about what we did, and then we'll get in huge trouble."

"But nothing happened," I said, matter-of-factly. "And

everyone knows you like Ben and that nothing would ever happen between us."

Her eyes widened in a warning look, like she was still worried someone might hear our conversation from all the way downstairs.

"I'm going to be sleeping in my room, okay?" she said, closing the subject of switching rooms.

And I knew I should probably stop teasing her. That I should do what my mom had said and not give Cambrielle a hard time for once in my life, but the devil in me just couldn't help himself. So I said, "Well, if you're in love with your room so much, I guess we could share." I pressed my lips together and studied the spot beside me. "I already know you don't snore, and I think this bed is big enough for both of us. Especially if we cuddle."

"Shhhh." Cambrielle flung herself across the bed and covered my mouth with her hand to silence me. "What don't you understand about the words 'stop saying things like that?'"

I wrapped my long fingers around her delicate wrist and removed her hand from my mouth so I could speak, and whispered, "If you wanted to cuddle with me before we go to bed, all you had to do was ask." I looked pointedly at the way her body was pressed against my side after her attempt to shut me up.

She looked down at our bodies, let out a surprised squeal, and was just trying to scoot away when Nash's voice sounded from the doorway. "Um, so is this the real reason why you haven't been talking to Ben?" His blue eyes were wide with shock as he stared at the compromising position his sister and I were currently in on her bed. "Was he just a decoy?"

"No, of course not," Cambrielle said as she clambered to the side of the bed and away from me. "Mack was just being stupid, and I had to resort to physical force to shut him up."

When she got to her feet on the floor, she smoothed her fingers through her long, light-brown hair and straightened her pink blouse as if she was afraid to look like we'd just been in some sort of romantic tussle.

Nash narrowed his eyes at his sister and then at me, as if trying to decide whether she was telling the truth. Then with a shrug, he said, "Just don't let Carter or Dad see you flirting like that."

"We weren't flirting," Cambrielle insisted. Then she glanced at me, her expression telling me I better back her up. "Tell Nash that you were just being a butthead and that it's not what it looked like."

I lifted my hand to my mouth, cleared my throat dramatically, and said, "I was being a butthead. And even though I'm sure Cambrielle would be fun to make-out with, we were not and nor have we ever done anything remotely close to that."

"Thank y—" she started.

But before she could finish thanking me, I added, "Though since I am under oath, I cannot, of course, testify as to whether Cambrielle has ever thought about kissing an amazing specimen of a human such as myself. But I will say that if she has, I wouldn't hold it against her since many girls have been susceptible to my tall, dark, and utterly handsome looks and—"

A fuzzy white pillow hit me in the face before I could finish my sentence.

"Hey," I said, pulling the pillow away. And when I looked to the side, Cambrielle was already grabbing another pillow to launch at me.

But before she could, I got to my knees and snatched it from her hands, tossing it at her instead.

It hit her on the side of the head, messing up her hair again. Fire instantly showed in her aqua-blue eyes as she reached for another pillow and yelled, "Take this," as she hit me with it repeatedly.

It didn't hurt, of course, but it did have me rolling to the other end of the bed so I could take cover on the floor.

I'd always thought Cambrielle had twenty different throw pillows on her bed because she had a weird addiction to them, but maybe she actually had so many because they doubled as ammunition against all the teasing she received from her brothers, and now me.

"Well, I was just grabbing something from my room to show Mom and Dad," Nash said, losing interest now that Cambrielle and I were about to have a full-blown pillow fight. "But you should probably head downstairs before they send Carter up to get you."

3

CAMBRIELLE

"YOU'RE THE WORST, you know that?" I said to Mack as we walked down the stairs together toward my family's dining room. We didn't have family dinner every night since we were all so busy with school and work and our extracurricular activities, but we did try to have a few nights during the week where we were all together.

Carter's girlfriend Ava joined us sometimes, and Mack was obviously here tonight, but usually it was just my parents, my brothers, and me. My older brother Ian even joined us occasionally now that he was living in the pool house.

"I am not the worst," Mack disagreed with my statement. "In fact, I think you like it when I tease you."

"And what would give you such a deranged opinion?" I asked, not sure how he could ever think I enjoyed constantly being on edge about whether he'd tell everyone about him staying in my room.

Mack shrugged as we made it to the foyer. "Just something about the way you keep coming back for more." He leaned close to my ear, his warm breath sending chills racing across my neck as he whispered, "And the way your eyes light up every time you see me makes me think all this banter is actually your way of telling me you like me."

I stumbled. But before he could get an even bigger opinion of himself, I promptly elbowed him in the side and said, "In your dreams."

"Hey," he said with a wince as he rubbed the spot where I'd hit him. "Have you been working out or something? Because that actually hurt."

"Just my usual yoga and horseback riding," I said. *Along with the few dancing sessions I'd snuck in while everyone was away from the house.*

But I wouldn't mention those until I was ready to tell everyone that I was considering taking up ballet again, since things hadn't exactly gone well the last time I'd been immersed in the dancing world.

We made it to the formal dining room where my dad and mom were seated by each other in front of the huge windows that overlooked the back terrace. My blond-haired, blue-eyed father sat at the head of the table still wearing his suit and tie from work. My brown-haired, brown-eyed beauty-queen mom wearing one of her designer dresses was seated beside him. Nash and Carter were at the other end of the table across from one another, leaving the spot across from my mom and the seat at the other head of the table open for Mack and me.

"Ah dang," Mack said under his breath. "Looks like I won't be able to play footsie with you during dinner after all."

"What?" I looked up at him, my eyes wide.

He bent closer again and spoke in a voice no one else could hear, "I told Carter to put me across from you since I like being close, but apparently he didn't like that idea very much."

"Yeah, I imagine not."

While Nash couldn't care less about which guys at school may or may not be interested in dating me, Carter on the other hand had always been super overprotective of me when it came to guys—so overprotective that I was pretty sure he scared most guys away from even thinking about asking me out.

Or at least that was what I told myself in order to feel better about the fact that I was a junior in high school and had yet to go on a single date.

Mack had picked up on Carter's whole protective-older-brother vibe a long time ago and frequently teased my brother about taking me to the falls—AKA "make-out point" —many times in the past. To which Carter would tell him to back off and never lay a finger on me, as if I was some porcelain doll princess who would break if I was ever taken out of the glass box I lived in.

The first time Mack had said he wanted to take me on a date, my heart had skipped a beat, because I'd naively believed that my middle-school fantasy about my brothers' hot best friend was going to come true—the one where he actually saw me as more than the kid sister he'd never had.

But when it happened over and over and it became clear that the thought of actually being interested in me was only a joke to Mack, I resented their banter more and more.

Like, was the thought of dating me, or having any sort of romantic relationship with me just comical to Mack?

I didn't know.

He probably never even thought about it that way. Probably only saw it as a fun way to get a rise out of my brother since Carter took things way too seriously sometimes. But since I had wanted him to see me differently at one point—to see me as a girl he would actually want to take on a date—him making a joke out of it stung a little.

———

DINNER WAS DELICIOUS, as usual. After dinner, my mom and I took our horses out for a ride while all the guys played a round of basketball with my dad.

After brushing down Starlight, my Camarillo White Horse, and chatting with my mom, I headed upstairs to get ready for bed.

When I made it to the top of the stairs, I noticed Mack sitting alone in the lounge area at the end of the hall.

"Where are Carter and Nash?" I asked, stepping into the room.

Mack looked up from his phone. "Carter just got a call from Ava and went to whisper his sweet nothings to her in his room." Mack made a face like he still wasn't sure how he felt about my brother and his newly found sister's relationship. "And I think Nash said something about running lines in his room to prepare for his audition."

"So why are you still up then?" I looked at the time on my watch. "It's ten-thirty. Isn't it past your bedtime?"

"Yeah, I know I should go to bed." He sighed and leaned

back to stretch with his hands behind his head, the bulge in his biceps accentuated with the movement. "I was just thinking."

"Thinking?" I asked, curious what might be on his mind. "About what?"

"My mom." He tossed his phone onto the cushion beside him. "I guess I'm a little conflicted about her going in for treatment tomorrow."

"You are?" I took a seat on the end of the large sectional opposite him. "What are you conflicted about?"

Mack rarely opened up to me about how things were going with his mom. He liked to put up a good front—put on a happy face for the world. But I knew it couldn't be easy on him.

He let out a heavy breath, his shoulders drooping. "I guess I'm not sure it's worth it to keep trying to find something that will keep her here longer."

"Y-you don't?" I furrowed my brow.

"Not that I don't want her to be here for forever," Mack hurried to say. "I definitely wish we could kick her tumor to the curb and say *sayonara*. But..." He rubbed his cheek with his palm. "I just don't know how fair it is to keep putting her through treatments." He sighed and glanced at his hand resting along the back of the couch. "Her headaches and seizures are only getting worse. She spends most days in bed. She's not really herself so much of the time and she's miserable. I guess it feels a little selfish to have her stay here for me and my dad when her quality of life is so low."

So it was worse than I thought.

"She's herself sometimes, too. Like today when she left with my dad, she was doing pretty well. She even made a joke about kicking my butt if I didn't behave while I was here. But..." He shrugged. "It's just hard to know what to do."

I tried to imagine what it would be like to be in Mack's shoes. To know he was only working with maybe a month or two to be with his mom if the new treatments didn't work.

"Do you think you're also conflicted because if the treatments don't work, then it means you're going to lose two extra weeks with her at home that you could have spent with her?"

He nodded slowly, his dark-brown eyes meeting mine. "I think so."

"But your dad wouldn't encourage it, if he didn't think it would help, right?"

"I'm not sure." Mack shrugged again. "I'd like to say that my dad is one of the best neurosurgeons in the world and so he should know what's best for my mom..."

"But you think he might be too close to the issue to be objective?" I guessed.

"I think so." His jaw muscles flexed. "There's a reason they don't recommend doctors treat their own family members."

I didn't really know what to say next—this whole conversation was kind of depressing, and I didn't want to say something that would just make it harder on Mack. I knew he already had a hard enough time sleeping, I didn't need to say anything that would bring up something to make him sleep even worse.

"Did you at least get better sleep the past month with your parents being at home?" I asked, curious if anything had changed in the last month since he'd stayed here.

"Not really." He peeked down the hall as if to make sure my brothers were still in their rooms. "I, um, I think the last time I slept through the night was when I was here."

"Really?"

"Yeah." He sighed, running a hand over his hair.

I watched him closely. He had been looking permanently tired the past few weeks. I'd assumed it was his worries over his mom's condition always being on his mind, but I hadn't realized his sleep was disrupted so much.

"Have you been sleepwalking, too?"

"Um, yeah. Just a few nights a week."

"A few times a week?" I said, surprised that it was still happening since he hadn't done it at all when he'd stayed here.

"But, um, I'm sure I'll be fine here." He waved his hand as if his sleepwalking was nothing to worry about. "I'll just lock Ian's room and I'm sure it will keep me from wandering around your house in the middle of the night."

"You think so?" I raised my eyebrows, wondering how a simple door lock would stop him when he'd gotten past his family's deadbolts before.

"I don't know." He shrugged, the fabric of his thin black T-shirt stretching over his broad shoulders with the movement. "Maybe I won't even sleepwalk at all. I mean, I didn't any of the times I stayed here last month. So..." He held his hands out at his sides. "Maybe the same thing will happen again. Maybe your house has some sort of magical sleeping powers."

"Do my parents know to be on the lookout for you tonight?" I asked, curious what his parents may have arranged with mine when they'd asked for him to stay here.

"I think so." He rubbed the back of his neck with his palm. "I think they said they'd have Duchess sleep in the hall so she could bark if I tried to leave in the middle of the night."

Duchess was my family's little rat-terrier who was definitely more bark than bite. She usually liked to sneak into my parents' room at night since she was addicted to my mom, but hopefully she'd stay in her bed by the door to keep watch for Mack.

"I guess we'll see what happens tonight, won't we?" Mack said.

I nodded. "I hope you get some sleep." I drew in a deep breath and sighed. "It sounds like you could use a good night's rest."

"I hope so, too."

AFTER LEAVING Mack in the sitting room, I headed to my en-suite bathroom to wash my face, brush my teeth, and work my long, brown hair into a side braid for the night. I changed into my pink polka-dotted pajamas with the button-up top and silky shorts, and then climbed into my bed, tired after a full day.

I was just dreaming about dancing with Ben at the Halloween dance when a soft tapping sound startled me from my sleep.

Tap tap tap.

I opened my eyes, noting the sound was coming from the door that led out onto the balcony I shared with Ian's room and not from my bedroom door.

I looked at my watch charging on my nightstand. It was just after midnight.

Tap tap tap.

Was someone on the balcony?

My heart raced at the thought of someone climbing up the tree out there to get to my second story balcony.

What did they want?

Should I check? Or should I ignore the sound and hope it was my imagination or that it would just go away?

Tap tap tap.

Who the heck would be out there?

A thief? A murderer?

But then, would a murderer really knock before entering?

Yeah, probably not.

I peeked over my covers, trying to see through the window beside the door, and my heart jolted when I saw a tall, dark figure.

Should I run and get my dad? Or Carter?

Carter's room was closer, just across the hall from mine. And he had been lifting weights more, he could probably take care of whoever might be out there.

Tap tap tap.

"*Cambrielle.*" I jumped when I heard my name, soft and muffled through the door. "*Cambrielle.*"

Mack?

I frowned as I pushed my covers away and climbed out of bed. I knew Mack had joked about sleeping in my room earlier, but had he been serious?

I turned on my bedside lamp so I could see where I was stepping. I peeked through the window to make sure it was actually Mack and not some psycho coming to kill me in the night. Sure enough, Mack was standing out there in his bare feet, wearing only a pair of gym shorts.

And even though I should probably pretend like I was sleeping through all of this and ignore him, I turned the deadbolt on my balcony door and opened the door to see what he wanted.

"Hey," I said, crossing my arms over my chest, realizing too late that I wasn't wearing a bra under my thin pajama shirt.

But instead of saying hi or explaining what he was doing outside my room in the middle of the night, Mack just stepped over the threshold, almost bumping into me with a dazed look in his eyes.

That was when I realized that he must be sleepwalking again because the vacant look was all too familiar from the times I'd found him wandering through the woods outside last month.

"Hey Mack," I said in a soft voice that hopefully wouldn't startle him. "Let's get you back to your room, okay?"

But he didn't hear me because he just kept walking around my bed and started pulling the covers down on the side opposite from where I'd been sleeping a moment ago.

"Oh, no, no, no, you don't." I hurried around the bed to stop him from climbing under the covers.

I grabbed his bare arm just below his bicep to tug him away from my bed. But he didn't budge. Instead, he just kept trying to climb in.

"Mack, you can't sleep in here," I whispered. "Just come with me back to your room."

But as I pulled on his arm with all the strength I had in my barely five-foot-two-inch frame, his feet might as well have been cemented in the ground.

Usually, I didn't mind being so much shorter than the giants in my life since lots of girls were short, but Mack being over a foot taller and outweighing me by almost a hundred pounds did make it hard to have any sort of physical power over him.

I pulled on his arm one more time, but he straightened his elbow at the exact same moment. Instead of pulling him back, my hands slipped over his long, toned arm and I fell backward with the force, crashing into the wall.

Nothing like a huge thudding sound to alert my whole family to the fact that I had a teenage boy trying to climb into my bed.

My heartbeat thundering in my ears, I hurried to stand back up. Rubbing my elbow where it was tender after hitting the wall, I rushed to my door—the one that led into the hall I shared with my brothers—and put my ear against the small gap between the door and the doorframe to listen for the sound of someone coming to check on what had made the clattering noise.

My heart was beating so fast, my breathing coming in short bursts, that I could barely hear anything over it.

Deep breath in, long breath out.

Deep breath in, long breath out.

My heart rate slowed a little, but I still didn't hear anything.

That was a good sign, right?

Maybe no one had heard the commotion? Carter was probably the next lightest sleeper in the family after me, so he would be the first person to check on me if he heard anything.

After another ten seconds and still nothing, I turned the knob and opened the door slowly so it wouldn't creak. The hall was quiet and dark. Not a soul to be seen.

Thank you! I said to no one in particular.

Then, after carefully closing the door and locking it, I turned around to deal with Mack. But he wasn't standing near my bed anymore. Instead, he had climbed under the covers and was currently fast asleep on his side, with a peaceful expression on his face.

What am I supposed to do now?

I definitely couldn't carry him to his bed like I would a child. And I'd already learned a few weeks ago that waking Mack from sleep was a noisy thing. The first time I caught him walking off into the woods, he had yelled at me when I'd woken him up.

I sighed as I looked at his sleeping form in the dim lighting of my room. He really did look peaceful. And from what he'd said earlier, I knew he hadn't been sleeping well lately.

Should I just let him stay?

He was hugging the side of the bed, so it wasn't like we'd even be touching once I got in on my side.

I chewed on my lip as I considered it.

No one usually came in my room in the mornings. I usually didn't see anyone until I went downstairs for breakfast.

I glanced over at the door. It was still locked.

It would be okay to let Mack sleep here just one night, wouldn't it?

Nothing was going to happen.

I sighed.

Was my level of tiredness just making me lazy? The logical part of my brain wasn't exactly functioning at peak performance after midnight.

I walked over to the balcony door, which was still wide open, and gently swung it shut before locking it.

This would be fine. Mack had slept in my room before and nothing had happened.

Sure, he was in my *actual* bed this time, instead of sleeping on the trundle bed. But...it was fine.

Right?

My eyes caught on the pile of throw pillows I had tossed to the floor when I'd first climbed in bed. I could create a barrier. It would be almost like sleeping in separate beds.

Deciding that was probably the best way to handle this, I started picking up the white and pink and gold decorative pillows and set them in a nice long line down the center of the mattress.

There. I put my hands on my hips as I studied the small mountain of pillows and decided that it was safe enough. I climbed onto my side of the bed and switched off the lamp.

This was fine.

I totally wouldn't get into huge trouble for sleeping in the same bed as my brothers' best friend.

I hoped.

4

MACK

THE ALARM on my phone startled me from my sleep. But since I always hit snooze three times before dragging myself out of bed, I reached over to my nightstand to push the button on my phone to silence the upbeat music.

Only, instead of touching something hard and cool, my fingers landed on something soft and silky.

What the?

When I opened my eyes, I saw that I was not in the same bed that I'd gone to sleep in last night.

I was in Cambrielle's bed.

And yeah, she was there, too.

She moaned tiredly and rolled onto her side, her hand reaching for her phone to turn off the alarm.

She seemed pretty drowsy still. I glanced at her balcony door, my heart pounding in my ears. Maybe I could slip out before she was fully awake and she'd never know that I'd somehow ended up in her bed last night.

I looked at her again. Her breathing seemed even

enough, and her back was turned to me now. I might have a chance at avoiding an awkward situation.

So I carefully rolled off the bed, bracing my fingers on the floor to slowly lower myself on to the carpet. Then ever so slowly, I crawled on my hands and knees past the foot of her bed. I was just reaching for the deadbolt on the door when Cambrielle's voice broke through the quiet room, saying, "I know you slept in here, Mack."

Busted.

I froze for a second, my hand hanging mid-air before I cringed and looked back at her. "How bad was it this time?"

Had I made it out of her house? Had she chased me through the woods again?

"Aside from the fact that you decided to get into my bed and make yourself at home, it wasn't that bad." Cambrielle scooted up to rest her back against the padded white headboard of her canopy bed, pushing some of her brown hair away from her face.

"Yeah?" I rolled from my knees to sit on my butt against her wall, resting my arms around my legs. "And how did I get in here exactly? Did I just come in and you found me next to you sometime during the night?"

Because from the wall of pillows down the center of her bed, she had to have noticed me at some point and decided to protect herself from any accidental cuddling in the night.

I didn't know if I was a cuddler, since I'd never shared a bed with anyone overnight—well until last night, apparently—but I hoped I hadn't tried spooning her in her sleep.

She would've screamed and woken me up if I had, right?

"You came to my balcony door." Cambrielle gestured at the French doors beside me. "At first I thought a murderer was knocking, but then I realized murderers probably don't knock before they come in. That's when I realized it was you."

I dropped my head and shook it, feeling the warmth of embarrassment creeping over me.

Why couldn't my body just stay where it was supposed to be at night? How was it possible for me to get so detached from reality in my sleep that I could wander around aimlessly, completely unaware of where my dreams were taking me, and then have absolutely no recollection of it in the morning?

Maybe I should have my dad take a closer look at my brain. Maybe my mom wasn't the only one who needed his and his colleagues' expertise.

I drew in a deep breath and sighed. "Sorry my subconscious is weird," I said. "I'm starting to think I need to have someone handcuff me to the bed, so I'll stop doing stupid stuff like this."

"Handcuffs?" Cambrielle's eyes widened, and a faint glow of pink colored her cheeks.

I shook my head. "Get your mind out of the gutter."

"Hey, you're the one climbing into my bed without a shirt on." Cambrielle laughed, a light, tinkling sound that always made me smile because it was cute and fit her midget size perfectly. "What am I supposed to think?"

I looked down at myself and quickly realized I'd been sitting here half-naked this whole time.

I grabbed one of the gold throw pillows still on the floor and hugged it to my chest. "There, is that better?" I asked. "Because I promise I wasn't trying to seduce you with my rippling ab muscles, even though I know how much you like looking at them."

She threw a pink pillow at my head. "In your dreams."

"Apparently." I chuckled, tossing the pillow right back at her. "Since my dreams are what led me here last night."

Cambrielle pushed back the covers and slipped her bare feet on the floor, drawing my attention to her tanned legs that I could see quite a bit of, thanks to her pajama shorts.

Though I knew better than to think of her as more than the kid sister of my best friends, or even as a friend herself, I still couldn't help but notice how grown up she was looking these days.

She was still tiny, her brothers having apparently stolen all the tall genes from their dad, but instead of being all hard angles like she'd been when she ate, drank, and slept ballet, she now had curves in all the right places. And yeah, I might have noticed them more and more in recent weeks as we'd been seeing more of each other.

I let my gaze linger on her curved booty and follow the line up along her torso as she started making her bed. And for a moment, I wondered why I'd never tried to make something happen with her.

Oh yeah, because she was like the sister I'd never had, and Carter would kill me if I tried to touch his innocent little sis since he knew all about my escapades to the falls on the weekends.

Not that I did anything more than kissing during those trips to the falls—the farthest I'd ever made it was second base. But from the things I'd heard here and there, I wasn't sure Cambrielle had even made it to first base yet...not sure she'd even really been up to bat.

She had a great personality and was pretty enough—the girl was gorgeous, actually. But she was also shy around guys.

Plus, the fact that Carter glared at any guy who looked at his sister the wrong way wasn't exactly making it easy for guys to approach her. I'd overheard a few guys in our biology class talking about wanting to take her out, but then someone would mention her big brother's protective nature and it always ended the conversation.

For which I was actually kind of glad, since most of those guys weren't good enough for Cambrielle anyway—she deserved better than a guy who just wanted a random hookup.

But it was still pretty crazy to me that she didn't go on dates more.

"What?" Cambrielle said when she turned to pick up a pillow from the floor, bringing me back to the present. "Why are you staring at me like that?"

She looked down at herself, like she thought something might be wrong, and then hugged the pillow to her chest.

"Nothing's wrong." I blinked my eyes and shook my head. "I, uh, I just zoned out for a sec."

She furrowed her brow and held out a hand, pointing to the pillow I was still hugging. "Well, you should probably get out of here before Carter or Nash try going into your room and find that you aren't in there."

"You're probably right." I stood and handed her the pillow. "Can't have them finding out about my sleepwalking."

She took the pillow and tossed it onto her bed before looking at me thoughtfully. "You sure you don't want to just tell them? It's nothing to be embarrassed about."

"Nah, that's okay." I rubbed a hand over my short, curly hair. "The fewer people who know about my issues, the better."

She gave me a skeptical look, tilting her head to the side. "So you'd rather have them discover your secret when they find you curled up in bed next to them one morning?"

My eyes widened at the thought of sleepwalking into Nash's or Carter's room.

Or their parents' bedroom.

Yikes, that would be a nightmare.

Had I just been really lucky that I ended up in the room of the one person who already knew all about my night wanderings?

I rubbed my cheek. "I guess I didn't consider that possibility."

"My brothers are cool," she said. "They wouldn't care if you told them you've been having trouble sleeping. It's completely understandable, especially with everything that's going on right now."

I sighed as I considered what she was saying. Of course her brothers knew I was a huge mess right now. They'd planned extra guys' nights where we just played basketball, went hiking, or played video games so I could blow off steam. But even though they'd probably be cool about it, I just didn't want them to know that I sometimes did crazy things in my sleep like going swimming with the fish in their pond, or wandering through the woods at midnight and walking until my feet were all bloody from the rough terrain.

I knew the only thing sure in life was that it would eventually come to an end. So the logical side of my brain wondered why I was having such a hard time accepting that my mom's passing was just coming a couple of decades sooner than we'd originally expected.

People died at a younger age all the time. Why should it cause such a disruption to my psyche when death was just a part of living?

But I knew the answer.

It was because it was *my* mom who was dying and not someone else's. It was *my* mom who was getting one day closer to never waking up again.

A feeling of dread filled me with those thoughts, and that "going crazy" feeling that I always got every time I thought about a future without my mom started creeping over me.

Suddenly, I couldn't breathe. My chest tightened, as if something was pressing down on me.

"Mack?" Cambrielle's voice sounded alarmed just as the edges of my vision turned black with the onset of another panic attack. "Are you okay?"

I shook my head and tried to catch a breath, but I couldn't through the pressure in my chest.

Breathe.

Just breathe.

I bent over with my hands on my knees, hoping the panic attack would subside, but my vision just blurred more as the pounding in my head started.

I was going to die.

It felt like I was going to die.

"Mack?" Cambrielle's voice was panicked. "What's happening?"

"I can't...breathe..." I said, clutching a hand to my chest. "I can't..."

I closed my eyes, feeling my muscles go weak as I surrendered to the feeling taking over me.

"Mack!" Cambrielle stepped in front of me, grabbing my shoulders in her hands. "Tell me what's going on. Are you having a heart attack? Do I need to call nine-one-one?"

"No," I gasped, shaking my head. "...panic attack..." I let out a labored breath. "Just give me a..." I gulped some air. "...minute..."

I sighed again and focused on Cambrielle who was now smoothing her hand along my back in a soothing gesture.

"It's okay," she said in a gentle tone. "You're going to be okay. Just breathe."

I sucked in a deep lungful, and after a moment, the pounding sensation that had taken over my whole body subsided. My vision cleared and I no longer felt like I was going to die.

I lifted my eyes to Cambrielle's worried face. "Sorry about that," I said, slowly standing back up to my full height and leaning against her wall for support.

"Don't be sorry," she said, running her hand up and down my arm. "Are you going to be okay?"

"Yeah, I just need a minute." I drew in a shaky breath, feeling wiped out and like I could take a nap.

Seeming to sense that I was indeed going to not die on her, Cambrielle patted my arm and then stepped back. She leaned against the side of her bed across from me so we were facing each other.

"Have you had a panic attack before?" she asked, her voice quiet as if afraid that if she spoke too loudly I might break.

I clenched my jaw and nodded. "A few."

"Was it something I said that made it happen?" she asked. "Because you don't have to tell my brothers about your sleepwalking if it's that bad. I just thought they might be able to help you better than I can."

I shook my head, and before she could worry she was at fault, I said, "It wasn't that." I bit my bottom lip. "I just started thinking about my mom and um..." Tears pricked at my eyes. I cleared my throat before my voice could wobble. "And my thoughts just went on this downward spiral."

She nodded, like she understood the exact kind of thoughts that would trigger a panic attack in me. "I'm so sorry you have to worry about this. I wish I could just make everything better for you."

I nodded solemnly. "Yeah, me too."

She looked away, and when she wiped at her eyes, I noticed her unshed tears.

Great. I was bringing her down already. And it wasn't even six-thirty in the morning.

This was why I didn't like telling my friends about the panic attacks or the sleepwalking. I hated being a buzzkill.

"Anyway," I said, pushing myself away from her light-pink wall and walking toward the French doors to sneak back to my room. "I really should go now."

I was just turning the door handle when there was a knock on Cambrielle's door, followed by Carter's deep voice. "Hey, Cambrielle, can I use your balcony to get to Mack's room? I've been knocking on his door and calling him, but he's not answering."

Crap!

I quickly opened the door and ran onto the balcony just as Cambrielle called out, "S-sure. Um, just a minute."

I made it to the French doors that led to Ian's room, but just before I stepped inside, I realized that I couldn't go in there because Carter would find me and wonder why I'd been ignoring him.

Thinking fast, I closed the door that I'd apparently left open last night and set myself on the porch swing that sat along the wall between Cambrielle's room and my temporary room.

I had just leaned back with my hands behind my head when Carter stepped through the balcony doors, already wearing his school uniform with the navy-blue blazer and tan slacks.

I pretended to look surprised when I saw him.

"There you are," he said when he saw me, relief showing on his face. "I've been knocking on your door and trying to call you."

"Oh you were?" I said, hoping to seem like I hadn't just heard him tell Cambrielle that very thing. "Sorry, I just thought I'd..." I scrambled for an excuse to explain why I was outside so early in the morning. Then it came to me. "I was just practicing my meditation. I must be getting pretty good at it since I didn't hear a thing."

Yeah, my mom would be so disappointed at how easily lying came to me these days. But it was kind of a necessary evil.

"I guess that explains the whole no-shirt thing you've got going on." He narrowed his eyes at my bare chest as if he thought all meditation enthusiasts preferred to meditate with the warmth of the morning sun directly on their skin. Well, who knows, maybe that was a thing. The Hastings family were the ones who did regular meditations on

Sundays. "It's a bit chilly to be hanging out here like that though, isn't it?"

"Eh, maybe if you're a wuss."

Carter rolled his eyes. "Whatever."

Though now that he had brought it up, I could feel the cold bumps prickling all over my skin from the chill in the late autumn air.

"What did you need from me, anyway?" I stood, deciding to head inside Ian's room since it was actually cold and if I started shivering, I might totally give myself away.

"I was just wondering if you wanted to go four-wheeling with Ava and me after school today." Carter followed me into my room. "I thought it might be nice to get out there before the weather gets too cold."

"You want me to be the third-wheel and get secondhand embarrassment from how bad you flirt with my sister?" I cocked an eyebrow.

Carter pushed his hands into his pockets. "We're not that bad. And yes, I think it would be fun. We could invite the rest of the crew, if you want."

It would be good to have something to do to keep my mind off of what might be happening with my mom's treatment. I could only study so much before my brain turned to mush.

So I said, "Okay. I guess that sounds fun."

"Cool. I'll text everyone. Should we plan on starting around four?" he asked.

"Sure," I said, knowing that as soon as he was done here, he would schedule the event into his beloved bullet journal— he was obsessed with the thing for some reason.

"Perfect." He glanced at the bed that I'd left at who

knew what time last night, and after taking in the tangled mess of sheets, pillow, and comforter, he furrowed his brow and said, "Restless night?"

"Yeah." I shrugged, hoping he couldn't tell it had been reckless in addition to being restless.

"Well." He swung his hands at his sides, like he wasn't sure if he should ask why it had been so restless. Like he worried it might have something to do with my mom and he wasn't sure if I wanted to talk about it. Then, after seeming to decide to leave the subject alone, he hooked a thumb over his shoulder to point to the door that led to the hall. "I'll just see you downstairs. I think Marie made my favorite crepes for breakfast, so I wanna make sure I get some before you and Nash attack them."

"Great, see you down there."

And once he left, I collapsed on the bed, thinking about how close of a call that was.

I needed to find a way to make sure I stayed in this room tonight.

5

CAMBRIELLE

"I HEARD Mrs. Johnson is assigning us new lab partners today," Elyse said as she slid into the seat beside me in our Culinary Arts class. "Think she'll let us stay partners?"

"I wish," I said, looking around the room at the rest of our classmates filing into the tables. Everyone wore their number two uniforms—the girls with their cream-colored blazers over their white shirts, pink and burgundy skirts and neckties, and maroon socks. And the boys with their navy blazers and slacks, and pink and burgundy ties.

I hated that I had to wear the same school uniforms every day since I much preferred the clothes in my own closet, but at least they'd gone with cuter uniforms this year. Last year's were just atrocious and the boxy fit had done no favors for my somewhat fragile body image.

Mack walked into the room a moment later, his tie already loose around his neck as if it had been a long, rough morning even though it was only second period. He stopped at the first table and said something to Porter Cunningham about basketball tryouts being next Monday. After Porter confirmed that he still planned to try out for the team, Mack gave him a fist bump and then started chatting about what they'd done to improve since last season.

I was about to turn back to Elyse and ask her who she wanted to pair with for the lab when my attention was drawn to the door as the tall, dark, and handsome soccer player I'd had a crush on since last spring walked into the room.

Yes, I was staring at Ben Barnett.

"Looks like Ben cut his hair," Elyse whispered, seeming to notice how my attention had been immediately captured by the senior god walking toward the back corner where his buddies sat.

"He did. And it looks so good," I whispered back with a sigh.

Just yesterday, Ben had been sporting an afro. But now his hair was shorter on the sides, making him look almost exactly like Regé-Jean Page who played the Duke of Hastings in the first season of *Bridgerton*—the show that I was so obsessed with that I'd had my mom help me throw a *Bridgerton*-inspired soirée just a week and a half ago.

"Don't you think he looks just like Regé-Jean Page now?" I whispered to Elyse who was a fellow *Bridgerton* fan.

Elyse furrowed her brow and studied the six-foot-four athlete. With a shrug, she said, "Kind of." She turned back to me and spoke in a lowered voice. "I mean, I always thought Mack looked more like him, but I guess I can see it now."

"You think Mack looks like Regé-Jean Page?" I raised my eyebrows, surprised at the comparison.

"Yeah." Elyse nodded. "I mean, can't you see the resemblance? It was kind of the first thing I thought of when I met him."

I turned to look at Mack who was still talking to Porter, trying to see what Elyse was talking about.

"They have similar jawlines and eyebrows, don't you think?" Elyse leaned closer to whisper about the boy whom she'd had a crush on before she found out he was her half-brother. "And when I first saw him, his hair was almost identical to Regé-Jean Page's. Plus, don't you think that if Mack didn't shave for a few days that his scruff would look exactly like the Duke of Hastings'?"

I narrowed my eyes, trying to picture the boy I'd known since we were kids as the Duke of Hastings—as the guy wearing an old-fashioned suit and cravat that I sometimes daydreamed about riding horses with when I wasn't daydreaming of Ben.

And sure, now that Elyse mentioned it, they did look a lot alike. I guess Mack might even resemble my celebrity crush slightly more than my real-life crush did.

But that didn't mean Ben didn't look amazing with his new haircut.

Because he did. He looked downright gorgeous.

I shrugged dismissively and said to my friend, "I still like Ben more."

"Well, I never said you needed to like Mack just because I think he looks more like Regé-Jean Page than your beloved Ben," Elyse said with a chuckle, amusement in her amber eyes.

"I would hope not," I said with a smirk.

I considered teasing her about how I wouldn't dare move in on the guy she'd just been crushing on but stopped myself just in time—making her even more embarrassed over what had been a completely innocent crush at the time wouldn't do our friendship any good. Even though Elyse hadn't even been at our school for two full months yet, I didn't want to do anything that would hurt our friendship.

I'd always wanted a sister, and even though her identical twin was the one who would probably end up marrying my brother Carter someday, I'd gotten close enough to Elyse over the past few weeks that she really did feel like a sister to me.

The bell rang a minute later. Our teacher, Mrs. Johnson, who taught all of the family and consumer-science classes at our school told us about how we'd be switching up our cooking lab partnerships and that all the people on the first two rows would be coming up to draw their new lab partner's names from a bowl she had prepared with names of the students on the last two rows.

"Looks like being partnered up together is out of the cards for us," I said to Elyse with a sigh.

"Sadly," she agreed.

Then looking around at the eight students who sat on the last two rows and seeing Ben among them, I turned back to Elyse with a half-smile on my lips and whispered, "But maybe the universe will smile down upon me and I'll draw Ben's name."

"Well," Elyse said. "If you get that lucky, then I better get partnered with Addison because I'm pretty sure she's the only one back there who can follow a recipe."

Mrs. Johnson had the front two rows gather in a line. One by one, we each pulled a small slip of white paper from the glass bowl she held to determine whom we'd be sharing a kitchen with for the rest of the semester.

I was third in line, and as the red curly-haired guy ahead of me pulled out his partner's name, I made a wish in my head.

Please let me pick Ben. Please let us be partners so he's forced to notice me.

After the guy ahead of me moved away from the line, I reached into the jar with a slightly shaky hand. Touching a few slips of paper with my fingertips, I closed my eyes and pulled out the one that felt right to me.

I didn't look at the paper right away. Instead, I went back to my seat so I could open it without all eyes on me. Once seated, I opened the folded-up slip of paper. And written there in Mrs. Johnson's elegant cursive were three letters that made up the most wonderful name in the world as far as I was concerned.

Ben.

My stomach immediately flipped, and I couldn't keep a huge smile from taking shape on my lips as I caressed his name with my gaze, hardly believing my wish had come true.

I get to work alone with Ben for over an hour every other day for the next several weeks.

The universe had finally heard my wish of getting on my dream guy's radar. And I hadn't even had to use my Kelana costume to do it.

If I didn't have a whole classroom full of people around me, I'd probably jump around and do a little dance to celebrate how excited I was to finally, *finally* spend some one-on-one time with Ben.

Elyse slid back into her chair beside me and after looking

at my face, a knowing smile slipped on her lips. "You picked Ben, didn't you?"

"Yes!" I whispered, my smile widening. "Who did you get?"

Elyse unfolded her paper, revealing the name.

"You got Mack?" I said with a smile, figuring he was probably the next best choice in our class after Addison since Elyse and Mack knew each other.

But when I looked at Elyse's face to catch her reaction, it had gone pale. Under her breath, she whispered, "No."

I frowned. "You don't want to be partnered with Mack?" I asked in a low voice, glancing around us to make sure Mack was oblivious to our exchange. He was currently leaning back in his chair and talking with the guy next to him.

Elyse just shook her head, a solemn look on her face as she said, "Things are just kind of weird right now."

Oh.

Yeah, I guess they probably would be.

While she and Mack hadn't ever gone on a date or anything like that, they had flirted a ton before they found out they shared the same father.

They were making the best of the situation right now, and I knew their parents were trying to help make the transition to integrate their families go as smoothly as possible given all the circumstances. But I could understand how it might be a little weird to work alone with a guy whom you were trying to see in a different light than you had originally.

Elyse folded up her paper again and released a long sigh. "Maybe it'll be okay. Maybe it'll turn out to be some good brother-and-sister-bonding time."

But when I studied her eyes, I knew she wasn't quite ready for something like this.

"Now if you will all go introduce yourselves to your new lab partners—" Mrs. Johnson's voice sounded loudly from the front of the room after everyone had finished drawing their names, "—then we can get started baking."

Elyse scooted her chair away from our table as everyone else on the front two rows made their way back to their new partners. But before she could stand, I snatched the paper with Mack's name on it from her hand and slipped the piece of paper with Ben's name into its place.

"What are you doing?" Elyse stared at me, her eyes wide.

"I'm helping you out," I whispered back.

She reached over to try to give me the paper back. "You don't need to do this, Cambrielle."

But I just shook my head and closed her fingers over her new lab partner's name. "It's fine."

"But it's Ben," Elyse said with a shake of her head. "You can't give him up for me."

"It's really fine, Elyse," I insisted. "I don't mind working with Mack."

It would probably be way less awkward for me to work with him instead of Ben, anyway. I was bound to get all anxious and mess up all the recipes if I was worried about impressing my lab partner.

Elyse seemed to study me for a moment, as if gauging whether I was really sincere. And then after a long pause, she swallowed and said, "Thank you. I promise to return the favor."

"Don't even worry about it." I waved the thought away.

But she said, "I'll talk you up to Ben. I'll tell him how awesome you are."

"Please don't." My eyes widened and I put my hand to my chest. "That'll only make it obvious that I like him."

Elyse nodded. "Okay. But I'll pay you back somehow."

I stood from my chair. "Just find out what costume he's planning to wear to the Halloween dance, and we'll call it even."

"Done."

———

"I SAW you traded Elyse names before coming back here," Mack said in a low voice near my ear once we made it to our cooking station. "You traded Ben to be with me?"

"You saw that?" I asked, surprised that he'd been watching us.

"And here I thought you just told Nash last night that you were going to talk to Ben." Mack grabbed two aprons from one of the drawers, handing me the red one while keeping the black for himself. "This was your chance. Why'd you chicken out?"

"I-I didn't chicken out." I took the red apron and put it over my head.

"You didn't?" He arched an eyebrow, clearly not believing me. "Then why the last-minute partner trade? You can't tell me it was because you have secretly always wanted to make fantastic dishes in the kitchen with me. Because if that's the case, we could have just done that at your house this week."

"Yeah, it's not that," I said. "It's, um..." I tried to think of an excuse that would cover up the real reason—that Elyse didn't want to be *his* partner. But when nothing came to mind, I sighed and said, "I guess I might have been overwhelmed by the thought of cooking with him for the rest of the semester."

Overwhelmed with joy, that is.

But I couldn't tell Mack that now, could I?

Mack glanced at the station across the room where Elyse and Ben were currently reading over a recipe together.

He turned back to me. "You really like the guy?" His deep, brown eyes looked skeptically at me, like he couldn't understand why I would like someone who was tall, gorgeous, and popular like Ben.

"Yes," I whispered, since it was dumb to deny it when he'd already heard the truth yesterday in my room.

"Well, then how about I help you out?"

"Help me out?" I asked, suddenly worried he was going to walk right over there and ask Ben and Elyse if they wanted to trade back partners.

"Yeah." Mack shrugged as he started tying his apron behind his lower back, the muscles in his triceps bulging against the sleeve of his white button-up. "I mean, I personally think you could do better than him, but if you really want to get to know Ben better, I can set something up."

"Really?" I furrowed my brow, wondering if there was some sort of catch.

"Sure," he said. "Carter talked about riding ATVs on the trails with everyone after school. Want me to invite Ben? I'll be your wingman."

My heart raced at the thought of Ben coming to my house.

He'd come to the back-to-school barbecue we'd thrown at the first of the year, and then I'd totally stared at him all night at the soirée a week and a half ago. But those had been big and more crowded events. He'd had all his other friends around him the whole time to keep me from going up and talking to him.

Having him come riding with us would be a lot more intimate. He might actually make eye contact with me for the first time, since it would be harder to make myself invisible in the crowd.

My fingers went tingly as I thought about it. Was I really ready to be forced to talk to him?

Because up until now, I'd been able to imagine that the only reason why Ben wasn't asking me out was because he just hadn't noticed me yet or had the opportunity to see how amazing I was.

But once we talked and actually said a few words to each other, what if he went right back to ignoring me again? I'd know for sure it was because of me.

"Why the hesitation?" Mack sounded like he couldn't imagine why I had to even consider this golden opportunity he was offering me.

"I'm just thinking," I said.

I looked over at Ben and Elyse. They had already started pulling together the ingredients for today's chocolate chip oatmeal cookie recipe and he looked super adorable with his eyebrows squished together as he seemed to be trying to figure out which measuring cup to use for the flour.

Mack leaned closer, and in a low voice that sent chills racing down my spine, he said, "I think I heard Ben say something about preferring brunettes over blondes. You could be exactly his type."

My heart swooped in my chest at the thought of Ben actually being attracted to someone like me. He'd always seemed to go for the taller girls with long legs before—which was how you'd describe my friends Scarlett, Elyse, and Ava way more than how you'd describe me.

I was barely five-foot-two, and sadly for me where my previous dreams of being a prima ballerina were concerned, I was much more torso than legs.

You miss all the shots you don't take. I heard my dad's voice in my head.

And so far, I was excellent at stalling at the free-throw line instead of shooting my shot.

So after taking one more look at Ben who was handing Elyse a silver measuring cup I sighed and said, "Okay. If you don't mind, then I'd love for you to be my wingman."

6

CAMBRIELLE

I GAVE Elyse a ride to my house in my red Mercedes after school got out. She'd never driven an ATV before and wanted to get the hang of it before everyone else arrived at four.

"We just keep the ATVs in here," I pointed to one of the buildings off to the north side of the house near the horse stables.

Elyse nodded and followed behind me, our boots crunching on the leaves that had fallen recently from the tall trees above.

I typed in the code to the garage door, and it slowly lifted to reveal the rows of ATVs. There was a side-by-side that my parents mostly drove, and then parked beside that were a dozen four-wheelers that we had for outings like we had planned today.

"Does it matter which one I use?" Elyse asked, her wide eyes telling me she was somewhat surprised at how many options we had in here.

While I'd grown up with everything I'd ever dreamed of as the daughter of the seventh richest man in the U.S., Elyse and Ava's mom hadn't made her fortune until very recently. So it was always interesting to see how my world looked from a newcomer's eyes.

"I'd probably pick one of those." I pointed to the black four-wheelers closest to us. "They're automatic and should be less complicated to drive."

"You have manual four-wheelers?" Elyse furrowed her brow. "Why?"

I chuckled. "Nash and Carter had a dumb rivalry going a couple of years ago where they wanted to prove who was more macho than the other. For some reason, they decided that having to shift gears while driving through the woods meant you were more manly or something."

"Really?" Elyse asked, the look on her face telling me she, too, thought they were ridiculous.

"I think being the same age has made them extra competitive sometimes," I said. "Though I think Mack had his parents get him a manual four-wheeler too, so maybe it's just a guy thing."

"Boys are weird," Elyse said.

"Yes, they are."

"Well," Elyse said. "I just want to be able to drive this thing without crashing into a tree, so I'll happily put aside my tough-girl card and drive the wimpy automatic."

I smiled at my friend. "Smart."

I walked to the cabinet where we kept all the helmets and pulled out a purple one that should fit Elyse's head. Then I grabbed my pink one with glittery gold star stickers on it.

Yeah, I'd never met a pink and gold thing I didn't like.

I helped Elyse with her helmet and showed her the basics of how to drive the ATV, and then we went on a quick ride to the pond. She picked things up quickly, and after riding down the trail that passed the blueberry fields and the greenhouse, I figured we should probably get back to the house so we could be ready for Ben to arrive.

Yes, Ben was coming over.

My heart fluttered just thinking about him coming over and finally noticing me. Sure, I was going to have helmet hair when I saw him, but hopefully he'd remember seeing me in class and know I knew how to brush and curl my hair like regular girls did.

On second thought, maybe I should hurry upstairs and tame my hair real quick so I'd at least look presentable when he first showed up.

Elyse and I were on our way back to the garage when I spotted Mack driving his four-wheeler through the clearing of trees between our houses, wearing his black riding suit with red stripes down the sides.

He only ever wore his riding suit when he planned to splash through a bunch of puddles and splatter everyone around him with mud, so I made a mental note to steer clear of him during our ride today.

I usually didn't mind getting splashed when I went riding with him and my brothers because splashing them right back was half the fun, but Ben would be here today, and I didn't want to be caked in mud when I finally spoke to him.

Elyse and I parked our ATVs in front of the garage and

were just taking our helmets off when Mack pulled up beside me.

"You guys get started without me?" Mack asked after he removed his black helmet and rested it on his knee.

"We just went around the pond and down to the greenhouse," I said. "This is Elyse's first time."

"And how did it go?" Mack turned to his sister. "Was Cambrielle's lesson any good? Because if you're looking for pro tips, you should ask me."

"I think I've got the basic idea of it," Elyse said, her gaze flitting briefly to Mack before looking back at me.

There was an awkward silence as we all tried to think of something to say.

This would usually be the time when Mack would say something flirty to Elyse, but since that wouldn't be happening anymore, we all just sat there trying to figure out what to say next.

Man, I really hoped the awkwardness between Mack and Elyse went away before long. Hopefully one of them would find someone new to flirt with so everyone could just move on and forget they'd ever liked each other.

Mack cleared his throat and looked toward the house. "Think everyone else will be here soon?" He glanced at me. "I told Ben four o'clock, so he should be here in a few minutes."

"Ava was going to text me when she and Carter were on their way," Elyse said, pulling her phone out of her back pocket. She looked at the screen briefly, and after reading whatever messages were on her lock screen, she nodded. "Yeah, looks like she and Carter finished their tutoring session and should be here any minute."

"Cool," Mack said. "I think I'm gonna grab a drink of water before we start."

I turned to Elyse. "Wanna go inside to wait for everyone?"

Elyse shook her head. "I think I'll ride a little longer, if that's okay."

"Sure." I climbed off my four-wheeler. "We'll be back out in a few minutes."

As Elyse headed off toward the pond trail again, I walked inside with Mack.

I was just about to head up the stairs to comb through my hair real quick when the front doorbell rang.

"That must be Ben," Mack said as he grabbed a glass from a kitchen cupboard and started filling it with water from the fridge. "Think you're brave enough to answer the door?"

I looked at the entryway, my heart rate suddenly skyrocketing with the anticipation of coming face to face with my crush without all his other friends to distract him.

We had rain-glass windows on both sides of the double front doors, and through them I could see a blurry figure of what looked very much like Ben's tall form.

"You going to be okay?" Mack asked after taking a sip from his water. "Because while I did invite him for you, I'm not planning to do much more."

I sucked in a deep breath, hoping it would calm me. "I can do it."

So when Regina, our head staff member, went to open the front door, I told her I could get it. But just as I was reaching for the handle, I remembered that I still hadn't tamed my helmet hair. I rushed to the mirror we had on the wall close by and started combing my fingers through my hair.

The doorbell rang again, and I jumped.

Mack's footsteps sounded in the hallway. "Are you just going to ignore him?"

I looked back at Mack, and in a quiet voice, I whisper-shouted, "I'm just fixing my hair real quick."

"You look fine." Mack leaned a broad shoulder against the wall. "Just open the door."

But I shook my head and went back to taming my hair.

There was a knock at the door then, like Ben assumed no one was answering because the doorbell was broken.

Why did he have to show up early?

"If you don't open that door right now, I'll open it for you and tell Ben the reason why he got stuck standing out there is because we were making out and it got so intense that I couldn't help but tangle my fingers through your silky hair."

What?

"You wouldn't dare." I narrowed my eyes and glared at him.

"Dare make out with you?" Mack pursed his lips into a pout as if considering the thought. Then he shrugged. "I don't know. It might be fun."

And when he waggled his eyebrows flirtatiously, my heart had a momentary lapse in judgement and flipped.

Yes, my heart actually flipped at the thought of kissing my brother's stupid best friend. But I told it to calm down because kissing Mack was the last thing I should be thinking about.

Especially when my *actual* crush was standing on my

doorstep and probably wondering why no one was answering.

Instead of responding to Mack's flirtatious comment, I gave my reflection one last glance in the mirror and opened the door.

Standing on the doorstep with the late afternoon sunlight hitting him in just the right way to make him look like he'd just stepped off an action-movie set was Ben.

He wore a long-sleeve, yellow-and-black shirt with a Fox symbol on it, like he was ready to go motorbiking. And suddenly, all the annoyance I'd felt toward Mack a second ago for all his teasing ways disappeared because he'd made this happen.

Mack had gotten Ben to come to my house.

"H-hi," I managed to say after staring at Ben's defined jawline for just a moment too long. "C-come in."

I stepped back to let him in.

"Thanks," he said, his boots thudding on the marble floor. "Mack said we were going four-wheeling, is that right?"

I nodded, and after loosening my tongue again, I managed to say, "Yes. We're just waiting for Carter and Ava and a few others now."

I glanced at where Mack had been standing a moment before, hoping he might help me welcome Ben to my house, but he must have already disappeared back into the kitchen because he was nowhere to be seen.

I cleared my throat. "D-do you want to go out back to pick out your ATV? Elyse is there already and everyone else should be here soon."

"Elyse is already here?" Ben's eyes lit up.

"Yeah, she's just out back." Was he more excited to see

Elyse than me? A jealous pit formed in my stomach before I reminded myself that Elyse would never break the girl code and flirt with my crush.

"Cool." He pushed his fingers into the pockets of his black pants and followed me through the kitchen where I hoped Mack would be.

But when we walked through the kitchen toward the doors that led to the terrace out back, Mack was still nowhere to be found.

Where did he go?

I knew I'd wanted to talk to Ben and let him know I existed, but I was so not good at hosting people on my own. I liked being around people enough that I wasn't a complete social disaster most of the time, but I was not the natural extrovert that Nash and Mack were. So I did always appreciate when one of them was there to help take some of the pressure off when I was around people I didn't know very well.

I mean, sure, I knew all kinds of things about Ben—like how he was from North Carolina and had two older sisters and liked to do motocross when he was home for breaks—because I totally stalked his social media accounts over the summer. But I couldn't exactly strike up a conversation about any of that since it would give away how much I'd learned about him online.

So instead of making small talk as we walked across the stone terrace and down the steps to the grass below, I stayed awkwardly quiet.

Ben followed me across the freshly cut lawn and soon we were at the garage with the ATVs.

"Do you prefer manual or automatic?" I turned to Ben after raising the garage door again.

"Let's go with automatic," Ben said.

"Good choice," I said. If he'd said manual, I probably would have said the same thing.

I showed him which four-wheeler to use—the big green and black one my dad often took out when he wasn't using the side-by-side. After giving him a helmet, I looked around the grounds wondering where Mack had disappeared to.

Was he purposely trying to give Ben and me some alone time? Because after the past few minutes of uncomfortable silence, I really wouldn't mind having Mack or even Nash show up and talk about whatever random subject popped into their minds. At least then I might be able to relax.

I was considering heading back into the house with the excuse that I needed to go to the bathroom when Ben asked, "So, do you guys go riding very often?"

"We go about once a week when the weather is nice," I said, relieved that he'd broken the ice with a question I could answer.

"That's cool."

"Yeah, it's fun." I pointed to his racing gear. "What about you? Did you just go out and buy that gear for this, or do you race?"

"Oh this?" He looked down at his shirt and pants, like he'd forgotten what he was wearing. "I'm pretty big into motocross when I'm home."

"That's awesome," I said, pretending like I didn't already know that about him. "Do you compete?"

"I've been in a few races, but nothing too big yet."

"Oh, that's cool," I said.

Even though I knew it from his photos online, I actually didn't know very much about the sport. I was about to ask him how everything worked when Carter and Ava, holding hands, came around the corner, along with Nash, Scarlett, and Hunter trailing behind them.

Elyse appeared out of the forest at the same time as well.

Oh well, I guess I would just have to ask Ben more about his racing later. It would at least give me a topic to bring up the next time I had a chance to talk to him.

Everyone greeted Ben and welcomed him to the house—everyone aside from my brother Carter, who seemed to tense when he realized my crush and I had been alone.

But Carter recovered from the surprise of seeing me actually talking to a guy quickly enough and started giving a rundown of where we'd be riding today.

As Carter pointed to the trail that went around the golf course and back to the very west end of the property, Mack finally rejoined us.

Where had he disappeared to for so long?

His gaze met mine as Carter asked everyone if they wanted to ride all the way through the secret trail we had that led to the falls. And I didn't know what it was exactly, but Mack looked like there was something off with him. He usually had an enigmatic energy about him that you couldn't help but be drawn to—like how he'd acted when he made that comment about telling Ben we'd been making out. But now he was broodier.

Had something happened in the past few minutes to change his mood?

I studied him as everyone agreed that going to the falls

sounded fun, and when our eyes met, I mouthed, *Everything okay?*

He gave a non-committal shrug before looking away.

I furrowed my brow, confused. I started walking over to ask him what was going on, but before I could reach him, he climbed on his ATV and pulled onto the trail directly behind Carter and Ava—who were of course riding the same ATV because they were in the inseparable stage of their relationship.

Why was Mack rushing off?

Had *I* done something wrong?

I had no idea.

But since he obviously wasn't going to tell me what was going on right now, I just climbed onto my ATV and managed to claim my spot directly behind Ben who had taken off after Elyse.

I'd just have to figure Mack out later. Right now, I would focus on enjoying this ride and the chance I had to hopefully make a somewhat good impression on Ben despite being tongue-tied earlier.

We passed the golf course and drove into the more heavily wooded part of my family's thousand-acre property where the land hadn't been developed yet aside from the dirt trail we were driving on.

As we went over the small bumps in the road here and there, I let myself sink into the present moment and appreciated the view I had of Ben from behind. He was handling the ATV well, his body anticipating all the dips and curves in the trail.

I should probably be embarrassed at how much I was staring at his backside, my gaze running over the shape of his tall, toned body under his fitted gear, but since no one—my brothers included—could see my eyes under my helmet and goggles, I just let myself enjoy the view. Checking out his broad shoulders and narrow waist, I imagined what it would be like to share a four-wheeler with him, the same way Carter and Ava were.

I usually liked riding alone, since driving the four-wheeler was where most of the fun was for me, but I could certainly appreciate the idea of sitting behind Ben and wrapping my arms around his torso for safety. I would scoot up close with my chest against his back, letting the side of my face rest between his shoulder blades.

Yeah, that would be nice. I could just breathe him in and see if being close to him felt as good as my imagination had made it feel during my daydreams. He probably smelled and felt really good.

I sighed, wistfully thinking about living in a reality where that fantasy actually came true.

Would it be totally obvious if I pretended like I ran out of gas and needed him to give me a ride?

Probably.

Ben turned a corner on the road, and I was forced to look at the beautiful, forested scenery around me for a moment. The trees looked like they were on fire from the bright orange and red leaves. There was a place where the road divided, giving the option of taking an offshoot path through the trees that would eventually meet back up with the main trail. I slowed down since I wasn't quite sure which way everyone had chosen to go and scanned the area to see which way Ben had gone.

I spotted him on the underdeveloped trail a moment

later, his ATV leaving a cloud of dirt behind it about fifty feet ahead of me. I was about to head in his direction when out of the corner of my eye, I caught sight of a figure dressed in a black riding suit with a red stripe down the sides driving his four-wheeler down the side road.

Was Mack trying to race ahead of Carter and Ava? He was going so fast.

The road he was on sloped up into a hill, and for a few short seconds, he was air-bound after taking a jump. My heart stopped as I watched him fly through the air. A sudden surge of panic filled my chest when I saw that just when his four-wheeler was supposed to hit the ground, it hit something on the road that was hidden from my view instead.

And then Mack was flying off his machine.

7

MACK

"HEY, YOU OKAY, DUDE?" a voice—Ben?—called from behind me.

I was lying on my back in the middle of the Hastings' woods and feeling like I'd just been hit by a train.

One minute I'd been pushing my gas pedal to the floor and driving down the road as fast as I could, and the next thing I knew, the sun was blinding me, and I was flying through the air after hitting a tree that had fallen across the road.

"I'm okay," I said, slowly sitting up and brushing some dirt and leaves off my arms and legs, my body already groaning in pain from the movement. "I guess I kind of blacked out there."

"Blacked out?" Ben's dark eyebrows knitted together, like he was worried I was drunk or something.

Which, no, I wasn't—even if I sometimes considered breaking into my dad's liquor cabinet on the days when I wanted to numb myself from reality.

"I mean—" I cleared my throat and removed my helmet, setting it on the ground beside me. "The, uh, the sun blinded me, and I guess I didn't see the tree in time."

Ben looked skeptically at me, but then seeming to decide it wasn't his problem to worry about, he shrugged and offered me a hand up.

"Thanks," I said.

I had just gotten to my feet when Cambrielle's four-wheeler rushed toward us. She jumped off the ATV when she was ten feet away and called, "Are you okay, Mack? What happened? Are you hurt?" as she yanked off her helmet and goggles.

"I'm fine," I said before she could get too worked up. "Just decided to make things exciting for a minute."

"You did this on purpose?" Cambrielle's voice raised an octave, her eyes widening. "Do you have a death wish?"

"No."

Not seriously, anyway.

Nothing that lasted more than a few seconds here and there, that is.

"It was an accident."

Sure, I'd been driving way too fast and wasn't exactly in the best frame of mind, but I hadn't purposely tried to off myself today.

Cambrielle stepped closer and reached for my arm to inspect me, like she was looking for a visible sign that I was hurt. "Did you break anything?" she asked, her hands feeling along my arm before moving to the other one. "I saw you flying through the air. There's no way you're not hurt."

She touched my wrist, and I instinctively pulled it away.

"Ouch," I said, noticing the dull throb.

"Is it broken?"

"I don't know." I pulled the sleeve of my riding suit up to look at it. It looked normal. No bones protruding or anything. "I probably just sprained it when I landed or something."

There was the sound of four-wheelers driving on the main trail below, which were probably Nash, Hunter, and Scarlett driving by.

Ben glanced in the direction of the sound, seeming eager to get back to the trail now that it looked like I was going to live.

"You need me for anything?" he asked, looking between Cambrielle and me.

"I'll be fine," I said at the same time Cambrielle said, "You're leaving already?"

Ben looked between the two of us, like he wasn't sure he could go. But then Cambrielle said, "Never mind. I've got this."

"Okay, cool," Ben said.

Before he could leave, Cambrielle said, "Will you at least tell everyone that we'll see them back at the house? I'm pretty sure we're gonna have to send someone out for Mack's ATV, but I'll take him back to the house so he can get some ice and maybe a bandage for his wrist."

Cambrielle was planning to stay with me while her crush rode off into the sunset with everyone else?

That didn't seem very fair.

"Sure," Ben said, lifting one leg over the seat of his four-wheeler to sit down. "I'll tell them what happened."

I touched Cambrielle's arm. "You don't need to stay back. I'll be fine," I said in a lowered voice, not wanting my reckless driving to keep her from spending quality time with Ben. "I can just walk back."

"You're gonna walk back two miles after getting flung off your four-wheeler?" Cambrielle stared at me like she thought I might have hit my head too hard. "Yeah, I don't think so."

I tried to tell her with my eyes and a nod of the head that she should let me walk so she could be alone with Ben.

But she didn't seem to understand my eye signals or head nodding because as Ben started his machine again, she just waved goodbye and then watched him drive back toward the main road.

Once he was out of view, she turned to me again and said, "Let's get you back to my house."

I turned off my four-wheeler's motor which was still miraculously running after everything it had gone through, and then climbed onto the back of Cambrielle's ATV with her.

"You sure you don't want me to drive?" I asked, after sliding up behind her on the seat, not sure exactly where I should place my hands. The last time I'd ridden on the back of a four-wheeler was when I was like nine, before my parents trusted me to drive by myself.

"And have you wreck my four-wheeler, too?" She scoffed. "I don't think so."

"I know you have this whole feminist thing going, but it just feels wrong for me to be back here and you to be up there."

"It feels wrong?" She turned to look back at me. I couldn't see her face through her helmet and goggles, but from the tone in her voice I figured she was probably rolling her eyes at me. Hard.

"Okay, so it just would look weird to have such a masculine guy like myself holding onto a girl who's over a foot shorter than me."

"Well, lucky for you, everyone's already gone, so no one will be around to witness you setting your man card aside for a few minutes."

I'd already humiliated myself enough by wrecking, did she really not want to leave me with any shred of dignity?

She pushed the button to start the vehicle. I knew for a fact that she didn't care about my ego whatsoever.

With a sigh, I tentatively placed my hands on her hips and said, "Fine. Take me back to your castle, Your Highness." And since making jokes was my preferred coping mechanism when put in an uncomfortable situation, I scooted closer and wrapped my arms around her stomach, then added, "Just don't get any ideas about this, okay? I'm only snuggling up to you because I don't want to fall off the back with your crazy driving."

"Says the guy who just drove into a tree."

She put her thumb on the gas, and then we were headed back toward the barn we'd left only ten minutes earlier.

8

MACK

I WAS MORE sore than I expected to feel as I followed Cambrielle up the steps to her house, the muscles in my legs groaning with each motion, and I wondered if I'd be covered in bruises tomorrow.

Cambrielle led me through the sitting room inside the back door and into the dining nook just off the kitchen.

"Have a seat." Cambrielle gestured at the table and chairs where we had eaten breakfast this morning. "I'll be right back with the first-aid kit."

But instead of sitting like she asked, I walked into the kitchen where Marie was busy cooking what smelled like spaghetti and washed my hands in the sink she wasn't using.

"What happened to you?" Marie asked when she looked up from stirring the spaghetti sauce on the large stove. "You fell off your four-wheeler?"

"Crashed into a fallen tree." I winced as the warm water stung the small cuts on my hands. "But don't worry, Dr. Cambrielle is planning to bandage me all up."

Marie shook her head and muttered something under her breath about teens being too reckless these days. Then she said, "You need to be more careful. Your parents don't need a son in the E.R."

"I know," I said, feeling my cheeks heat as I thought about how stupid my reckless driving had been.

But after the phone call with my dad right before the ride, I hadn't exactly been in the most responsible frame of mind.

Didn't really see the point in being safe and responsible when Fate did what she wanted with you, anyway.

I finished washing my hands and went back to the table again. I was just sitting down when Cambrielle returned with a big plastic container with the words *First Aid* written on it.

"You know you're lucky that the only injury you got is a sprained wrist, right?" Cambrielle said as she turned her chair toward me and sat down.

"I know." I sighed, feeling tired all of a sudden.

She studied my face for a moment. "That's all that's hurt, right?"

Physically? Probably.

Emotionally and mentally?

Well, I had a feeling things were only going to be getting worse for the next while.

I cleared my throat and tried to push the thoughts of impending doom away. "I'm sure I'll be really sore tomorrow morning and probably bruised, but I think my wrist got the worst of it."

She nodded and pulled out a new tan elastic bandage from its box. "Why were you driving so fast, anyway?"

I shrugged. "Ava and Carter were going too slow for my taste, so I figured I'd take a shortcut to get ahead and get to the falls first."

"You know not everything needs to be a race, right?" She gestured for me to hold out my arm so she could start wrapping it with the bandage. "Sometimes life is about the journey and not the destination."

"I guess." I gave a non-committal shrug. But since I didn't want to get into a deep philosophical conversation about how sometimes bad things happened to good people to help you grow and all that crap, I decided to tease Cambrielle instead. I said, "But sometimes the destination really is where all the fun happens."

Cambrielle arched a perfectly shaped eyebrow at me. "So you were expecting something fun to happen at the falls tonight?"

"You know the falls is one of my favorite places to have fun," I said.

"But it's too cold to swim in the water."

"True."

"So what were you planning to do at the falls then?"

"Well, I'm surprised it's a mystery after all these weeks of me hinting. But..." I slipped a mischievous smile on my lips. "I was hoping to sneak behind the waterfall before anyone else got there and wait for you in case you got bored with Ben and wanted to finally take me up on that date."

She groaned. "Are you ever gonna let that joke drop? We both know you've never once been serious about that."

I narrowed my eyes, lowered my voice to my most seductive tone, and said, "You can't tell me it wouldn't be fun to try just once."

I glanced down at her full lips for effect, and when I returned my gaze to her bright blue eyes, I imagined I saw a hint of anticipation in them.

Did that mean that me taking her to what was known as Eden Falls' "make-out point" wasn't exactly the worst idea to her?

My stomach swirled with heat as I imagined kissing someone again—kissing Cambrielle.

She was pretty—one of the prettiest girls I'd met, actually. And getting lost in a moment like that would be a nice way to distract my mind from everything that was going on. I never got lost in the moment more than when I was kissing a beautiful girl.

An image of Cambrielle and me kissing in the cave behind the waterfall came to mind, her back pressed against the rock wall with her legs wrapped around my waist as I pinned her there and kissed her until I forgot everything.

It wasn't a bad image, actually.

But then I imagined Carter finding us and punching me in the face for defiling his sister, and all happy feelings were gone.

"Sorry." I shook my head, hoping Cambrielle couldn't read my mind. "I think I hit my head too hard when I crashed. Forget I said any of that. Apparently, I have a problem with taking jokes too far and obviously none of that would ever happen. Especially with your feelings for Ben and everything."

Her gaze seemed to relax, and she nodded. "You don't have a concussion, do you?"

Was I really acting that weird?

"I don't know, are my pupils dilated?" I leaned closer so

she could look at my eyes.

As she inspected my eyes, I decided I really must have hit my head hard because all I could think of was how she had the most beautiful blue eyes with little turquoise flecks that reminded me of the beaches in Hawaii.

How had I never noticed her eyes before?

Or how she smelled like an angel?

I blinked my eyes shut. What was happening to my brain? This was Cambrielle I was thinking about. The girl who made mud pies with me in the backyard when I was eight.

I must be going into shock or something.

The news from my dad combined with my accident must be making me delusional.

But Cambrielle leaned back with a shrug and said, "Your eyes seem normal."

"That's good," I said.

She went back to wrapping the bandage around my hand and wrist, and my skin warmed under her delicate touch. She had nice hands. Her fingernails were painted a light-pink that appeared nice against her tanned skin.

Cambrielle's dad was white like my dad, but her mom had slightly darker features—my mom once mentioned that Mrs. Hastings had some Native American blood in her.

And even though Nash—her only full-blooded sibling— was blond-haired and blue-eyed like their dad, Cambrielle was a perfect mix of both. Smooth, tanned skin closer to Carter's coloring, bright blue eyes like her dad, and brown hair like her mom.

It was always interesting to me how different traits showed up differently in families. I myself looked almost identical to my father aside from being a lot darker and my hair having a much different texture. I had his straight nose, the Aarden family's defined jawline, his long fingers and big hands that helped me handle the basketball on the court.

We both wore size fifteen shoes—which meant that we had to special order those in most of the time. We even had the same long lashes that my mom was always so jealous of.

I'd liked taking after my father, since he was the male parent and what guy wanted to resemble a woman?

But now that my mom was only going to be here a short while longer, it made me wish I had more than just her curly black hair, ears that were slightly pointy on top, and what our friends call our mega-watt smiles.

I wanted more of her in my genes, so I could pass them on to my future children who would never get to meet their grandma.

I drew in a deep breath and tried to focus back on the present moment where my mom was still alive and Cambrielle was simply bandaging my arm.

She wrapped the end of the bandage over the back of my hand and secured it with two silver clips.

And then, since Cambrielle seemed to read me better than anyone else these days, she took my hand between hers and said, "What's really going on, Mack?" She had that look in her eyes that sometimes made me wonder if she could see into my soul. "When you came down before the ride, something was wrong. Is that why you were driving so fast? Did something happen before you came out?"

I looked down at our hands, lifted my pointer finger so my nail brushed against the inside of her wrist, and debated on whether to tell her about my dad's call. But since she'd be finding out soon anyway, I sighed and said, "My dad called me right before the ride."

"He did?" she asked, anxiety in her voice.

I lifted my gaze to hers. "I guess my mom had another seizure. A pretty bad one this time and..." I swallowed the lump forming in my throat. "And they're reconsidering the treatment." My tongue felt heavy with the words. "They're talking about driving back after she's rested so she can live out her time at home."

Even though I'd known about this for an hour—known the end had been drawing near for months—tears still pricked behind my eyes.

I pinched my eyes shut, pushing the tears away before they could fall.

Cambrielle let out a tiny gasp. In a soft voice, she said, "I'm so sorry, Mack."

I nodded and turned my head to the side to look out the window, hoping that if I didn't see the sadness I knew would be in Cambrielle's expression, it would help me keep things together.

I hated crying in front of people. Call it what you want—toxic masculinity, or that I'd been born in a world where guys were told to be tough and not to cry—but I hated getting emotional in front of people.

I was the funny guy at school. The one who always cracked a joke to ease the tension. The one who used the smile my mother had given me to brighten other people's day.

I wasn't the one who broke down and made people feel sorry for me. I saved up my tears for when I was alone in my room so no one would see Mr. Congeniality breaking down.

I knew the facade I tried to put on didn't really fool anyone—that all my friends knew I'd been different lately. But I appreciated that they went along with it. Had fun with me when I needed it and let me take time away when I needed that, too.

Cambrielle slid her hand up my arm in a soothing gesture. "I won't pretend like everything's going to be okay, because I know what's coming is a nightmare. But..." She sighed and squeezed my forearm. "But I'm going to be here for you. My whole family will always be here for you and your dad."

When I met her gaze, her eyes were as watery as mine. And even though I hated that my pain seemed to spread like a virus to everyone around me, I appreciated her words.

Appreciated that she always seemed to know just what I needed to hear.

"Thank you," I said.

We were quiet for a beat as I tried to think of something more to say. But when nothing came to mind, I sighed and said, "I think I'm going to go lie down for a bit. Tell everyone I'll see them later?"

"Of course."

We both stood. Before I could leave, she said, "Can I at least give you a hug?"

"Sure. You know I'll never turn down a hug," I said, opening my arms to her.

She stepped closer and I let my arms go around her back. She was so short that the top of her head only barely reached my chest when her arms wrapped around my waist.

I was a pretty affectionate guy and frequently hugged my friends. But for some reason, Cambrielle and I had never hugged a ton. Probably something to do with the glares Carter gave me anytime he caught me looking at her for more than two seconds.

But it was nice. She felt nice.

She was tiny. Short enough that I was pretty sure she could still shop in the kids' section if she wanted. But she was also soft in a way that was comforting. She'd been skin and bones when she'd come home from the ballet academy in New York a while back—like the stress of being away from her family had kept her from eating a full meal. She'd gotten some meat back on her bones since then and was looking much healthier now. And not only did she look and feel healthier, but she also had those curves that I'd noticed earlier in her bedroom this morning—curves that also felt nice pressed against me.

Really nice.

In fact, it was kind of hard picturing her as the girl who played night games with me in the woods while growing up, or the girl I used to prank, like that time I'd snuck a snake into her bed. Not when she felt like the kind of girl I'd take to the prom or make out with under the bleachers before a basketball game.

Or...

Okay...enough with the make-out-with-Cambrielle fantasies.

How was it possible that I could go from the verge of a breakdown one minute to considering feeling up my best friends' sister the next?

Teenage hormones were weird.

I stepped away before my imagination could get carried away again.

I must have done it too suddenly though, because when she looked up at me, she frowned in confusion.

And since I was in idiot, I said, "Sorry, your hands moved a little too close to my butt."

"They did not!" Her jaw dropped, like she was shocked I would suggest such a thing.

"I know I look a little too good in this jumpsuit of mine." I gestured to the boxy, zip up suit. "But I can't have you getting distracted by me."

"I wasn't trying to touch your butt." She smacked my shoulder.

I couldn't keep a grin from my face because riling Cambrielle up was one of my favorite pastimes.

"It's okay, Cambrielle." I patted her shoulder. "I know it's hard to ignore our crazy chemistry when we're together. But we don't want to make Ben jealous. So I'm going to go upstairs, and you're going to remind yourself of all the reasons why it could never work out between us."

"Maybe we should have your dad check your head after all," she said. "Because I think you're delusional."

But from the way she was fighting back a smile, I knew I hadn't pushed her too far. Which made me happy that I was at least able to end on a lighter note to make up for the past thirty minutes.

I started toward the staircase that would lead to my temporary room. But before heading up, I turned back to Cambrielle who was closing the first-aid kit.

"In all seriousness though, I'm sorry I ruined your afternoon with Ben," I said, feeling bad since I'd known how much she'd been looking forward to it. "I'll find a way to make it up to you."

9

CAMBRIELLE

AFTER PUTTING the first-aid kit back in the closet, I told Regina about Mack's four-wheeler in the woods and asked her to arrange for someone to take care of it. Then I headed upstairs to change out of my dirty riding clothes and into a cute light-green blouse and jeans that I'd bought on a trip to Paris with my mom this summer.

And since I still had a while before everyone returned from their ride, I decided I might as well fix my hair so I could make the most of the time with Ben before he headed back to the school.

I saw Hunter and Scarlett on their four-wheelers through the balcony doors, and a moment later, Elyse, followed by Nash and Ben, came into view. My heart skipped in my chest at the sight of Ben's tall form and broad shoulders, but I told myself not to get nervous because being nervous would not do me any good.

I gave myself one more glance in the mirror and then went down the grand staircase that led to the large entryway of my home. I considered sitting on the couch in the living room to wait for everyone, but since I wasn't sure if they'd be coming in or if Ben would be using the gate at the side of the house to return to his car, I decided to head back down to where everyone was parking their ATVs in the garage.

"How was it?" I asked Elyse when she came out of the garage, running her fingers through her long, brown hair to smooth it out. "Did you have fun?"

"It was so fun." She grinned. "I'm so jealous that you get to do this anytime you want."

"Hey, you can totally ride any time you want to," I said, happy she'd liked the new adventures she was having in Eden Falls.

"Really?" Her golden-brown eyes brightened at the prospect. "Like even tomorrow after school?"

"Even tomorrow after school." I laughed, loving her enthusiasm. "You can ride them every day up until it snows. And then after that, I'm going to teach you all about snow-mobiling."

"Snowmobiling?" Her eyes brightened even more.

"Yes," I said. "Basically, if you want to have fun outside any time of year, we've got you covered."

My parents were firm believers in playing just as hard as they worked, and so they had equipped our estate with everything under the sun to keep us busy building memories together.

Elyse headed inside to wash up and Ben came out of the garage next.

He had a little more dirt and mud on his clothes than the last time I'd seen him, but I was happy to see that he had a smile on his face as he approached.

"You missed a fun ride," he said when he reached me.

"Yeah?" I asked, my chest feeling somewhat heavy with the feeling of missing out. But I tried to push it aside and said, "I'm glad you had fun. And, uh, if you ever want to go out with me again, just let me know."

"Go out with you?" he asked with what I could only interpret as a flirtatious curve on his lips.

"Um, I didn't mean like go out with me...like on a date," I hurried to say, feeling my cheeks flush red hot. "I, um, of course I didn't mean that. I wasn't even really there for the first ride and um..."

"I knew what you meant." He chuckled, seeming to find my flustered ramblings comical. "And that sounds fun. Maybe next time we can even leave Mack behind, so he doesn't try to pull you away again."

"You think he crashed on purpose?" I asked. "Just so we could be alone?"

"Not exactly." Ben shrugged. "But it would kind of go with the theory everyone at school has about you two."

"There's a theory about Mack and me?" I pulled my head back, not having any idea what Ben was talking about.

Ben looked behind us to where the rest of the group was just coming out of the garage and heading up to the house.

He waved me closer to him so we could let everyone pass, and my heart throbbed in my chest as I wondered what he was going to say about this theory I'd never heard of.

Once Ava had dragged Carter around the corner with everyone else and onto the terrace above, I asked, "So what is this theory?"

Ben cleared his throat, a hint of unease in his dark-brown

eyes. "Everyone thinks you two have a secret relationship going on."

"What?" I nearly shouted. I quickly glanced around to make sure no one was coming back. Then in a lowered voice, I said, "People think Mack and I are dating?"

"Well...yeah," Ben said, like it should be obvious. "We all know about how protective Carter is of you, and well, we figured that was why you and Mack never came out with it."

"But we're not dating." I shook my head, feeling shocked by this whole thing. "Like, we're friends and help each other out and stuff...but we are not and have never been like that."

Sure...he had slept in my bed last night, but that was *so* not because we were secretly dating.

Ben narrowed his eyes, as if he thought I was just covering up some huge front Mack and I had been putting on. He said, "Then why did you switch partners with Elyse in class today? You switched papers and ended up with him."

I let my head fall back as I blinked my eyes closed. *Had everyone in the entire class seen that?*

I never knew I was interesting enough for anyone—let alone two of the most popular guys in the school to watch.

I looked back at Ben and said, "Believe me, I didn't want to switch partners today. I just..." I stopped, knowing I couldn't tell Ben the real reason why I had switched because it would embarrass Elyse. So I said, "I get kind of nervous around people I don't know well sometimes, and so Mack seemed like a safer choice."

"A safer choice than me?" Ben furrowed his brow. "Should I be offended or glad that I'm not what you would consider a safe choice?"

"Um, just..." I sighed and tried to think of a way to let him know that I had actually *wanted* to be partnered with him without coming out and saying I'd had a huge crush on him for months. I twisted the ring on my index finger. "Let's just say you kind of make me nervous."

"Because I'm scary?"

"No!" I said. "Of course not."

I was making a mess of this, wasn't I?

And since I knew it was unsafe for me to really say anything else, I simply said, "I didn't switch to be partners with Mack because we have a secret relationship going on. And I didn't give Elyse your name because I *didn't* want to be your partner. I did it for other reasons that I can't tell you."

"So you don't think I'm gross then?"

"Of course not." I couldn't help but laugh a little at Ben thinking that I thought he was gross. "Y-you're the opposite of gross."

"Well, good," he said, a half-smile on his full lips. "For the record, I've never thought you were gross, either."

Really?

I knew he hadn't said he liked me, just that he didn't think I was gross...but my whole body felt light over the fact that Ben had even thought about me in the first place.

Which meant he'd noticed me.

Our eyes caught, and for a moment, I was weightless, my body floating away from the earth and into orbit among the stars with Ben.

He broke eye contact first. After looking down at his black boots and licking his lips, he met my gaze again some-what nervously and said, "Uh, my buddies and I were planning to go to this haunted house on Friday night. Maybe you should come."

Ben was inviting me to hang out with him?

I discreetly pinched the skin just above my ring to make sure I wasn't still floating off in the universe somewhere.

And yep, from the sting in my finger I knew this was real.

Ben Barnett, the hottest guy on the soccer field, was inviting me to hang out with him this weekend.

"That sounds fun," I hurried to say before he could think I'd forgotten how to talk.

"Really?" he asked, the look in his eyes telling me he hadn't fully expected me to accept his invitation.

"Yes," I said. "Halloween is my favorite holiday, and so I'd love to go to the haunted house."

"Cool." Then after a short pause, he added, "We're planning to meet there around eight."

"Eight. Got it." I had to fight to keep my whole face from lighting up with a smile and making me look too eager.

"Y-you can bring your friends too, of course." He gestured at my house where everyone had disappeared into. "But if you hang out with Mack the whole time, consider your secret out."

I scrunched up my nose. "Yeah, that won't be happening."

Ben laughed, a deep sound that made my insides melt a little. "See you at school tomorrow, Cambrielle."

Why did my name sound so good on his lips?

I cleared my throat. "See you then."

And when he walked out the side gate to head toward his car, I could not keep the biggest grin from filling my whole face because Ben freaking Barnett just invited me to spend time with him.

MACK ENDED up taking dinner in his room, so it was just my parents, my brothers, and me eating together today.

Nash helped Marie put the spaghetti and the steamed veggies on the table, and soon we were all sitting around chatting about our days and what we had coming up.

"Your Halloween dance is this weekend, right?" Mom asked as she twirled some pasta onto her fork, using the spoon to keep it in place. "Are you all ready for that?"

"I think so," Carter said after taking a sip of his water. "Ava and I finally decided on our costumes anyway."

"Yeah?" my mom asked. "And what did you decide on?"

"We're going to be a fireman and his Dalmatian." Carter shrugged.

"Oh, that's a cute idea." Mom smiled.

"I guess," Carter said. "I mean, I was really pushing for the sumo wrestling costumes, but apparently, Ava thought I'd look better as a fireman."

I bet she did. I loved Ava—she was spunky and fun, and we actually got along really well. But she was also a little too good at feeding my brother's ego over how hot they both thought he was. So it wouldn't surprise me in the least if Carter's fireman costume included a *very* tight T-shirt to show off the muscles he'd grown since last summer...if she had him even wear a shirt at all.

And before I could picture their costumes in too much detail, I pushed the thoughts away. Because even though all my friends growing up had told me how lucky I was to have such hot brothers, I did not have the same kind of feelings as them since, yeah, gross.

"And we already know Cambrielle wants to keep her costume a secret," Mom said, glancing at me with a twinkle in her eyes since she was the only one who knew what it was. "So I know better than to ask about that. But do you have any other things going on over the next few weeks? Still considering auditioning for the play?"

"I, um..." I looked down and straightened my napkin in my lap. "I'm still thinking about it."

"You're auditioning?" Nash furrowed his brow, like he hadn't heard me mention it before. "For which part? Not Christine, right?"

"And possibly have to kiss you if you get the part of the Phantom?" I laughed. "Yeah, no."

"Good." Nash let out a long breath. "Because that part better go to Elyse. She was made to play Christine."

"Don't worry," I said. "I'm not going to ruin your plans."

Did I think his plan to wait for their romance to blossom on stage instead of just asking her out on a date was a bit ambitious? Yes. Of course. Especially since technically, Christine was supposed to end up with Raoul and not the Phantom.

But Nash seemed to believe that his plan would work, and I knew better than to tell him not to try. Once Nash was set on a path, there was usually no way to convince him to try something else—no matter how unconventional it may be.

And really, I guess it wasn't that much different from my

plan to wait until the Halloween dance to possibly set things in motion with Ben.

But now that he'd invited me to the haunted house, hopefully I wouldn't need that plan anymore.

"You still considering being one of the dancers, honey?" Dad asked, his bright blue eyes showing a hint of concern, like he was worried I might fall back into old habits if I picked up dancing again.

But I nodded and said, "I think I'm going to try at least. I think I can handle it."

"Then I wish you the best of luck," Dad said. "Miss Crawley would be crazy not to cast you."

"Yes, she would," Mom added. And when I saw a little sparkle of pride in my mom's brown eyes, my chest warmed because I liked having my parents' support.

I knew I'd put them through a lot of stress when the pressure of everything at the ballet academy got the better of me my freshman year—what should have been my first and not my last year at the school. And I knew I needed to be careful and always watchful so that I didn't fall back into old habits. But I really had missed dancing so much and didn't want my fears over what might happen keep me from something I loved so much.

After dinner, I finished up an assignment from my AP Biology class. Usually, Mack and I worked on our homework for that class together since we were the only ones in our friend group taking that class and science was more his forte than mine. But Mack still hadn't come downstairs since this afternoon, so I decided to finish up on my own.

Before heading upstairs for the night, I made myself some chamomile tea. I made Mack a cup as well, knowing that the news from his parents would probably only make sleeping more difficult for him tonight. I carefully carried them up the marble staircase to the second floor.

Carter and Nash were just leaving Mack's room and shutting the door behind them when I got there.

"How's he doing?" I asked my brothers in a hushed tone that I hoped Mack wouldn't overhear.

"He's trying to put on a good face, but I think he's really struggling," Carter said with a solemn look in his eyes.

"Did he tell you about the latest with his mom then?" I asked, my gaze darting back and forth between my brothers' faces, which were so similar most people thought they were twins when they found out they were the same age.

"Mack told us they're probably going to come back tomorrow." Nash swallowed. "That they're probably going to be saying goodbye sooner rather than later."

Tears pricked at my eyes at the confirmation of what Mack had hinted at before. And the helpless feeling that flooded my insides made my heart squeeze so hard in my chest, because I knew there was nothing we could do to protect Mack from the pain of losing his mom this early in his life.

His dad could be the best neurosurgeon and be best friends with the seventh richest man in the world with all the possible options for care at their fingertips. And yet, we couldn't fix this.

We couldn't do a single thing to prevent the worst from happening.

Carter's eyes filled with unshed tears as well, and I knew he felt as helpless as I did with how to protect Mack from the future.

"Is that tea for Mack?" Carter wiped the corner of his eye, probably wanting a change of subject. I knew that as hard as this was for all of us, Carter was the only one who actually understood what Mack was facing since he had actually lost his mother. He'd already had to live without her for most of his life.

I watched the steam rising from the mugs. "I thought it might help him sleep at least."

Carter patted my shoulder. "That's very thoughtful of you. I'm sure he'll appreciate it."

"You're not just using it as a cover up to spend more time alone with him, are you?" Nash narrowed his eyes at me. "Because I'm already onto you two, if it is."

"What?" Carter straightened up, suddenly on high alert. "What are you talking about?"

"Nothing," I hurried to say before Nash could say something that was closer to the truth than he knew.

But Nash being Nash and being addicted to drama, he said, "I caught them cuddling on Cambrielle's bed yesterday before dinner."

"Are you serious?" Anger instantly flashed in Carter's eyes when he looked at me. "Is that the truth?"

"Nash is exaggerating," I said quickly before Carter could do something stupid like go and yell at his best friend on the other side of the door. "We were not cuddling. Mack was teasing me, and I was trying to shut him up."

"Oh, so that's what we're calling it these days." Nash waggled his eyebrows suggestively, a smirk on his lips.

And if I wasn't holding two mugs with scalding hot tea right now, I would have smacked him.

Instead, I drew in a calming breath and looked up at

Carter. "Mack was trying to get me to switch rooms with him because he thought my bed was more comfortable, and Nash just came in at the wrong moment."

"You were practically on top of him," Nash said.

"I was not!" I lifted my mug in the air. The crazed feeling I used to get when I was younger whenever I fought with my brothers came over me. "Do you want me to pour this hot tea on your head? Because if you don't start telling the truth, I might just do it."

"Fine." Nash gripped my wrist to protect himself. "So maybe you weren't cuddling. But I just wanted to make sure your crush wasn't coming back, and that Carter and I didn't need to keep a closer eye on you two."

My cheeks immediately burned at his mention of my old crush on Mack.

I could smack him.

I really could.

I glanced at Mack's door to make sure it was still closed. Between clenched teeth, I said, "I don't like him like that anymore. You know I like Ben. Stop saying stupid things."

Nash just laughed. Carter, seemingly over this conversation, rolled his eyes and said, "I'm going to bed. I'll see you in the morning."

"Goodnight," I said.

Once Carter had disappeared down the hall and into his room, I glared at Nash and said, "Why are you such an idiot sometimes?"

"Just watching out for my little sis." He patted the top of my head. "In fact, do you need me to help deliver the tea? Perhaps I can act as a chaperone to make sure no monkey business is happening under Mom and Dad's roof."

"Can you just drop it?" My cheeks flamed hot. "You know we're not like that."

"Okay, fine." Nash lifted his hands in the air. "But remember, I'm just across the hall and can see everything."

"Oh my gosh!"

I was considering setting the mugs on the ground so I could duct tape Nash's mouth shut, but he quickly bent over and planted a brotherly kiss on my cheek. "Love you, sis. Just making sure you know Carter isn't the only brother who cares about you."

I rolled my eyes. "If you really cared about me, you would have shut up about five minutes ago."

"We all show our love in different ways, don't we?"

"I guess."

Nash finally went into his room. After taking a few calming breaths, I knocked on Mack's door.

He opened it a few seconds later, saying, "I was wondering when you two were going to stop fighting."

"You heard all that?" I asked.

He chuckled. "I'm not exactly deaf."

"And you didn't consider coming out and saving me?"

A half-smile lifted his lips. "I was waiting to hear if your crush had changed from Ben and back to me." He winked.

"Ugh," I groaned, blushing for about the thousandth time today. "You boys are the worst sometimes."

"Can't help that I think I'm a much better option than your Ben." Mack smiled widely, showing off his perfect teeth. "But I guess everyone has their thing."

"Just like you have your thing for Ariana Grande."

"Too bad she'll never love me back." He sighed, putting a

hand to his chest dramatically. "Anyway, I'm guessing you wanted to come in?"

"Sure."

He held his hand out for one of the mugs, and after handing him the one with *The Avengers* characters on it, I followed him into his temporary room.

"Thanks for the tea, by the way," Mack said after sitting on the black chair in the corner. "I was thinking about fixing myself a cup, so that was really thoughtful of you."

I sat on the bench at the end of Ian's bed, facing him. "I hoped it might help you sleep better."

I took a sip of my own tea. I didn't exactly love the flavor of it and always had to add a splash of vanilla creamer to make it palatable, but since sleeping through the night had never come as naturally to me as it did to others, I'd turned it into an evening routine.

"Are you feeling any better?" I asked, studying him. He wore a plain white T-shirt and joggers that could pass for pajamas if I didn't know from experience that he usually slept in gym shorts and no shirt.

"Physically?" He arched an eyebrow after taking another sip of his tea. "I think I'll be pretty sore tomorrow." He lifted his arm. "Probably wear this bandage to get some attention over the next few days." He winked.

Yeah, like he ever needed a bandaged wrist to get attention from girls.

"And not physically?" I asked.

"About the same." He set his mug on the nightstand beside him, using one of the coasters from inside the drawer. "I guess you probably know that I told your brothers."

I nodded. "They said you did."

He pulled on the thighs of his pants and adjusted his position. "So I guess everyone is all worried about me now."

"We just care about you," I said. "We just want you to know that we'll be here for you and help you in whatever way you need."

"In whatever way I need?" he asked, something I didn't understand passing across his face.

"Within reason, at least," I hurried to say before he could ask for something crazy.

"Well, if you're offering favors." He rubbed his freshly shaven jawline. "I was just thinking about how much better I sleep in your room."

This again?

"Are you trying to sleep in my bed again?" I asked. "Because I don't know if you heard my brothers out there, but Nash is already suspicious and I'm starting to think that we got *very* lucky no one caught us this morning."

"I know," he said. "You really don't have to." He waved the thought away. "I was mostly joking."

Mostly joking.

Which meant part of him was serious.

I remembered the look in his eyes this afternoon when he told me about his parents and the specialists thinking his mom only had a short time left.

He really did seem to sleep better when he was in my room for some reason.

I couldn't deny him a good night's rest after the news he'd gotten today, could I?

It wasn't like he was going to do anything other than sleep.

So I sighed and said, "If you think it'll help you actually sleep tonight, I can pull out the trundle bed again."

"Really?" he asked, seeming surprised I was actually offering. "But what about your brothers?"

"We'll just have to be quiet," I said. "Which means no more teasing me, okay?"

He sat up straighter and saluted me with his bandaged arm. "Yes, ma'am."

"Okay." I sighed again, hoping I wasn't making a huge mistake. "Just give me a few minutes to get ready and I'll text you when you can come over."

10

MACK

AFTER CAMBRIELLE LEFT MY ROOM, I took a quick shower. I changed into gym shorts because I usually got hot in the night, and joggers would only make me sweat more. I typically slept without a shirt too, but since I would actually be conscious when I walked into Cambrielle's room tonight, I grabbed a white V-neck. I didn't want to make Cambrielle uncomfortable with the sight of my shirtless body like earlier this morning.

I was re-bandaging my wrist when the text from Cambrielle came through my phone.

Cambrielle: **You can come over now. Just lock your bedroom door so no one can go in and find you're missing.**

I brushed my teeth, and then after grabbing my phone charger from Ian's nightstand, I locked the bedroom door and snuck out the balcony to go into Cambrielle's room.

She was just opening the French doors when I made it across and I quickly slipped inside.

I locked the door behind me. When I turned around, I took in Cambrielle's room. The main lights were turned off—only the string lights she had strung across the ceiling were lit, giving a slightly magical ambiance to the room. She'd already pulled out the trundle bed that was usually stored underneath her queen-sized bed.

"Thanks for doing this again," I said as she climbed onto her mattress, slipping her legs under the covers.

"No problem," she said, leaning into the pillows propped up against her white headboard. Her long, brown hair was braided down the side of her head and resting over her shoulder, her makeup from earlier washed away.

I knew some girls were self-conscious of how they looked without makeup on, but Cambrielle was beautiful. I liked the smattering of freckles on her nose and cheeks. Liked that even though we were growing older, she still resembled the girl I'd known ever since my family built our house next door.

I walked around the beds and set my phone to charge on the nightstand opposite from where Cambrielle slept. It was already after ten, so I knew I should probably just go to sleep. But I wanted to put it off for a minute. So I sat on the side of Cambrielle's bed, turned toward her and said, "You never told me if you were able to talk to Ben after bandaging me up."

"Oh," she said in surprise. She cleared her throat. "I talked to him a little."

"And?" I arched an eyebrow when she didn't offer any more information.

"And he invited me to go to the haunted house with him on Friday."

When I saw the excitement in her expression, the slightest twinge of jealousy pricked at me. But I pushed it away because since when was I jealous of Cambrielle hanging out with another guy?

I mean, I'd known all about her obsession with the actor from that *Bridgerton* show she watched and had never once been jealous of him.

"So, is it like a date?" I asked, wondering how it had come about and if Ben had agreed to come over because he'd already been interested in her.

"Oh, no." She shook her head. "At least I don't think so. He said his friends would be there and that all our friends could come too, so it's probably just a friend thing."

Why did that make me feel better?

She liked Ben and wanted him to like her back. Was I a bad friend for being relieved that it wasn't a date?

"Wanna know something funny, though?" she asked.

"What?" I asked, turning to face her a little better.

"You're not going to believe this," she said, a hint of amusement in her bright blue eyes. "But Ben said a bunch of people at school think we're secretly dating."

"Think you and him are dating?" I furrowed my brow, wondering how anyone had come to that conclusion when I was pretty sure they hadn't talked until today.

"Noooo." She stretched out the word like I was missing something. "Not me and him. They think *you* and I are secretly dating."

"Us?" I pointed at her and then back to myself.

"Yeah."

I scrunched up my face. "Why would they think that?"

"I guess because we're friends and do homework together." She shrugged, like she was as confused as I was about the assumptions. "I don't know...he said something about everyone thinking we were sneaking around behind Carter's back because he's so protective."

"What?" I pulled my head back.

"I know!" She laughed. Then, realizing we were supposed to be quiet so her brothers wouldn't find me in her room, she lowered her voice to a whisper and said, "Crazy, right? Me and you actually dating?"

"Not that crazy," I said. "I mean, you did have that crush on me in middle school."

"Yeah, back when I didn't know any better." She laughed quietly.

I didn't know why, but for some reason, Cambrielle laughing over the idea of ever having feelings for me burned a little.

Like, was the thought of dating me laughable to her now?

From the way she was reacting, I guess it was.

I decided to return to the trundle bed below, but I must have made a face before turning away or something because she stopped laughing. She touched my arm and asked, "Did I say something wrong?"

"No." I shook my head, not looking at her. "Of course not." I bent over to pull down the covers on the trundle bed.

But she must have sensed that she had in fact ruffled my feelings because she scooted across her bed and tugged on my bicep to stop me from slipping off her bed. "What did I say?"

"Nothing," I tried to insist, but my voice didn't come out

nearly as believable as I wanted. Instead, I sounded more like a kicked puppy.

I turned back to her and didn't realize how close she'd scooted up behind me until I was looking at her face from only six inches away.

My gaze darted down to her blue eyes that were so big and soft and full of concern that she'd done something wrong.

But really, she hadn't done anything wrong at all, had she?

Just bruised the ego of a guy who apparently thought every girl who'd ever liked him in the past should continue to pine after him until the end of time.

"Are you frustrated Ben thought we were dating?"

"No." I sighed, making my gaze meet hers even though I felt completely awkward with all these weird emotions coursing through me. "Of course not."

Her eyes tightened with confusion. "Then what is it?"

I rolled my bottom lip between my teeth before saying, "I guess I wasn't expecting you to laugh so much over the possibility of us ever dating."

"Oh." She said the word slowly, like she hadn't considered it.

Which of course she hadn't.

We had only ever been friends.

Sure, I'd known about her crush on me in middle school. And yes, I teased Carter all the time about taking her out. But I had never once been serious about following through with that threat.

I'd only ever seen Cambrielle as a friend.

But if I only saw her as a friend, why was my heart

suddenly beating so fast right now? Why was I noticing how smooth her skin was and wondering what it would feel like to run my thumb across her cheek?

Why was I noticing how soft and full her raspberry-colored lips looked and wondering what they would taste like?

Our eyes locked, and I didn't realize I'd been holding my breath until she slowly relaxed her grip on my arm and pulled her hand away.

Did she know I was thinking about kissing her?

And did that thought scare her?

Her eyebrows knitted together. "Us secretly dating is a crazy idea, right?" she asked, her eyes darting between mine, like she was worried I might actually be considering something like it.

And since I wasn't—at least I didn't *think* I was interested in dating Cambrielle—I blinked, gave my foggy head a slight shake, and said, "Of course that would be crazy. We would never do anything like that." I swallowed. "Y-you like Ben and I, uh, I'm still waiting for Ariana Grande to show up on my doorstep."

"Right." She leaned back and narrowed her eyes at me, as if she wasn't sure she believed what I was saying.

"Anyway." I cleared my throat. "It's getting late and we have school in the morning, so I better let you get to bed."

"Good idea." She scooted back toward the left side of the bed where she usually slept while I climbed under the covers on the twin-sized trundle bed below.

She used a remote to switch off the twinkle lights above our heads, and after rustling around on her bed to get comfortable, she said, "Goodnight, Mack. I hope you can get some sleep tonight."

I sighed, letting my body relax into the mattress and pillow. "Goodnight, Cambrielle. Thanks again for letting me stay in here."

11

CAMBRIELLE

I WOKE up early Wednesday morning and Mack had somehow slipped out of my room without me noticing. I showered and got ready, and when I didn't see him downstairs at breakfast, I started to get a little worried.

I brought my savory crepes to the table. "Have you seen Mack yet today?" I asked Carter who was just finishing up breakfast.

"Yeah," he said after swallowing his bite of food. "He said his dad texted him that they'd be back this afternoon. I think he decided to take his stuff home before school so he could just spend time with his parents after school today."

"Oh."

Carter took a sip from his water then picked up his plate to take back to the sink. "I think he's planning to spend more time at home over the next month. Get as much time with his mom as he can."

"Makes sense." I nodded.

"Anyway, I'm gonna head to school. Ava wanted me to help her review for our Stats test before school."

I considered pulling a Nash and asking Carter if his study session was code for a make-out session, but instead of doing that, I just asked, "Things still going well there?"

And the smile that he got on his face at my mention of his new relationship told me everything I needed to know. He was smitten. Happier than he'd been in a long time.

"Things are great. Ava keeps me on my toes, but I wouldn't have it any other way."

"Well, I'm happy for you. You deserve it."

He nodded. "I saw you talking to Ben after the ride yesterday. Is there anything you need to tell your big brother?"

"Just that I actually talked to him," I said. "Nothing you need to get all *protective older brother* about."

"Yeah?"

"Yep." I rubbed my finger along my napkin and in as nonchalant a voice as I could manage I said, "He invited all of us to the haunted house this weekend."

"The one at the old Richardson mansion?" he asked.

"I think so," I said. I hadn't exactly clarified. But that was the only haunted house in Eden Falls that I knew about.

"Well, I'll ask Ava if she feels like getting scared Friday night, so I can keep an eye on you and Ben."

"You do remember that this isn't the eighteenth century and that I really don't need a chaperone whenever I'm with a guy, right?"

"I know." He shot me a half-smile. "But I also have a little insight into the mind of a teenage guy, and so you can't blame me for wanting to keep you safe."

"Does that mean Mack should be chaperoning you and Ava every time you get together?" I raised an eyebrow, letting him know that the double standard wasn't fair.

But he just smiled and said, "I'm a complete gentleman so Mack's services are not needed."

Yeah...sure he was.

I'd caught him and Ava making out once before, and while I was pretty sure they didn't take things any further than kissing when they were alone, it was definitely not the kind of kissing you'd find in a Hallmark movie.

I pushed the image away. I really didn't need to picture my brother kissing one of my friends before I'd gotten my breakfast down.

Carter rinsed his dishes off in the sink, and then after pulling his backpack over one shoulder, he said, "I'll see you at lunch."

"See ya." I waved goodbye, and then focused on finishing my breakfast before I was late for school.

MACK and I had our biology class together later that day. When I asked him if he'd sleepwalked last night, he said that the magical powers of my room had kept him in the bed all night. So I figured that was a win.

He didn't come to any of our group study sessions after school and the next two days were pretty similar. I only saw him in the two classes we had together or during lunch, and I worried that I might have said something wrong the night he'd stayed in my room. He'd been acting slightly off after I'd laughed at the thought of us secretly dating. Then again, it was probably just him worrying about the things going on with his mom, so I tried not to think too much about it.

On Friday night, all our friends were climbing into Carter's truck and Nash's car to head over to the haunted house together when Mack suddenly appeared in the driveway beside Carter's black Ford Raptor, asking, "Got room for one more?"

"Of course," Carter said. He pressed the button to unlock the truck doors. Since Elyse and I were both sitting on opposite ends of the backseat, I scooted toward the middle to make room for Mack.

When he climbed in beside me, I was reminded of how he was basically a giant compared to me because while I had plenty of room for my legs back here, his knees pressed right into Carter's seat in front of him and he had to duck to keep his head from touching the roof.

"Want me to trade you seats?" Ava asked from the passenger seat, noticing how smushed Mack looked next to me.

"Naw, it's fine." Mack waved away her offer as he pulled his seatbelt around him. "I wouldn't dream of coming between you and your boyfriend. Carter might get confused by the family resemblance and try holding my hand."

Everyone laughed because while we'd noticed a few similarities between him and the twins since finding out they were half-siblings, there was about zero chance of anyone ever confusing Mack for his very feminine-looking sisters.

He finished buckling in, his fingers accidentally grazing against my hip in the process, and then we were following the lime-green BMW carrying Nash, Scarlett, and Hunter toward the old Richardson mansion on the other end of town.

"I didn't think you were going to come," I told Mack as we drove through the dark neighborhoods of Eden Falls.

He shrugged, his broad shoulder brushing against mine. "My mom went to bed early tonight, so I decided I might as well distract myself for a couple of hours."

"H-how is she doing?" I asked, not sure I wanted to know the answer in case it was worse than I thought.

He let out a low sigh. "Her headaches have been worse the last couple of days and so she's been sleeping a lot."

"Yeah?" I asked, not really sure what else to say.

"Yeah." His Adam's apple bobbed as he swallowed. "She's been quieter than usual and sometimes she talks to people who aren't in the room."

"Like hallucinations?" I asked, not sure what he meant.

"My dad and the hospice nurse say its normal and that we should just go along with it." He shrugged. "But I don't know, maybe someone is there. Maybe my grandpa Jackson is keeping her company."

His mom's dad had died a couple of years ago.

"Anyway," he said. "Enough about that. I'm hoping to have fun tonight, so don't let me bring you down."

"Then let's have fun tonight," I said. And when Ava turned the conversation to the last time she and Elyse had gone to a haunted house, I leaned my head against Mack's shoulder because it just seemed like the right thing to do for some reason. When he seemed to relax beside me, I slipped my hand into his, giving it a squeeze. He squeezed my hand back.

A few seconds later, I thought about pulling my hand

away because I'd never held Mack's hand before, but when he didn't make a move to let go, I decided to just let it be.

And it was kind of nice. His hand was so much bigger than mine, his fingers long with calluses from the work he'd done in his mom's flower gardens this summer and fall.

They were the hands of a boy who was going through something most people my age wouldn't have to face until they were grown and had families of their own.

The streets passed by in a blur, and I didn't realize we'd made it to the haunted house until Carter turned off his truck. Our eyes caught in the mirror.

His blue-eyed gaze seemed to tighten when he saw my head on his best friend's shoulder, and for a moment, I thought he might be upset.

But instead of saying anything to us, he turned to Ava and said, "Ready to hold me while I scream?"

"Ready," she replied before climbing out.

"I guess we better go find Ben now, shouldn't we?" Mack asked in his deep voice when we were the only people left in the truck.

"Oh, yes. Of course." I sat up straighter and let go of his hand, remembering why we were here in the first place.

Mack opened the door and I climbed out after him. After shutting the truck door and gazing around the parking lot for a moment, I saw one of Ben's friends walking toward a group of guys just leaving the ticket counter and getting in the long line that led into the entrance of the 150-year-old Victorian mansion that had always creeped me out even when it wasn't Halloween.

The home was three stories tall, with a big turret on the north corner where it had been rumored that Mr.

Richardson and his wife had been murdered shortly after it was built. Neighbors had allegedly reported to have seen their ghosts through the windows whenever there was a full moon.

My dad had told me all those stories were made up and that Mr. Richardson's wife had actually died during childbirth. That Mr. Richardson had simply moved away from the house afterward because he believed the house to be cursed. But the house had given me the creeps ever since I heard the story in first grade, and I was pretty sure I had seen something through the windows when I'd driven down this street with my mom and Ian a few years ago.

The full moon wasn't expected until next week though, so hopefully, the only ghosts I'd be seeing inside tonight would be wearing costumes.

I scanned the crowd for Ben and soon found his tall frame among a group of familiar senior guys from school.

"We should hurry and get our tickets, so we can get in line." I pointed to the small circle of guys from school, my stomach fluttering at the thought of approaching Ben. We'd said hi in the halls at school the past couple of days, so the four-wheeler ride had helped him acknowledge my existence at least. But I wasn't exactly sure how to let him know I was here.

Should I go stand by him, so he'd see that I'd come? Or just get in line with my friends and hope he'd notice me?

We hadn't exactly touched base after the initial invitation, so it was completely possible that he'd forgotten even mentioning it to me.

And suddenly, I wasn't completely sure I hadn't imagined our entire conversation.

"Go get in line by Ben." Mack nudged me with his elbow, as if reading my thoughts. "I'll get your ticket."

"Get in line by myself?" My eyes widened and my heart jumped to my throat. "With all his friends?"

"Take Elyse or Scarlett." Mack shrugged.

A woman in her mid-thirties with two elementary-aged kids got in line behind Ben's group. He'd never see me if the line behind him kept getting bigger.

So, deciding to use Mack's idea, I slipped between Elyse and Scarlett and said, "Come get in line with me. Ben will never see us if we wait."

"But we need to get tickets first," Elyse said, pointing to the ticket counter.

"You got theirs, too?" I called to Mack.

When he nodded, I turned back to them and said, "Mack's taking care of it."

We trudged up the grassy hill and made it to the line before anyone else could separate us too much from Ben's group.

Before I even needed to figure out how to get Ben's attention, one of his friends looked our way. Casey Elliot, who had the reputation for being a bad boy, called, "Are you stalking us, Caldwell?" to Scarlett.

"Of course," Scarlett called back. "I heard you'd be here, so I wanted to see you scream when the killer clown popped out."

Their back-and-forth must have gotten Ben's attention because he looked back at us in that moment. And when his eyes caught mine, a pleased smile slipped onto his lips.

Stay cool. Act cool. Now is not the time to freak out over the fact that the boy you've been obsessed with for months saw you and smiled.

But my nervous system was not getting my "act cool" memo because suddenly, I was so jittery with excitement that when I tried to smile back, the muscles in my mouth shook.

"Ben's coming our way," Elyse whispered quietly beside my ear.

And sure enough, he was saying something to his friends and then walking around the mother and her kids to join us.

As I watched his tall, handsome form approach, I made myself take a deep breath. Acting like an idiot was something I could so not afford to do right now.

I felt him step up behind me. "Hey Cambrielle," he said. "Looks like you made it."

Okay, it's officially go-time, I told myself.

I turned around to face him and slipped my most confident smile on my lips. "Yeah, who can resist a haunted house this time of year?"

"I see you brought your friends." He glanced at Elyse and Scarlett behind me, his lip quirking up slightly as he took them in. "Is it just you three?"

"No." I looked down the grassy lawn to where the boys and Ava were just finishing up buying the tickets. "Everyone is down there." I pointed. "We just wanted to save a good spot in line."

"Ah, cool." Ben's eyes narrowed, like he was trying to make out the faces of my friends and brothers below. Then he turned back to me with a half-smile on his lips and said, "Looks like your buddy Mack is here, too."

"Yeah, he decided to join us at the last minute."

"You know, that isn't exactly helping convince anyone that you don't have a secret relationship going on." Ben winked.

"What?" I felt the blood drain from my cheeks. "We're just friends."

Had he somehow seen Mack and me in the back of Carter's truck?

I'd only held Mack's hand because it seemed right at the time, but had Ben somehow noticed how close we'd been sitting and thought there was more to it than there really was?

But then Ben laughed and playfully touched my shoulder. "I'm just teasing you. I was watching you two in class this week, and even though you seem close, I'm taking you on your word that there's nothing going on."

He'd been watching Mack and me during class?

Should I be flattered?

Or self-conscious?

The rest of our friends joined us before I could decide. Mack handed Elyse, Scarlett, and me our tickets.

"Here, let me pay you back," Elyse told Mack, pulling out her wallet.

But he just waved her away and said, "I got it. The money is from Dad, anyway."

"Oh, okay. Thank you," Elyse said. And from the somewhat surprised expression on her face, I realized this was probably one of the first times Mack had referred to his dad as her dad, too.

Mack went to stand by Hunter and Nash who were at the back of the group behind Carter and Ava.

And seeing that everyone was here now, Ben suggested

that the family between our two groups of friends move ahead of us so that we could all be together in one big group.

The line slowly inched forward as small groups of haunted-house goers handed their tickets over and went through the front door. Soon we were on the large front porch, getting ready to go inside.

"Wanna be my buddy?" Ben offered when it was our turn. "That way we can keep each other from getting kidnapped by Mr. Richardson's ghost."

"S-sure," I stuttered, caught off guard by his offer. "That would be great."

12

MACK

"DO you think we should be worried about Cambrielle?" I asked Carter and Ava. We were sitting at a picnic table behind the Richardson mansion and had been waiting for her and Ben to show.

"Just give her another minute, and if they don't show we'll send out the search party," Carter said, not nearly as concerned about his sister's well-being as I thought he should be.

Wasn't he the one who was usually bent out of shape anytime a guy so much as hinted at taking his sister out?

But then again, he and Ava were currently cuddled up together on the bench beside me, so of course he wasn't worried about anything.

I looked back at the mansion's back door where we'd exited about ten minutes ago.

Had they gotten lost in there? It was a big house with about fifteen different rooms.

I'd kept a close eye on Cambrielle and Ben for most of

our walk through, since her brothers had been too busy flirting with Ava and Elyse to notice the way Ben had slipped his arm around her waist and was getting much too friendly with her for my liking.

They'd only just talked for the first time this week. Was it too much to ask that Ben hold off on the PDA for a while?

I mean, sure, his arm had only been around her waist, but her waist was very close to her butt. With the booty jeans she was wearing tonight, I knew all too well how tempting it would be for him to just casually slip his hand into her back pocket.

I pushed the image away. I didn't need to imagine Ben getting all touchy-feely with the girl whom I'd considered my honorary sister for over a decade.

I scanned the windows on the second floor, wondering which room I'd last seen them in. I'd been with them when we walked into the room with the volunteers dressed up as Dr. Frankenstein and his monster, but then Frankenstein's Bride had jumped out of a closet with a chainsaw and the whole room had turned into chaos.

I'd assumed we were close to the end and that we'd all just catch up when we got outside, but what if something had happened to them?

Ben wouldn't take advantage of Cambrielle, would he?

He didn't necessarily seem like a creep or anything, but you never knew. Serial killers were usually able to commit multiple crimes because of how friendly and charming they came off.

Cambrielle was tiny compared to Ben. If he did have dark motives, she'd be no match for his strength and size.

My leg bounced as I looked at the time on my watch. I

was pretty sure we'd come out just before nine and it was already nine-thirteen.

Had Frankenstein's Bride offed them with the chainsaw?

I was just about to call Cambrielle's phone when she suddenly appeared at the exit. But instead of walking to where our group was waiting for her, she bolted to the side of the house and started running down the hill.

What the heck?

I jumped up from my seat and chased after her. "Cambrielle!" I called, jogging down the path that led down the side of the house. "Cambrielle, wait!"

Either she didn't hear me or she was ignoring me, but she didn't stop. She just kept running down the grass lawn toward the road.

Had she gotten scared by something in the house and was just trying to put distance between herself and whatever monsters she'd come across?

But if she was running for her life, why wasn't Ben chasing after her? He'd seemed to enjoy comforting her every time she screamed when I was behind them—eager to put his arm around her and take the opportunity to pull her close.

Why wasn't he with her now?

She slowed her run into a walk when she hit the sidewalk, but instead of stopping or heading to Carter's truck like I expected, she headed toward the park next door.

"Cambrielle, wait," I said, jogging the last few steps to reach her. "What's going on?"

"I just need to get away from there," she said, her short legs speed-walking as fast as they could down the path that led toward the park's playground area, the sidewalk lit by streetlamps and the moon.

"Did you get scared or something?" I asked. "Because it's all pretend. None of that was real back there and you're safe."

"I'm not scared." She sighed. "I just..." She lifted her hands in the air. "I just need to disappear right now."

"Why do you need to disappear?" I frowned, so confused about what was going on.

"It's too embarrassing." She shook her head. "I just need to never see Ben again."

She couldn't see Ben again?

Had he done something to her?

"Did Ben hurt you?" I asked as images of Ben putting his hands places where they didn't belong flitted through my mind.

"No." She shook her head again and glanced up at me. "He didn't hurt me."

"Then what's going on?" I asked, frustration building inside my chest at her vague replies. "Because if I need to go beat Ben up for you right now, I'll do it."

"No. Don't do that." Surprise filled her expression. "You definitely don't need to do that."

"Then why can't you see Ben again?"

"I really don't want to talk about it." She glanced back the way we'd come and shuddered. "It's too embarrassing."

"Did he violate you?" I gripped her arm, making her stop so I could figure this out without having to chase her down. "Did he do something inappropriate?"

"No. Not really." She started pacing back and forth on the grass. "I don't know. He just..."

"Did he touch you?" I looked her over carefully. She didn't seem any different than she had earlier—her hair wasn't messed up. Her clothes were still intact. "Should I call the police? Do Carter, Hunter, and Nash need to hold him there so the cops can take care of him?"

"Of course not!" she said, seeming to realize that by not saying what was going on, she was making me jump to the worst-case scenario. She stopped her pacing and looked at me. "He tried to kiss me and I..." She covered her face with her hands. "Oh, man, it's too humiliating."

I flexed my hands into fists at my sides, wondering who I needed to punch.

She continued, "I've never really kissed anyone before—like nothing bedsides Spin the Bottle—and so when he stuck his tongue in my mouth, I got all grossed out and..." She dropped her head, ashamed. "And I wiped off my tongue, and then wiped my hand on his shirt."

"What?" I asked, not understanding what she was talking about.

"Like this." She licked her hand and wiped it on my shirt.

It took me a minute to even understand what she was doing, and when it clicked, I still wasn't sure I understood her at all.

"So let me get this right." I furrowed my brow. "You're saying that Ben tried to French kiss you and you were so surprised and grossed out by it that as soon as you felt his tongue, you immediately licked your hand and wiped it on his shirt...like you were trying to wipe off his germs?"

"Yes!" She groaned, staring down at her designer boots.

And I knew theoretically that this would be a really bad

time to laugh, but as I imagined Cambrielle doing that to Ben and then pictured how shocked he must have been, I couldn't keep from chuckling.

"I knew I shouldn't have told you," she said.

"Sorry," I said, bending over as I tried to stop laughing. "I just wasn't expecting that."

"Yeah, neither was Ben."

And when she said that, I couldn't keep another round of giggles from bursting out of me.

She turned on her heel and started walking away. "I'm never going to live this down."

"Stop trying to run away." I chased after her and tugged on her arm to stop her before she could climb up the ladder that led to the top level of the playground equipment. "I'm sure it will be fine."

"He's going to tell everyone."

"Maybe not," I said. "I mean, he's probably still here. You could go find him again and ask for a re-do."

"He's not going to want a re-do," she said, glaring at me like I was an idiot for suggesting such a thing. "And even if he didn't run when he saw me, who's to say I wouldn't just do the same thing again?"

"You won't." I took both of her shoulders in my hands and drew in a deep breath, hoping she'd follow suit so she could calm down and realize this wasn't the end of the world.

She took a few breaths with me, and for a second, I thought it was working. But then she squeezed her eyes shut, leaned her head back, and said, "This is a nightmare." She straightened and met my gaze. "The hottest guy at school just kissed me and I basically gagged over it."

"I don't know if I'd say he's the hottest guy at school," I said, unable to let her remark go without comment.

"This is not the time to get into a debate about how you think you're hotter than Ben." She glared at me. "I'm seriously going to have to go home and convince my parents to let me do homeschool."

"You're going to let one embarrassing moment keep you from attending school?" I asked. "Come on, I embarrass myself in front of people all the time. It's not the end of the world."

"You didn't see Ben's face." She looked at me seriously. "He one-hundred-percent thinks I'm crazy."

"So just go back and explain what happened and ask for that re-do."

"Sorry, but I can't face him again." She shook her head. "It was too horrifying."

"So you're just going to skip out on the rest of your junior year? What about the Halloween dance tomorrow?" I asked, knowing how much she'd been looking forward to it. "You've been planning to surprise everyone with your costume, haven't you? Are you really going to miss out on all the fun things in high school just because of a bad kiss?"

At my mention of the Halloween dance, something sparked in Cambrielle's eyes. Then she whispered, "That's it. I can still go to the Halloween dance." Her whole countenance brightened, and before I knew it, she was hugging me and saying, "You're a genius, Mack. Thank you!"

13

CAMBRIELLE

"SO, um, how exactly am I a genius?" Mack asked when I pulled away from my impromptu hug.

"You just reminded me about my plans for the dance tomorrow and, um..." I tucked some hair behind my ear. "And I think everything might be okay."

I'd originally planned to use my Kelana costume to be brave and talk to Ben at the party. But things had changed a little since I'd made those original plans—I'd actually talked to Ben a couple of times and gotten on his radar.

But sadly for me, things were not any better than they'd been before I'd gotten up the nerve to talk to him.

In fact, they were worse. So much worse because he knew exactly who I was, and at my first chance to really make something happen, I'd blown it.

Blown it to smithereens, as my grandpa Hastings would say.

When Ben had first pulled me into a storage closet on the second floor, my heart had been beating so fast because I could feel something was going to happen. And when he told me he'd had a crush on me for a while and had just been too nervous to talk to me, my heart had nearly leapt out of my chest because I couldn't believe that Ben actually liked me back.

I hadn't expected him to kiss me, since we were in a creepy closet standing next to a fake corpse—not my idea of a romantic atmosphere. But when he slipped his hand to the nape of my neck and slowly bent closer to kiss me, I tried to ignore our surroundings and focus on what Ben was doing.

I'd managed to stay in the moment and tried to kiss him back in the way I'd seen people kiss in the movies, but that was the funny thing with movies. You didn't always see everything that went on, the camera lens only caught so much. And so when he slipped his tongue inside my mouth, I'd been so surprised by it that I'd done what I always do when something gross gets in my mouth. I completely ruined everything.

I could still see the look on his face when I wiped my hand off on him. His shocked eyes. The look of horror.

The look that said that on a scale from one to ten, Ben thought that I was a level twenty-five crazy.

And when I'd run out of the room without saying anything, he hadn't even tried to follow.

He was probably happy to see me go.

But maybe all hope wasn't lost quite yet. I might be able to salvage this.

Sure, Ben was likely to run the other way if he saw me coming toward him. But he wouldn't run from someone he didn't recognize. He wouldn't run from a faerie queen he'd never seen before, would he?

And if I could somehow kiss him as Kelana—and do a much better job of it tomorrow night—I could then reveal my true identity and say, "Ta-da, it's me, Cambrielle. I didn't mess it up this time, right?"

And then he would know that what happened tonight was just a really unfortunate mistake and he could give me another chance.

It would work, right?

If he really had liked me for a while like he'd said, he'd be open to giving me another shot, wouldn't he?

My chest lightened, and I started to feel a little better as I thought about how I might save everything tomorrow night... until I remember that I had, like, zero experience kissing guys.

How was I supposed to convince him that things were all better when I didn't know what the heck I was doing?

Mack's phone buzzed in his pocket, bringing me back to the present. And while he was looking at the message that had come through, the craziest idea popped into my head.

"Carter just texted to see if you're okay," Mack said, swiping up on his phone to unlock it. "I'll tell him we're on our way back."

"Wait, stop." I grabbed his wrist before he could respond to Carter's text.

"Why?" Mack frowned, a line forming between his dark eyebrows.

"I need you to help me with something first."

"You do?" The confused look on his face deepened.

Before I could talk myself out of asking him, I said, "So you know how you said you'd make things up to me after I took you home from the four-wheeler ride and missed out on time with Ben?"

"Yeah?"

"Well, I think I figured out what you can do."

A look of intrigue filled his expression. "I'm listening."

I glanced around the dimly lit park to make sure no one was around and said, "Just come over to the gazebo with me first."

I wanted a little more privacy from the cars driving past for what I was about to ask him to do.

Then I grabbed his hand and pulled him toward the wood gazebo that could use a new paint job.

"What's going on?" he asked as I pulled him behind me.

"Just a minute," I said. "I'll tell you when we get there."

We walked up the small, grassy hill that the gazebo was built on, and then once we stepped onto the wooden planked floor, I let go of his hand and turned to face him. In a voice that was slightly out of breath, I said, "I need you to kiss me."

"What?" He took a step back, obviously not expecting me to say that.

So I drew in a deep breath and said, "I was just thinking about everything, and I want to try to make a re-do happen with Ben tomorrow at the Halloween dance like you suggested."

"I didn't say anything about the Hallo—"

"Yes, you did," I cut him off. "And if I'm going to make this re-do happen, I need to know what I'm doing. So I need to practice first."

"And you want to practice with me?"

"Yes."

"Why me?"

"I don't know." I shrugged. "You're here and I'm desperate?" Did I need more of a reason than that?

Mack's jaw dropped. "Should I be offended that you'd only kiss me out of desperation?"

"That's not what I meant," I hurried to say, suddenly feeling nervous.

"Then what did you mean?"

"I don't know." I lifted my hands in the air. "I guess I figured that since we're kind of friends, you might be willing to help me out with this."

"*Ooooh*," he said, drawing out the word. "So this is what friends do?"

"Sometimes." I scrunched up my face. "I mean, out of all my friends, you probably have the most experience. So why not ask the pro?" Mack liked having his ego stroked, so I hoped the last part might help.

The smile I'd hoped he'd get at my flattery lifted his cheeks. "Oh, you think I'm a pro?" He brushed off his shoulders like he was proud.

"Well, I mean, I can't really verify that statement unless you actually help me out," I said, still not believing I was even saying any of this.

Since when did I ask Mack to kiss me?

Since I completely humiliated myself with my last kiss, apparently.

Mack seemed to study me for a moment, his dark-brown eyes narrowing as if he wasn't sure I'd actually be up for a practice kiss with him.

And under normal circumstances, I wouldn't dream of asking him to do something like this. He'd always been

Carter's and Nash's friend first—on a slightly different level from me that made him seem untouchable.

But we'd become closer the past several weeks. He'd opened up to me in ways he hadn't opened up to the rest of our friends, and so he seemed like the right person to help me through this.

He wouldn't judge me if I was really bad at kissing.

He'd be patient and make me feel safe.

Yes, he might have laughed when I told him what I'd done to Ben's shirt, but he wouldn't laugh at me for this. Because under his fun and outgoing exterior, there was a deep-feeling guy underneath.

A guy who would help out a friend without judgement.

And because of all those things, and because I really was desperate and had apparently left my pride back at the haunted house, I pushed my bottom lip into a pout and said, "Please, Mack. I really like him, and I don't want three stupid seconds to have ruined everything."

Mack must have understood that I was in fact desperate for him to save me because after a beat, he nodded slowly and said, "So you want me to French kiss you? Is that what you're asking me to do?"

"I think so," I said. "I mean, I guess? Like, that's what I failed at fifteen minutes ago."

"And you're not going to bite my tongue off?" He arched an eyebrow like he thought it was a real possibility.

"I'll be expecting it this time, so while I can't make any promises, I'll definitely try my best not to."

"How reassuring."

"Please," I whispered, starting to feel deflated. "This is already humiliating enough."

"Okay, fine," he said. "But just so you know, I'm not exactly the 'shove my tongue in a girl's mouth from the get-go' kind of kisser. There's an art to this so...it might take a bit to work up to it."

"Okay." I swallowed. "Just, um, just pretend we're, I don't know, at the falls and that you're finally kissing me there like you've been teasing Carter about all this time."

"Okay," he said, letting out a low breath.

We looked at each other for a few seconds, and for the first time, I wondered if the thought of kissing me made him nervous, too.

"Should we just, um, go for it then?" he asked after a long moment, taking a slight step closer.

"Yeah."

After another awkward pause where he seemed to look for any signs that I wanted to back out, he took another step closer and whispered, "Just don't smack me."

I knew he was just trying to lighten the moment, but I couldn't laugh right now because my whole body pulsed with nerves. Even though I liked Ben and was doing this for a re-do with Ben, there had been a time when I'd dreamed about doing this very thing with Mack.

While I knew this practice kiss meant nothing to Mack, I really didn't want to be bad at this with him, too.

He came even closer until we were toe to toe. After searching my eyes again for a sign that I wanted to run, he gently cupped my face in his hands and guided my lips to his.

The touch of his lips against mine surprised me at first—not because I hadn't been expecting them, but because I hadn't expected them to feel so soft when they slowly grazed against mine. And when he coaxed my mouth to move in rhythm with his, I was surprised by the butterflies that swarmed low in my belly and the heat that spread from the center of my body and out to my fingers and toes.

I didn't really know what I was doing, since the few kisses I'd had before had only lasted a few seconds, but Mack didn't seem to mind. He didn't seem like he was in a hurry to get this lesson over with. Instead, he slowly slid his fingers to the nape of my neck, curling them into my hair and whispering, "Is this what you wanted me to do?"

And even though we hadn't gotten to the part where he was supposed to deepen the kiss and teach me how to respond, I found myself nodding and saying, "Yes. This is perfect."

Because it was.

It actually felt really nice.

Better than I'd expected a kiss to feel from someone I didn't currently have a crush on—so much better than my train wreck of a kiss with Ben.

"Am I doing okay?" I whispered back, wanting to make sure that I was responding correctly. If I was going to try this tomorrow with Ben, I really wanted to make sure the whole experience was better.

I felt Mack's lips curl up into a half-smile against mine before he nodded and said, "You're doing just fine, Cambrielle."

"That's good." I sighed.

We kissed like that for a while, settling into an easy rhythm. And it felt nice. But after another minute, I started to wonder if Mack had forgotten the purpose of this practice kiss because so far, he was keeping his tongue a safe distance from mine.

He'd said something about not being the kind of guy to shove his tongue down a girl's throat, which was probably how I actually preferred things myself. Else I wouldn't have reacted the way I had with Ben. But since the purpose of this was to prepare me for my next kiss with Ben, I really did need to explore that side of kissing, didn't I?

Otherwise this kiss would be for nothing.

"You're distracted," Mack said, pulling away. "Is something wrong? Are my kissing skills actually not on a pro level like you said and you want me to stop?"

"No, they're fine," I said. But when it looked like I'd offended him, I hurried to add, "They're good. Um...yeah, I'm not complaining about your skills. It's just that, I thought you were going to teach me to French kiss, and I don't know I..." I let my voice drift off as I shrugged.

"You just want to get it over with?"

"Yeah." I let out a shaky breath, searching his brown eyes. "I guess that's what's going on."

He chuckled. "Are you expecting to hate it then?"

"Well, kind of." I shrugged. "I mean, the last time someone French kissed me it didn't exactly end well."

"Which is why I was trying to work my way into it," Mack said. "Give us time to get used to each other before I take you there." He narrowed his eyes at me again. "But we can stop if you want. I don't want to do this if it's torture for you the whole time."

I didn't know exactly what it was, but there was something behind his words that I hadn't expected.

Was it possible Mack was interpreting my impatience to mean that I thought the whole kiss had been a chore?

Because it hadn't been.

It had been nice. In fact, it probably would have swept me off my feet if the whole purpose was just to kiss without another goal in mind.

But that was the problem I had sometimes. I sometimes focused so much on the end result that I didn't really let myself just get lost and enjoy all the moments that led up to it. I didn't always enjoy the journey.

"Should we just head back then?" Mack asked. "Everyone's probably waiting for us."

He looked over his shoulder at the direction of the mansion.

He wanted to leave?

Disappointment filled my chest as I felt this opportunity slipping through my fingers.

When he started walking back to Carter's truck, I pulled on his hand to stop him and said, "Can we just try one more time? I promise I'll be a better student."

"We can try once more." He met my gaze again. "But if it's a chore, or if it makes you uncomfortable, I'll stop. It might hurt my ego a little if I find out that my kissing skills don't have a universal appeal, but I'll try not to cry about it if you absolutely hate it."

Okay, he was totally interpreting the last few minutes wrong because I had most definitely not hated kissing him. I'd just been focused on wanting one particular aspect too much.

But since I didn't want his head to get too big over the

fact that kissing him was the only time I'd ever actually enjoyed a kiss, I just said, "I'll let you know if that happens."

"Okay." He looked behind me. "Let's just fix one thing."

He gently walked me backwards, and before I knew what was happening, he was lifting me up and setting me on the rail that went around the gazebo, with my feet dangling in the air.

"This will make it easier on my back, shorty," he said with a smirk, placing my hands on his shoulders so I had something to hold on to.

Then he stepped between my knees, wrapped one arm behind my waist for extra support, and then lifting his other hand to trace a thumb along my jawline, he whispered, "Try not to think too much." His breath was warm against my face. "Just feel." And then he was dipping his head down and kissing me. His lips were tender and slow against mine.

And instead of overthinking and anticipating what I thought might be coming, I tried to empty my mind of all thoughts and expectations and just let myself feel.

To feel the way his thumb on my cheek sparked my skin to life.

To let myself feel his strong shoulders under my hands, let one hand explore its way down his shirt and along his chest, reveling in its muscular definition. Let the other hand travel up the back of his neck to feel the coarseness of his short, curly hair.

I'd secretly always wanted a reason to touch his hair like this, to feel the tight, black curls on the top of his head against my fingertips. It was so different from my own long hair, and I loved it. Loved that this moment allowed for this familiarity that we didn't usually share with each other.

I moved my hand back down and rubbed my fingers along the back of his head where his hair was buzzed so short it was mostly skin.

"That feels nice," he mumbled against my lips when my nails grazed against the nape of his neck.

And when I did it again, he moaned lowly into my lips.

Shivers of pleasure raced down my spine.

I'd never made a guy make a sound like that before. Never had a guy make my lower belly swirl with heat the way Mack and his slow kisses were making me feel.

"Still doing okay?" Mack asked in a husky voice, like he worried my trembling meant something was wrong.

But I shook my head and whispered, "So far, so good."

As in, this kiss was so good that I really didn't mind anymore if it took forever for him to finish the lesson.

His hand moved up my back and along the sides of my ribcage, and I liked that even though there was a layer of fabric between his skin and mine, I could still feel the warmth of his hand on me.

I'd danced *pas de deux* several times during my year at the ballet academy and so I should have been used to having a guy's hands touching my sides for lifts, but for some reason, it felt different with Mack.

Warmer.

Nicer.

More intimate.

And I liked it. Liked the heady sensations coursing through me and making me feel like I was drifting away to the clouds.

He smoothed his hands against my back, pressing his palms and fingers firmly against me. And since he was letting his hands wander, I decided to do a little more exploring of my own.

I let my hands move across the tightly corded muscles in his shoulders and down his chest before sliding them under his jacket to feel the muscled contours of his back.

He was tall and had the body of a basketball player, but unlike a lot of guys my age, he had also filled out in the past year. He was no longer the lanky teenager with hunched-over shoulders who was still trying to get used to his sudden growth spurt. Instead, he looked more like a man than a boy.

His fingers slid into my hair, and just as I was pulling myself closer to him to erase all space between us, his tongue slid ever so lightly against my lips.

It was so light that I wasn't sure it had even happened, but then he did it again, and my stomach contracted and all I could think was, *I like that.*

I never thought I'd want something like that, but mmm, I really did like it.

He pulled away briefly, checking me for my reaction, and when I pulled him closer again, he chuckled lightly, like he was enjoying the fact that I wanted more.

His tongue flicked against mine again, and even though I'd never done this before, my instincts took over—when he deepened the kiss further, I joined him in the give-and-take. Our tongues danced together, and my entire body flooded with an exhilarating heat that I'd never experienced before.

As I got lost in the moment and allowed myself to feel everything, to feel what it was like to be in Mack's arms and experience this moment that was more intimate than anything I'd ever shared with anyone before, I couldn't help but wonder how it was possible that I'd been so afraid of this earlier.

Because now that I was experiencing this kind of kiss with Mack, all I could think of was that I wanted more.

More time alone with him to practice. More time to feel all the feelings this moment was causing to swirl inside of me.

More of his hands in my hair and his lips pressing hot kisses down my neck.

More moments where I was gasping for air because I didn't want to stop kissing him long enough to draw in a full breath.

I wrapped my legs around his waist and was just pressing myself closer when Mack suddenly pulled away from the kiss, as if he only just now realized that he'd been making out with me.

He stumbled back and his eyes were slightly dazed when he said, "Okay, so um, I hope that helps you know what to do tomorrow with Ben."

Ben.

That's right. I'm kissing Mack like this because I wanted to kiss Ben.

"Yeah." I tucked some hair behind my ear. "I-I think that will help," I said, not really knowing what else to say since I'd completely forgotten that we'd only been doing this because I liked Ben.

He let out a long breath. "Good."

We stared at each other for a long moment. And then, seeming to realize something, Mack said, "Here, let me help you get down from there."

And when he put his hands around my waist to lower

me from the railing, I was not expecting the sudden surge of electricity that came with his touch.

Or the way I wanted to stay close to him forever when he set me on my feet.

"T-thanks for your help," I said, looking up at him, wondering if he was feeling any of the same sparks I had flickering through my body.

"No problem." He cleared his throat, and when our gazes caught, I imagined I saw something like wonder reflected in Mack's eyes.

Like he, too, was trying to process what had passed between us.

Was it possible that he'd also momentarily forgotten it was just a kissing *lesson*?

That he'd forgotten who we actually were to each other —just friends who most definitely should not be thinking of excuses to have another practice kiss before tomorrow night?

I shook those thoughts away. Just because "practice makes perfect" was a saying I'd heard on repeat during my days at the ballet academy, it didn't mean I needed to apply it here as well.

Because asking Mack to give me a second kissing lesson would be weird, right?

"Anyway." He clasped his hands together. "We better get back to everyone. They're probably worried Mr. Richardson's ghost found us out here."

"Yes," I said. "That's probably a good idea."

I just hoped when we walked up to everyone that it wouldn't be obvious what had just happened. Because if my brothers had any idea that I'd just made out with Mack, they'd never let us out of their sight again.

14

MACK

WHAT JUST HAPPENED? I wondered as Cambrielle and I walked back to Carter's truck.

Had I seriously just made out with Cambrielle?

Did that really just happen?

When she asked me to help her practice kissing so she could have her re-do with Ben, I'd thought she was joking at first. And then when I found out she was serious, I'd decided that even though it might be completely awkward, I did owe her. She'd helped me with my stuff a lot this school year, so it was only fair that I help her out in her time of need.

Kissing my best friends' little sister wasn't exactly something I'd ever thought I'd end up doing, but it seemed harmless enough since it wasn't like we were going to make it into a weird thing because we didn't actually have feelings for each other.

But now that we'd done it, I wasn't so sure. Because even though it had started out as a purely platonic exchange, somewhere in the middle I'd forgotten the goal and had lost myself in the kiss.

Had she noticed?

Could she tell that I'd let go of reality for a few minutes there, that I'd forgotten that the girl I was holding and kissing and getting lost in the moment with wasn't someone I should have ever touched in the first place?

Cambrielle turned to me before we reached Carter's truck. "So um, I'm sure it goes without saying, but we're just going to keep that back there our little secret, right?"

"Of course." I cleared my throat that was suddenly froggy. "It'll just be another one of our secrets."

"Good." She sighed, as if she'd been worried I would actually tell everyone that we'd just been making out.

I quickly looked her over to make sure her hair hadn't gotten too messy from when I'd ran my fingers through it.

"Here, let me just..." I reached over to tuck some disheveled hair behind her ear, trying not to notice the way my fingers tingled as they grazed against her skin. "There, that's better."

Her eyes widened. "Is it obvious that we were kissing?"

"No. I don't think so." I narrowed my eyes to look her over again, and though I felt different standing beside her than I had an hour ago, she didn't look much different. "You look fine."

Even as I said it, as I met her gaze, my mind instantly told me that she didn't look *just fine*. It told me the more correct description would be to say that she looked beautiful —stunning, really.

But I'd just have to keep that little observation to myself.

"Where did you guys disappear to?" Nash asked when

we reached the group. He was leaning against his lime-green BMW convertible, with his legs crossed at the ankles.

"Um, I just got really scared and needed to get away," Cambrielle said. "Thought I saw Mr. and Mrs. Richardson's ghosts, and Mack had to convince me that it was safe to come back."

"It was pretty creepy in there," Nash said, thankfully seeming to buy Cambrielle's story. "That room full of clowns and mirrors was the worst."

"It really was," Cambrielle said. She looked around at everyone else. "Anyway, sorry for the hold up. I guess we can leave now."

Hunter and Scarlett climbed into Nash's car with him, and I was about to get into the back of Carter's truck with Cambrielle and Elyse when I noticed Carter eyeing me suspiciously.

"How about you ride with Nash this time," Carter said. "That way, you're not so squished back there."

I glanced at the backseat of Carter's truck to where Cambrielle was already scooting toward the middle and making room for me.

"It wasn't that bad," I said with a shrug.

But Carter stepped closer, put a heavy hand on my shoulder, and said, "I think you'll be more comfortable with Nash."

And when his steely gaze met mine, I had the feeling that we weren't really talking about me having enough room for my long legs.

Did he somehow know what had happened at the park?

Because if Carter knew what I'd just done with his sweet and innocent little sister, I was a dead man.

I DIDN'T SLEEP well that night. Which was normal, I guess. But instead of wandering through my house in my bare feet and boxers like I'd been doing since my parents returned home, I just tossed and turned and had vivid dreams of kissing Cambrielle again in the gazebo or in her bedroom, or behind the falls.

And the dreams were good. They were so good and offered relief from my usual dreams that centered around life without my mom. But then the dreams would take a twisted turn and Carter or Mr. Hastings, or even Mr. Richardson's ghost would find me kissing Cambrielle and I'd be running off into the woods to escape.

When I awoke more tired than I'd been when I'd gone to bed, I tried not to relive the good parts of the dream. Tried to put some other girl's face on Cambrielle's body while I fantasized about the kiss from last night. But it would immediately shift back to the girl with a heart-shaped face and aqua-blue eyes whom I really shouldn't be dreaming about, and I knew I was in trouble.

Because I couldn't like Cambrielle.

It was so not something that should be happening right now. Not when I had so many other things to worry about.

But as I did my Saturday chore of cleaning my bathroom, and while I sat next to my mom watching old episodes of *Good Witch*, my mind kept wandering back to last night in the gazebo and wondering if Cambrielle was thinking about it, too.

She had to be thinking about it, right?

I couldn't have been the only one to feel something, could I?

I mean, I'd kissed a lot of girls during my high school career—more than I could remember if I was being honest. And even though I'd thought they'd been great kisses at the time, a fun way to pass a lazy Friday night, I'd never been so distracted by a kiss or a girl that I couldn't concentrate on anything else.

And I couldn't freaking concentrate on anything else today.

"What are you thinking about?" my mom asked, her speech slower and more slurred than it had been a week ago.

"Nothing much," I said, not sure I wanted to get into it. My mom loved Cambrielle. In fact, Cambrielle was one of her all-time favorite people—the honorary daughter that she'd never been able to have.

But even though I knew she loved me more than Cambrielle, by at least a little bit, she probably wouldn't like to know that when I wasn't worrying about her, I was fantasizing about how to convince Cambrielle to forget her re-do kiss with Ben tonight and kiss me instead.

"You know it's not good to lie to your mother." She used her good hand to pause the show. "What's on your mind?"

I picked at one of the tiny pompoms on the throw pillow beside me. "It's nothing."

But my mom, apparently more perceptive today than she had been in recent days, arched an eyebrow and asked, "Is it a girl?"

"No." I ticked my gaze up to meet her warm brown eyes. "There is no girl."

At least, there shouldn't be one right now. And definitely

not the sister of my best friends.

"So what's her name?" Mom asked, her dark-brown eyes lighting up.

"Nothing."

The half-smile that had become her natural smile now, thanks to the paralysis, lifted her lips when she said, "So does 'Nothing' know you like her?"

I rolled my eyes, knowing my mom wasn't about to give up on this. "No, Mom. She doesn't."

"Ah, so there *is* a girl."

I sighed, feeling my cheeks warm with embarrassment. My mom had always been a hopeless romantic and trying to figure out who I may or may not like had always been a favorite hobby of hers.

But I knew I wouldn't have much longer to talk to my mom about my various crushes—even if it was sometimes embarrassing talking about these kinds of things with her. So I said, "Maybe I was thinking about a girl."

"I knew it." Mom's smile broadened again on the right side of her face, showing some of her ultra-white teeth. "Is it someone from school?"

"Yes."

"And does she know you like her?"

"No." I shook my head. "I mean, I never said I liked her. Just that I was thinking about her."

"Same thing." Mom laughed lightly, and I liked how it sounded. Light and joyful, like she wasn't in the process of dying. "Do you think she likes you back?"

Her question made me suddenly feel like I was back in elementary and passing notes to one of my crushes, asking her to check the box *yes* or *no* to see if she liked me.

But since I did know the answer to my mom's question already, I said, "She likes another guy."

"Likes someone more than my boy?" Mom tsked. "Is she blind? Does she even know who you are?"

"I'm as confused as you are by that." I chuckled. "I mean, there's no doubt that I'm the better choice."

"Of course you are." She patted my arm with the hand that wasn't paralyzed by her illness. "With two amazing parents like your father and me, there's no way you can't be the better choice."

"Yes, my special charm is all due to you and dad."

She looked like she was going to say something, but then she winced in the way she always did when a headache was hitting, and I knew our lighthearted conversation would be over.

She sighed. A look that I hated crossed her features—the look of defeat that showed how miserable she was and with no hope that the pain would go away while she was still living.

"I think I need to rest." Mom sighed heavily again. "Could you shut the curtains?"

"Of course." I leaned closer and kissed her gently on the cheek.

Then after squeezing her hand three times, I climbed off her bed and pushed the button on the remote to close the curtains.

When the room was darker, I asked, "Want me to help you get more comfortable?"

She looked down at her body. She'd been propped up on pillows for the past hour so she could see the TV on the wall in front of her and my dad's bed. "Yeah. I'd like that."

So I walked over to her side of the bed, and after pulling out a few pillows from behind her, I set one of my arms behind her knees and the other beneath her back so I could get her to a lie-down position.

I helped her get settled on her side—in case a seizure came while she slept. And because there was a part of me that always worried she might not wake up again, I kissed her cheek once more, letting myself linger beside her for a second to breathe in her familiar and comforting lavender scent. I whispered, "Thanks for being the best mom. I love you."

She opened her eyes and gently patted my arm with her good hand. "I love you too, Macky. But you really need to stop looking at me like I'm going to die today."

"Sorry," I said softly, my heart squeezing as I took in her face. "I'm not trying to. I just..."

"I know." And when her eyes met mine, there was an understanding in them that didn't need to be spoken aloud. We both knew that each day that passed just brought us one day closer to our last goodbye. "But the doctors promised I'd be here for Thanksgiving. And I'm determined to have my pumpkin pie."

I gave her a sad smile even though the prospect of only having her for a few more weeks gutted me. "I'll make sure we get the best pie you've ever tasted," I said. "Sleep well, Mom."

She nodded. "Show me your costume before the Halloween dance, okay? I need a photo with my baby."

"I will." I kissed her forehead and smoothed a thumb over the scarf she wore on her head. "We'll have a whole photo shoot if you want."

15

MACK

I DECIDED to take the slow cooker that the Hastings had brought over with soup back to them after I finished talking to my mom.

They'd been really awesome and had their cook, Marie, cooking enough food for my family, so my dad didn't have to worry about meals and could just focus on spending time with my mom and me when he was home.

I used the special stone path between our houses and rang the doorbell. When no one answered, I rang the door-bell and knocked again.

Usually, someone answered the door pretty quickly, since if one of the family members wasn't around, one of the staff members would come answer the door. But maybe they all had the afternoon off?

When no one came, I punched in the code for the door that they'd given me—a perk of being a best friend and neighbor—and then walked through the marble-floored entryway to the kitchen.

I expected to see Marie whipping up something in the kitchen, but even though something was cooking in one of the ovens, she was nowhere to be seen.

I set the crockpot on the granite countertop of the large kitchen island, figuring Marie or someone from the family would take care of it when they got back. I was about to head out the front door when I heard muffled music coming from the hall that led to the ballroom and conservatory.

Were they having a party I didn't know about?

My curiosity piqued, I headed down the wide corridor to see what everyone was doing.

Only, when I looked through the ballroom windows, I didn't see a party at all. Instead, Cambrielle, in a black leotard and pink ballet shoes, was dancing across the ballroom floor.

The music was loud and familiar—the melody reminding me of something she'd played in her bedroom one of the nights she'd let me stay in her room.

There were no vocals, just a slow instrumental song with a piano and cello carrying the melody. And the soothing tone of the music made me pause and brought me back to those few nights we'd stayed up late chatting and of how peaceful her room had been.

Cambrielle's back was turned to me as she leapt across the floor in her pointe shoes, her arms lifting up at her sides in the way I'd seen ballerinas gracefully move them in movies.

I'd never watched Cambrielle dance before, because I never paid much attention to her back when she spent hours in the dance studio with her ballet tutor. Playing basketball or video games with Carter and Nash had always been more my speed back then.

But even though I didn't know much about the art of dance and ballet, I could tell from the way Cambrielle moved across the dance floor that she wasn't just a rich kid whose parents forced her to be involved in an extracurricular activity. She wasn't a girl who had been accepted to the ballet academy because her billionaire parents had made a large donation.

No, I could tell she had a natural ability and talent that had been shaped and developed through years of dedicated practice. She was gifted. A prodigy any teacher would feel lucky to come across.

And as I watched her twirl and leap across the floor, I couldn't help but become mesmerized by the beauty of her art because I'd never seen anything like it.

I'd always assumed the reason she quit attending the ballet academy in New York after her freshman year was because she didn't like dancing anymore—I hadn't heard of her dancing or taking lessons the last year and a half at least. But this girl I saw before me was not a girl who hated dance. It was obviously part of her soul, and it almost took your breath away to witness.

She made it to the far end of the ballroom, doing some sort of quick step before standing on pointe and extending one leg up high behind her, showing off how impossibly strong and flexible she was. Then she pivoted until she faced the window I stood behind. And I realized a little too late that I probably should have stepped behind the wall so she wouldn't see me and get distracted. But her focus snagged on me almost immediately, and I knew I'd been caught.

Been caught admiring a girl I wasn't supposed to be feeling waves of attraction for.

Since being a creeper who snuck away after getting caught staring at her would only make me look creepier, I forced a smile on my lips and waved.

She glanced sideways, as if blushing over being watched. And since I really didn't want to interfere with her dancing session, I hurried to the large double doors that led inside the ballroom, poked my head inside, and said, "Sorry. I didn't mean to distract you. I just heard the music and wondered what was going on."

She frowned and used the dial on her watch to turn down the music's volume. "What did you say?" Her brow was furrowed, like she hadn't heard me over the music.

Which made sense. It had been loud.

Since I'd already interrupted her dancing session, I opened the door the rest of the way to step into the large ballroom. "I said I didn't mean to interrupt. I was just dropping off the crockpot your mom brought over when she came to visit my mom yesterday and heard the music."

"Y-you weren't standing there for long then?" she asked, the apprehensive look on her face telling me she was self-conscious of being watched without knowing it.

I could have lied and saved us both some embarrassment, but instead of hiding my admiration of her dancing, I said, "I was only here for a minute or two."

"Two minutes?" Her eyes widened and her cheeks colored a beautiful shade of rosy pink.

"Maybe only one?" I hurried to say before she could become too embarrassed, or self-conscious, or whatever emotion she was feeling. "I promise I wasn't trying to spy on you. I just..." I sighed, knowing I probably wasn't coming across very well. "I don't think I've seen you dance before, and I couldn't help but watch."

She looked down at her satin pointe shoes and swallowed. "I don't usually dance when anyone is around these days."

"No?" I couldn't help but ask. "Do you still practice a lot?"

She shrugged. "I usually dance in the studio downstairs when everyone is out."

"You do?" I wondered why she'd want to keep her dancing a secret when she was clearly very talented for a sixteen-year-old.

She rubbed her forearm. "Um, I'm thinking about auditioning for the winter musical. Thinking about being one of the dancers."

"Really?" I raised my eyebrows. I knew she'd helped with the stage crew last year but didn't know she'd been thinking about being part of the production.

"I know it's been Nash's thing..." She let her words taper off as she scratched her neck. "But I don't know, it sounded fun. And I love *The Phantom of the Opera*, so it just seemed like the right time to try dancing again."

"I think that's great," I quickly said before she could interpret my surprise as me thinking she shouldn't do it. "From what I saw, I have no doubt that you'll get the part. I mean, I'm not a ballet expert or anything, but I don't think I've ever seen anyone dance like that."

Her blush deepened, and I couldn't help but think that it made her look even more beautiful. And it made me want to ask more questions, so I could talk to her a little longer.

"Why did you quit dancing before?" I asked. "It sounds like you still love it."

"I do love it now." She shrugged and walked over to the wall where there were a couple of chairs. She sat down and started unlacing the ribbons around her ankles. "But it started feeling too much like a job when I was at the academy, and I needed time away to learn to love it again." She looked up at me. "Have it just be for *me* instead of all the pressure."

I sat in the chair beside her. "Is that why you came home after just one year at the ballet academy? Because you were burnt out?"

"Partly." She sighed heavily and pulled her dance shoe from her foot, tossing it onto the floor. "But I also wasn't taking very good care of myself while I was away."

I remembered how frail she'd looked when she came home that summer. "You did look like you had skipped a few meals here and there."

"Yeah." She started unlacing her other pointe shoe, looking like she was considering saying more.

I simply waited, just watched her unlace the thick ribbons from her smooth, tanned leg. I'd seen her wear shorts a lot, but it wasn't until now that I really noticed just how strong her calves were. She must have been practicing on her own for quite some time because the strength in her legs couldn't have just been built overnight.

She removed her pointe shoe and dropped it to the floor, and then looking up at me, she asked, "Did my brothers never tell you the real reason why I came home?"

"I don't remember." I frowned. "I don't really remember

talking about it aside from them saying you decided to join us at our school instead of going back."

"I guess that's one way to put it."

"So it's not the truth?" I asked.

She shook her head. "I was actually pretty sick."

"Sick?" I furrowed my brow. "Sick with what?"

She drew in a deep breath, like she needed it for strength. "I had an eating disorder, Mack." She stared at her hands where they rested in her lap. "I was anorexic and bulimic."

"Y-you were?" I asked, surprised for some reason even though now that she'd said it, it made complete sense. She had been so tiny. Barely more than skin and bones.

Wariness filled her eyes as if she was worried I was going to judge her for admitting it. "I was having a hard time being away from my family and my grades were slipping, and I was no longer the top dancer in my class like I'd been here." She shrugged. "So I decided that if I couldn't be the best dancer, or get the best grades, or be the prettiest and most popular, I would be the skinniest." She let out a humorless laugh. "And I was finally the best at something. I was so good that I actually ended up in the hospital after collapsing during a performance."

"I had no idea," I said, not really knowing what else to say.

"It's not exactly something I'm proud of."

"Is that when your parents brought you home?"

She nodded. "Once they found out what was going on, they checked me out of the school and had a few words to say to the school administration for not picking up on it sooner. Then I was in therapy and basically always had someone with me for a few months to make sure I ate and kept it down and didn't over-exercise to burn off the calories."

"Is that why you couldn't come to Prince Edward Island with my family that summer?" I asked. "Because your parents wouldn't let you out of their sight?"

Since I didn't have any siblings to go on trips with back then, my parents used to invite Carter and Nash to go on several summer vacations with us. That way, I had some buddies to hang out with and it gave my parents more space to do their thing without needing to constantly entertain me. And since Cambrielle was in high school that year and old enough to come with us, they'd planned to bring her to Canada with us, too.

Until the Hastings changed their minds a week before we left.

She nodded. "I tried to tell them that Carter and Nash would watch out for me, and I think your mom knew what was going on, but it was smart of them to keep me back because I totally would have taken advantage of them. I was really good at keeping my purging quiet."

"I remember you being really sad you couldn't go," I said. She'd come with her mom and dad when they dropped Carter and Nash off, and as she stood under the big tree by my house, tears were streaming down her cheeks.

I'd been confused as to why she'd cared so much about the trip, since she and I weren't as close then as we were now. But now that I knew, I guess having to be watched by someone 24/7 to make sure she didn't continue starving herself would feel pretty smothering.

"You seem to be doing a lot better now," I said, noting the healthy glow in her cheeks.

"I'm a lot better than I was." She nodded. "I mean, it's something I'll always need to watch out for, and I sometimes kick myself for eating too much dessert or compare myself to other girls and feel myself slipping again." She looked at me through her lashes, the vulnerability in her expression making my heart squeeze. "But I've mostly made peace with that part of me."

"I'm glad." I wanted to reach over and take her hand in mine. Do what she'd done for me last night in the truck. But for some reason, I hesitated.

I hadn't had a problem kissing her last night and letting my hands run along her back and in her hair. But right now, I just couldn't seem to close the distance between us.

Maybe because I realized I was starting to like her now and if she pulled her hand away from mine, her rejection would actually have the ability to hurt me.

But that was crazy, right?

Because I didn't actually have feelings for this girl, did I?

I couldn't suddenly go from seeing her as nothing more than the girl next door, who was my friend and a keeper of my secrets, to wanting her to be the girl whose heart I got to share a piece of, too.

But when I met her gaze and looked into her blue eyes that reminded me of the ocean, I knew that I did see her as more than that.

And I was starting to fall for her.

I was falling for a girl who had plans to kiss another guy tonight.

I tightened my hand into a fist at my side when I imagined Ben kissing her the way I had kissed her last night—the way I wanted to kiss her again.

Was she still planning to kiss him again? And would she let his hands roam over her body, let his tongue taste her sweet cherry lip gloss like I had?

I hoped not.

I hoped that maybe she'd been thinking about that kiss as much as I had and that her plans might have changed.

But if they hadn't changed, could I stand by and watch that happen? Could I sit back and watch her go after another guy when I was starting to want her for myself?

I didn't know if I could stomach it now.

But then again, I didn't know what her costume was for tonight, did I?

So maybe I wouldn't see it happen at all.

"Anyway," she said, breaking me away from my thoughts. "I hear not all guys like their girlfriends to be shaped like runway models and prima ballerinas, so I've also made peace with the fact that I got my mom's genetics and will always have a bit of a booty."

Did she just bring her butt into the conversation?

I wasn't expecting that.

But since she seemed self-conscious of it and I was one of those guys who actually appreciated a bit of a booty, I said, "It sounds like you see that as a flaw, but um, some of us guys actually like having something to hold onto when we're kissing a girl."

For a moment, it looked like I'd stunned her speechless with my comment. But then she said, "Do you usually grab girls' butts when you're making out?" Her jaw dropped, and I worried I might have said the wrong thing until she added,

"Does that mean I didn't get the full 'make-out with Mack' experience yesterday then?"

I coughed and pounded on my chest. Soon my cheeks felt all hot and tight, and I knew I was blushing.

Blushing so hard my face was as red as a kid waiting in line at the ice cream truck during a heat wave.

And I never blushed. Usually, *I* was the one making Cambrielle blush.

"I was trying to be a gentleman," I finally said when I found my voice. "I, um, didn't realize you were hoping for the full *Mack Aarden* experience."

"The full *Mack Aarden* experience?" she asked, and for a moment, it looked like she was trying to picture what it would have been like. Then she gave her head a slight shake and said, "I, uh, just for the record, I wasn't trying to say that I wished you'd grabbed my butt last night." She cleared her throat. "That would be so weird."

"Totally weird." I laughed awkwardly, wondering how in the world we'd gotten here.

But as I watched the pink bloom across her cheeks, all I could think of was how much I wanted to experience a make-out session like that with her. To really, really get lost in the moment with Cambrielle and not have it be practice for anyone else.

I just needed to decide if I wanted it badly enough—enough to possibly upset her older brother who had suggested I ride in a different vehicle last night, or if I dared interfere with whatever plans she had for her and Ben tonight. Because I knew if I didn't act fast and her plans worked the way she hoped, I might just lose my chance with a girl who might be perfect for me.

16

CAMBRIELLE

AFTER WALKING Mack to the front door, I grabbed a bite to eat and headed upstairs to shower. My mom had arranged for one of our friends, Deirdre, to come do my hair and makeup for the Halloween dance tonight, so I needed to get all clean and into my costume before she got here.

As I washed off the sweat from my dance workout, I couldn't help but think back to my conversation with Mack. I smiled to myself. Only in a conversation with Mack Aarden could I go from me telling him about my eating disorder to finding out that Mack preferred girls with a little junk in the trunk in the same minute.

It was so weird.

And yet, so natural at the same time.

Natural because it was Mack, and we could talk about all sorts of things with each other and not think the other person was a weirdo.

At least, I hoped he didn't think I was a weirdo now for

accidentally hinting that I'd wanted the full make-out experience with him last night.

I still couldn't believe I'd said that. Like, who says things like that to their friend?

I mean, yes, we'd kissed last night, and the kiss had been kind of amazing—a kiss that I might have stayed up really late thinking about and reliving. The type of kiss I'd probably compare all other kisses to from now on.

But it was a new day, and after only a slip up or two this morning where I'd caught myself fantasizing about pulling Mack aside during the dance and kissing him while I wore my Kelana costume, my head had come back down from the clouds. I knew that just because we had the kind of chemistry I'd always imagined we'd have, it didn't mean we were ever going to find a reason to kiss again.

That kiss had a purpose: to prepare me for my second kiss with Ben tonight—a kiss that would hopefully be much better than our first. And as long as everything went according to plan, the only person I would be kissing for the foreseeable future would be Ben.

At least that was what I was telling myself, because suddenly having feelings for Mack again after one unbelievable kiss would be crazy, right? Especially since I should know better than to harbor feelings for someone who had only ever seen me as a friend.

But future kisses aside, it had been nice feeling safe enough to open up to Mack about my past. I hadn't necessarily been keeping it a big secret on purpose for the past year and a half—it just wasn't something that popped up in random conversation. But it was somewhat freeing to let him know about that part of me that I'd never shared with anyone besides my family before. And nice that he hadn't seemed to judge me for it, either. He'd just taken it in stride and was even sweet about it.

After my shower, I changed into the dress I'd be wearing tonight—a pale-pink strapless dress with a full skirt that made me think of all the beautiful dresses from the fairytales I'd watched growing up. My mom and I even had the seamstress sew little butterflies and flowers onto the bodice and skirt, which made the whole dress look magical in my opinion.

Once dressed, I pulled the pink contacts I'd chosen out of the top drawer in my vanity and put them in.

I didn't normally wear contacts, so it took a while to get them in and my eyes watered a little at first, but then I got used to them and couldn't help but smile at my reflection. Because even without the purple wig and makeup and the glittery mask that I planned to complete the look with, I felt beautiful.

I just hoped Mack—I mean, Ben—liked the faerie-queen look as well.

Deirdre made quick work with my makeup and set a long, light-purple wig over my hair, making me feel like I could walk into the Seelie Court and charm any of the Dark Fae who tried to threaten my people. And once she added the finishing touches— pointed ear tips, a whimsical flower crown, and the masquerade mask—I barely recognized myself.

"Think anyone will know it's me?" I asked Deirdre as we both gazed at my reflection.

Her lips spread into a wide grin. "If your momma hadn't

arranged for all of this, I don't think even she would recognize you tonight," Deirdre said in her Southern accent.

I smiled back because I looked even better than I had imagined when I first came up with the idea for the costume.

And if my own mother wouldn't be able to pick me out in the crowd tonight, I hoped that meant that neither would Ben.

Until I wanted him to know it was me, that is.

17

CAMBRIELLE

I PURPOSELY ARRIVED LATE to the dance. So when I stepped into the school's great hall where we usually ate lunch, it was already alive with music and fellow students dancing to the beat in their Halloween costumes.

Our school was over a hundred years old and it had always felt a little like going to school in a castle, but tonight with all the candles hanging from the ceiling, the cauldrons with bubbling potions, and the gnarled trees with lanterns hanging from their branches—it almost felt like I had stepped into a scene from *Harry Potter*. It was spectacular to look at and made my heart thrill inside because of how magical it all was.

I walked around the edge of the large room, hoping to scope things out and find out where everyone was. I didn't know what Ben had decided to dress up as, because I'd botched up our kiss before I had the chance to ask him. But when I walked down the right side of the room, I did spot a few familiar faces dancing to the slow song playing through the speakers.

Carter and Ava were dancing about fifteen feet away, the top of his fireman helmet giving away their location in the crowd since he was one of the taller guys at the school. Their costumes were actually way cuter than I'd thought they'd be when Carter first told us about them. Ava had a headband with floppy, white polka-dotted Dalmatian ears and a fitted white mini-dress with black dots painted all over it. And I was glad to see that Carter was actually wearing a plain white T-shirt under his firefighter suspenders and that the shirt wasn't even that tight.

Maybe Ava didn't want everyone seeing her boyfriend's eight-pack abs—she'd bragged about them to me once, before remembering that I was his sister and not just her friend after all.

Hunter and Scarlett danced a few feet from them, wearing the astronaut and alien costumes Scarlett had talked about. And close to them was Nash in his *Phantom of the Opera* costume—made up of a black suit with a long cape and a white mask that covered most of his face. Dancing with my youngest brother was Elyse who was the perfect Elizabeth Swan in a pale-gold corseted dress that her mom must have spent hours designing.

I scanned the crowd to see if Mack was close by as well but didn't see his tall frame near the group.

Had he decided not to come tonight?

I hadn't thought to ask him earlier, but he was spending more time with his mom these days. Maybe she was feeling better this evening and he'd decided to stay home and take advantage of it.

I continued walking around the room, to see if I could spot Ben. And even though I didn't see anyone who immediately stood out as him in costume, I did have a few people gaze in my direction.

I smiled at my curious classmates, wondering if they could tell who I was beneath the mask, but no one seemed to recognize me.

Which was good.

I was just about to finish my circle around the room when I noticed a tall guy with broad shoulders wearing a cowboy hat, a plaid button-up shirt, and tight wrangler jeans leaving the great hall.

It was Ben.

My heart stuttered as I watched him walk into the hallway.

Was he leaving already?

Or just going to the bathroom?

I quickened my step and made my way through the crowd, hoping I wouldn't lose him. And just as I made it to the exit, I saw him slip around a corner down the hall.

I walked even faster, trying to keep my pink ballet flats as quiet as I could as I headed down the shadowy corridor. I turned the corner just in time to see him go through one of the doors that led outside.

Why was he leaving already? I wasn't that late to the dance, was I?

I made it to the back door where he'd exited from and was about to burst through when I saw a group of guys standing in a circle.

And since convincing Ben for a re-do kiss in front of his buddies wasn't exactly part of my plan, I scooted away from the door and leaned against the wall with hopes I could catch him alone soon.

"So did you complete the dare?" one of the guys asked, the sound of his voice slipping through a crack in the door.

"I sure did," another voice answered. "I did it last night."

It took me a moment to recognize the tenor voice, but then I realized it was Ben who had just spoken.

He'd completed a dare last night?

He'd been with me at the haunted house. Was he completing some sort of dare while we were together?

"And how did it go?" the first guy asked.

"She bought it hook, line, and sinker." Ben laughed. "It was so easy."

I frowned and inched closer to the door so I could see through the window. It was darker inside than it was outside, thanks to the exterior lights, so I hoped they couldn't see me.

"So did you kiss her?" a guy wearing a Thor costume asked.

"Yep," Ben said, raising his fist to bump knuckles with his friend. "For being one of the hardest girls to date at our school, she kissed me easily enough."

And with those words, my temples started pounding and I immediately felt sick.

Because he was talking about *me*.

He was laughing about kissing me with his friends.

"Did you make it to second base?" another friend in a zombie costume asked. "Third base?"

What?

Did they really think I'd do any of that with a guy I barely knew?

Even though they were only talking about it and I'd barely kissed the guy, I suddenly felt so violated.

So used because it had all been just some sort of sick game Ben and his friends were playing.

To think I'd actually believed him when he told me he liked me.

I was so stupid.

So naive and desperate for a guy I barely knew to like me that I believed everything he'd said just because it was what I wanted to hear.

I was going to throw up.

"First base was more than enough for me." Ben chuckled. "There's definitely a reason why she doesn't date much."

My face burned.

I needed to get out of here. I needed to get away from the school and put as much distance between me and these guys as possible. But before I could slip away, the guy dressed like Thor asked, "So how many girls do you have left on your list?"

There's a list?

Were there other girls who were going to be lied to and made fun of behind their backs?

How many other girls had he done this to?

Even though I wanted to run away, I knew I couldn't just leave now.

"I think I just have Addison Michaels and the new twin, Elyse, and I'll have made it through the initial list."

Elyse was on his list, too?

No wonder he'd always seemed happy to see her.

Well, he wouldn't have a chance to play with her heart

like he'd done with mine. As soon as I got out of here, I was going to tell everyone about his stupid dare and he would regret ever messing with me.

"I have English with Addison, so I'm sure I'll have her checked off the list in no time," Ben said. "And then I'll get Elyse last since she's hot, and I wouldn't mind dragging that out for a while."

"She is hot," Zombie guy, who I now recognized as Casey Elliot from my biology class said. "Her sister, too."

Though I knew I shouldn't take anything they were saying seriously, my cheeks burned with shame. I couldn't help but compare what they were saying about my friends to what they had said about me. Ava and Elyse were hot and actually interesting enough for Ben to really want a hookup.

They were the super skinny supermodels, and I was just chopped liver and a notch in the belt, not pretty enough to ever actually interest Ben.

I decided I'd heard enough. Staying here longer would probably only make me cry, so I pushed away from the wall and got ready to slip back down the hall and out to my car.

But then one of them said my name and I couldn't pull away from my hiding place just yet.

"So why was first base enough with Cambrielle?" Thor asked. "Was she that bad of a kisser?"

Ben chuckled and my stomach twisted because I knew exactly why he was laughing. Because it had been *that* bad.

Though really, it was *his* fault it went so badly, wasn't it? He was the one who basically gagged me with his slimy tongue.

"Let's just say that you're not missing out on anything,"

Ben answered his friend's question once he stopped laughing long enough to talk.

"Dang." Thor snapped his fingers. "I was actually hoping for sloppy seconds when it's my turn to complete the list since she's actually pretty cute."

Tears pricked at my eyes, and I knew it was time to go.

I walked against the wall down the hall so I could blend in and not bring any attention to my retreat. Once I turned the corner, I sped up and darted toward the doors that led to the student parking lot where my red Mercedes was parked.

I was looking behind me to make sure I wasn't being followed when I suddenly collided with something very tall and hard.

A guy.

A guy wearing a suit. And not just any suit but a black suit with a dark-blue vest and a charcoal cravat.

Nash?

I frowned. I recognized the vest and cravat that he'd worn to the soirée earlier this month.

But when I looked up closer, I saw the light-brown skin and face of the boy Elyse had said looked like a younger Regé-Jean Page.

Had Mack borrowed Nash's things and dressed up like a regency lord?

"Sorry I didn't see you," he said, gripping my arm before I could fall.

"It's okay," I mumbled, looking down before he could recognize me. "I-I wasn't watching where I was going."

He let go of my arm, and I made to move past him and toward the exit when my phone slipped out of my pocket and clattered to the floor.

I went to pick it up, but Mack was faster. And just as he was handing it to me, a text came through, lighting up the lock screen and showing a photo of me and my horse Starlight in the stables at my house.

"Cambrielle?" Mack asked, recognition lighting his face after seeing my photo. "Is that you?"

"Yes." I took the phone from his outstretched hand and slipped it back into my pocket. "Now if you'll excuse me, I need to leave." I was still on the verge of crying and knew that I wouldn't be able to keep things together for much longer.

He looked like he was going to let me go, but then voices sounded from the way I'd just come, and a moment later Ben and his buddies came into view.

Mack turned back to me with wide eyes. "Did something happen back there?"

"No," I tried to say, my voice coming out strangled. "I just need to leave."

But the protective glint from last night after the haunted house incident came into Mack's eyes, and I knew he was putting things together.

"Does Ben have anything to do with why you're running out of here so fast?"

"It's fine, Mack," I said before he could make a scene. "I was just leaving. That's all."

Before I could get away, he grabbed my hand and said, "What did he do this time?"

The memories from the past few minutes flitted through my mind, and I knew I was going to lose it right then and there with an audience if I didn't leave.

So I tugged on Mack's hand and said, "Just let me get out

of here and I'll tell you."

I led him out the door, but instead of going to my car like I'd planned, I pulled him under the gothic colonnade that trailed toward the dorms. We made it to the third archway before he stopped me. "What happened Cambrielle? Did you kiss him again? Did the same thing happen?"

"No." I shook my head. "I didn't kiss him."

Thank goodness.

"Then what happened?" he asked. "Did he or his friends do something to you?"

"They didn't do anything," I hurried to say before he could jump to the same conclusions he had last night. "I just..." I sighed and met his gaze. "I just overheard a conversation that Ben probably didn't want me to hear."

"What did he say?" Mack asked. "Because you looked like you were going to cry back there."

The tears pricked at my eyes again, a wave of emotion coming over me.

Mack took my hands in his, running his thumbs across my knuckles in a soothing way. "Please tell me, Cambrielle. Tell me so I can help make this better."

I looked down at our hands and let out a shaky breath. "I just overheard Ben telling his friends that he basically only pretended to like me for some sort of dare or bet that him and his friends have going." I lifted my gaze to Mack's again. "And he was making fun of me."

"What?" Mack asked, rage filling his eyes. "I knew there was something wrong with that guy. Now if you'll excuse me, I'm going to go and show him what happens when he messes with my friends."

"Don't." I gripped his wrist before he could leave. "Don't waste your time on him."

"But he hurt you," Mack said, turning back to me. "He shouldn't be able to play you and get away with it."

"I know," I said. "And I'm going to make sure he can't do that to anyone else. But..." I sighed. "I don't want you to get involved. I just want to go home and forget that I was ever stupid enough to like him."

"You're not stupid for liking him," Mack said. "He was manipulating you."

"But I fell for it."

"He was charming." Mack shrugged. "And sometimes we can't help who we like. It just happens."

"Yeah, well." I shook my head. "I definitely don't like him anymore."

"See, that's all that matters." A half-smile lifted his lips. "When you know better, you do better."

"And now you sound like an inspirational quote." I leaned against the stone archway behind me and sighed again. "I'm just glad I found out before I tried to make that re-do kiss happen. That would have made me look even more pathetic."

Mack leaned his tall frame against the other end of the arch. "Or make him rethink his whole plan because you're so good at kissing now."

When he winked, I couldn't help but smile.

How was it that Mack always knew just what to say to make me feel better?

It really was a gift that he had.

Since we were already on the topic, and my ego could use the boost, I said, "So I'm a good kisser then?"

Mack's smile broadened, and I liked the way his eyes crinkled at the corners. "With a teacher like me, how could you be anything but the best?"

And I knew he was essentially complimenting himself and his teaching skills but having him say I was a good kisser warmed my chest. Because if Mack Aarden, who was basically known as the "king of kissing" by a lot of girls at our school, thought I did okay, it must mean that I at least didn't completely suck at it.

"Are you really planning to go home now?" Mack asked, his brown-eyed gaze meeting mine in the moonlight. "Because I know how much you love Halloween, and it would be a shame not to show off your costume to everyone after keeping it a secret."

"You think it turned out okay?" I asked, glancing down at my dress and touching my light-purple wig.

Mack nodded. "Pretty sure you're the prettiest faerie I've seen all week."

Heat rose to my cheeks at his compliment, and while I was probably the *only* faerie he'd seen this week, I liked that he'd called me pretty.

I liked that when our gazes locked, I believed him.

And even though I'd been on the verge of tears and so ready to leave a few minutes ago, I suddenly didn't want to leave anymore.

"I guess I'll stay a little while longer." I tucked some of my purple wig behind my pointy ear. "My mom and I did spend a lot of time putting this costume together."

"You'll stay?" Mack's eyes lit up, and he looked genuinely happy that I wasn't leaving.

"As long as we promise not to talk about that jerkface Ben and his stupid plans to mess with girls' hearts for the rest of the night, I'll stay."

"Works for me." He stood up straighter and offered his arm to me. "Let's go find everyone else, shall we?"

18

MACK

WHEN CAMBRIELLE and I made it to our friends who were in a circle, dancing to a fast song, all the girls quickly surrounded her and gushed over how amazing she looked. And as they touched her purple wig and commented on her amazing dress, I couldn't help but wish I dared tell her all the same things.

To tell her that she wasn't just the prettiest faerie I'd seen all week, but that she was the most beautiful girl I'd ever seen.

Because it was true. Cambrielle Hastings was gorgeous, and I must've been blind to never really notice it before.

"Did you and Cambrielle drive here together?" Carter asked from beside me as we watched the girls rave over Cambrielle's dress and flower crown.

"No," I said, a hint of anxiety filling me over what he might be thinking right now. "I ran into her in the hall."

"Oh good."

Good?

I knew he'd had an issue with me sitting next to her on the drive home from the haunted house, but was I not allowed to ever drive in the same vehicle as Cambrielle again?

"You don't like the idea of your sister and me driving places together?" I asked, deciding to talk about the elephant in the room instead of speculating on what he might be thinking.

He took a sip of water from the plastic cup in his hand. "I'm just trying to figure out what's going on with you two."

"You think something's going on?" I asked, trying to hide the guilt in my voice and failing.

Had he noticed the way I'd been watching her? Had he somehow seen that kiss in the gazebo?

Or could he simply just tell from looking at my face that my feelings for his little sister were shifting?

Carter had always been too perceptive for his own good.

If he ever had the slightest hint that I'd started fantasizing about kissing Cambrielle again and holding her and telling her all my secrets, I'd be in trouble.

Because like it or not, Carter was protective of his little sister. And unfortunately for me, he knew all about my reputation for kissing multiple girls during the same weekend and never having plans to get serious with any of them.

So while it had been fun to brag about in the past when it had all just been a game, I had the feeling Carter wouldn't be so supportive of someone with a track record like mine getting involved with Cambrielle.

"We're just hanging out like we always have," I said with a shrug, hoping to come off as nonchalant. "We're just good buddies."

Good buddies who had practice kisses and sometimes slept in the same room when my parents were out of town.

So yeah...totally nothing to get worked up about.

He studied my face like he was weighing my intentions. After a beat, he said, "I hope that's all it is. Because I'd hate to see her get hurt."

I gulped.

"Good thing I don't have plans to ever hurt her."

"Yes, it is." He put a hand on my shoulder. "Because if I had to choose between you and her, I'd have to pick her."

Okay, so me having complicated feelings for my best friends' sister was not going to be an issue at all, was it?

I guess I'd just have to show Carter that things would be different if I ever did get a chance to be with Cambrielle.

Because I had the feeling if she ever did want me back, it would be different with her. Longer than a weekend fling.

No, if anything did happen with her, I might just want it to last forever.

19

CAMBRIELLE

A SLOW SONG started playing over the speakers after I'd been in the great hall for about ten minutes, and my friends all began pairing off.

Carter pulled Ava into his arms. Nash and Scarlett started doing the waltz together. And Hunter held out a hand to Elyse.

A tall senior girl wearing a 1980's aerobic exercise costume walked up to Mack, asking him to dance. And since there was nothing more awkward than standing in the middle of the dance floor by yourself with couples dancing all around you, I started doing what I always did during slow dances and walked toward the dark corner nearby to wait the slow song out.

I was just a few steps away from my sanctuary when someone tapped me on my shoulder.

I frowned as I peeked over my shoulder, almost expecting Ben to be there hoping to earn extra points for his stupid dare, but instead I found Mack.

"H-hi?" I said, confused at why he wasn't dancing with the senior girl right now.

"Why are you going to hide in the corner?"

"It's better than standing there awkwardly and watching everyone dance." I shrugged.

"Is that what you always do during slow songs?" He furrowed his brow, like he'd never heard of anyone doing such a thing.

Which made sense, I guess, since Mack had never not had a dance partner.

"It's kind of my thing," I said, hoping he'd just let it drop so I could go hide without having to explain to him that not all of us were in high demand the way he was.

He looked behind us, to where the rest of our friends were dancing. Then, pulling on my arm and guiding me even farther away from our friends, he said, "Would you be okay dancing this one dance with me?"

"You don't need to feel obligated to ask me." I glanced behind him at everyone else. "Just because the rest of our friends are dancing together doesn't mean you have to ask me. I'm fine standing over here."

"You think I'm asking you to dance out of obligation?" he asked.

"Kind of." I shrugged. "I mean, isn't that just how it works?"

"No," he said. "At least, I've never seen things that way."

"Then why do you keep looking over your shoulder at everyone like you're worried they'd be upset you didn't ask me to dance?"

"Oh that." A guilty expression covered his face.

"Yeah that."

"It's not what you're thinking," he hurried to say. "I didn't just follow you over here because I thought it was my duty, or as part of some unspoken friend pact."

"Then what's going on, Mack?" I crossed my arms, getting slightly frustrated that there *was* something going on besides him just asking me to dance.

Did he have some sort of dare going on, too? Was this just like the thing with Ben?

He pinched his eyes shut and squeezed the bridge of his nose. "I'm only looking over my shoulder to make sure Carter isn't paying attention to us."

What?

"Why would that be a problem?"

Mack shrugged his broad shoulders. "Carter just said something earlier and, um, I think his protective older-brother instincts have been alerted."

His older-brother instincts?

"What do you mean?" I frowned. "Are you saying Carter doesn't want us dancing?" I pointed between him and myself.

"Yes," Mack said. "At least, that's the vibe I got from him earlier when we walked into the dance together."

"That's weird."

Carter had never really liked Mack teasing me about going to the falls, since he knew kissing girls was just a game to Mack, but he'd never had an issue with us hanging out before.

Had he somehow found out I was done with Ben and worried that my old crush on Mack had instantly come back?

Because even if I had caught myself looking at Mack a few times over the past fifteen minutes and maybe noticed that he did in fact know how to pull off the suit and cravat just as good as any actor in a regency movie, that didn't mean I liked him in that way.

Mack had always been on a different level than me, and I had learned long ago that crushing on him would only leave me sad and frustrated.

"It's a little surprising," Mack said. "But since Carter worrying about me dancing with his sister while he's dancing with mine is a bit hypocritical, I don't think we need to worry about that."

I laughed. "Pretty sure you and me dancing is way less scandalous than what he and Ava do when they're alone."

Mack scrunched up his nose. "Yeah, not exactly something I'd like to picture in too much detail."

"You're lucky you don't live with your sisters," I said. "It's harder to accidentally walk in on a make-out session when you don't share the same house."

"I'll just take your word for it." He winked. "So leaving protective brothers out of the scenario, what do you say? Do you think it's okay for pretty faeries to dance with British nobility?" He gestured at his costume and mine. "Or is it more fun to hang out in that dark corner?"

"The dark corner is pretty underrated," I said with a shrug. "But since you asked so nicely, I'll leave it waiting just a little longer."

"I'll have to send it my apologies later." His mouth stretched into a wide smile, like he was actually glad I'd said yes.

He pulled me into the dance position, taking my right

hand in his and letting his other hand rest just under my shoulder blade to support my other arm. And even though we were just dancing as friends and there was definitely nothing romantic going on between us, as he pulled me closer, a slight spark of electricity shot through my body.

Oh no. It was happening again.

My body was having some sort of muscle-memory reaction where it thought it needed to act all jittery every time we were close now.

"Are you dressed up as anyone specific?" I asked, hoping that if I could distract him with conversation, he wouldn't notice how much my body liked being close to him.

"What?" He arched an eyebrow, a slight smile on his lips. "You can't tell?"

"Well," I said. "You do look like someone from a Jane Austen novel. Are you supposed to be one of her characters?"

"Did Jane Austen write *Bridgerton?*"

I laughed. "No."

"Then no. I'm not your beloved Mr. Darcy." He chuckled.

"So if you mentioned *Bridgerton,*" I said. "Does that mean that you're dressed as the Duke of Hastings?"

"He's your favorite character from the show, right?" Mack asked.

"Yes."

His smile broadened. "Then that's who I'm dressed up like."

Was he trying to say that he'd chosen this specific costume because of me?

I mean, *should* I be reading into the fact that he just asked if the Duke of Hastings was my favorite character?

"Well, it looks nice," I said.

Hot, my mind corrected out of nowhere.

What the heck?

Why in the world had I just thought that?

Was the punch I'd drank earlier spiked and just hitting me and making me delirious?

I'd never drank alcohol before, so I didn't know what it felt like, but why else would my mind suddenly be telling me that Mack looked downright sexy in his tailored suit, the crisp white shirt striking against his dark skin?

"I'm glad you like my costume," he said in a low tone near my ear. "I may have made a last-minute costume change after our conversation this afternoon—hoping it might impress a certain Bridgerton fan."

He was trying to impress me?

I nearly tripped over my own feet when his words and the warmth of his breath sent shivers racing down my spine. But thankfully, I only stumbled a little and didn't think he noticed.

At least, I thought I'd managed to cover it up. But then a knowing smile lifted his lips, and I knew he knew that I was suffering from the effects of being under the influence of a hot guy.

He bent his head close again and whispered, "I'd totally claim the title of *best dressed* tonight, but we all know that title belongs to you." He looked pointedly at my dress, letting his gaze slowly run the length of me. "That dress is amazing, by the way. Almost as beautiful as the girl wearing it."

My eyes widened when I looked up at him.

Was he flirting with me now?

And not in the teasing kind of way?

Was it possible that this guy, who had always been untouchable, was actually, seriously flirting with *me*?

I shook the thoughts away. He was just being a nice friend.

It was totally normal for friends to tell their friends they were beautiful and to give them the kind of looks that made their blood turn hot in their veins.

"H-how did you learn to dance so well?" I asked, needing something to bring me back to reality.

"My mom taught me. She made me practice with her in our living room when I started going to school dances. Said that I needed to learn the proper form since I was so tall and girls' arms would get tired if I didn't support them right."

"Really?" I asked, trying to picture him and his mom dancing in their living room.

He nodded.

"Well, your mom is a really good teacher."

"She is." He nodded. "I actually like to think that being a good teacher runs in the family."

"Is that your back-up plan if you don't make it to the NBA?" I asked. "To be a teacher?"

He shook his head, a wicked grin spreading on his lips before he said, "I was talking about what I taught you last night." He wiggled his eyebrows. "I mean, that wasn't a terrible lesson, was it?"

And suddenly, an image of us kissing in the gazebo popped into my mind.

Was Mack trying to tell me that he'd actually enjoyed the lesson?

That teaching me the art of the French kiss was something he'd be open to trying again?

No.

I quickly pushed that thought away. That lesson was a one-and-done thing.

He wouldn't want to try that again.

Would he?

But then my mind reminded me of the way he'd moaned when I'd grazed my fingers across the back of his neck and the look in his eyes when we'd broken apart, and suddenly, I was wondering if he would in fact not mind practicing again.

Mack was famous for kissing lots of girls—famous for it being one of his favorite pastimes before his mom got sick, actually. So it wouldn't be completely out there to assume that he would be open to the idea of kissing me again.

But was that something *I* was open to?

His hand smoothed along my spine, his fingers grazing against the skin just above the back of my dress. When he pulled me closer and I became aware of every point of contact between us both, I couldn't help but think that maybe I was open to another teaching lesson from my brothers' best friend.

That maybe there was something in me that actually craved it. Something that had actually secretly craved it for a long time.

So I answered his question by saying, "No. It wasn't a terrible lesson."

His eyes narrowed slightly as he studied my face, like he was measuring my reactions and trying to figure out just how much I may or may not have enjoyed the lesson from last night.

And after seeing whatever he needed to see, he pressed his lips together, dipped his face close to mine, and whispered, "If you ever feel like upgrading to lesson number two, just let me know."

20

CAMBRIELLE

I DANCED with Mack once more before the event ended, and even though I'd been sure the punch had been responsible for the jittery way I'd felt in his arms during our first dance, I continued to feel sparks of electricity every time we touched throughout the night—long after any spiked punch should have been affecting me.

So maybe the punch hadn't been spiked at all?

Maybe my body really did have that muscle-memory thing going and it now thought it needed to act like I had a crush on him again.

"Do you guys want to watch a movie in the common room?" Scarlett asked us when the dance was over. "Heather and Todd said we could stay up late and watch a scary movie instead of going straight to bed in honor of it being Halloween weekend."

Heather and Todd were the dorm parents for our house.

"I'm in," Nash said, draping his arm around Elyse. "Are you?"

She nodded, a faint blush rising to her cheeks that made me wonder if maybe my brother had been making some progress with my shy friend when I wasn't watching.

"Us too," Ava said, linking her arm through Carter's.

"What about you, Mack?" Scarlett asked. "Think you can stay?"

"I don't know." He looked at his watch and made a face like he was actually considering going home instead of staying. "It's past my bedtime..."

"We'll have popcorn," Scarlett said to bribe him, knowing he could eat a huge bowl by himself.

"Well, if there's popcorn..." He shot Scarlett a smile. "Then you know that I'm in."

"What about you, Cambrielle?" Hunter asked from where he stood across the circle.

"Yeah," Mack piped in. "Think you can handle a scary movie?" He shot me an ultra-white smile, almost like he was daring me to stay.

I bit my lip, trying to decide. Even though Halloween was my favorite holiday, I really was not a fan of scary movies.

Well, actually, I loved scary movies. Loved the suspense and the jump scares in the moment.

I just didn't like the nightmares and scary images that came to my mind when I was trying to sleep over the following days and weeks after watching them.

"I don't know..." I said. "It's kind of late and I—"

"I'll keep you safe from any monsters that might jump out of the screen," Mack said before I could finish my sentence. Then bending close to my ear, he whispered, "I'll even let you cuddle up to me if it gets too scary."

Was he saying he wanted to sit next to me during the movie?

Where everyone could see us?

Where my brothers could see us?

"So what do you say?" he asked more loudly so the whole group could hear this time. "Think you'll stay?"

And when he slipped his hand behind my back and rubbed the bare skin between my shoulder blades, something told me I couldn't say no.

So I nodded and said, "I guess I'll stay."

"Great." Scarlett clapped her hands together. "Let's go then."

Carter and Ava led us out of the great hall with the rest of us following behind them. As we walked toward the dorms, my stomach started twisting in knots of anticipation as I thought about the possibility of sitting close to Mack during the movie.

We'd watched hundreds of movies together through the years, but even though I'd totally wondered what it would be like to sit next to him during a movie back when we were in middle school, we'd never sat close enough that it would be considered cuddling.

Pretty sure the closest I'd ever sat next to him had been on Friday in the back of Carter's truck.

So the thought of actually cuddling with a guy that I may or may not be rekindling my crush on was slightly overwhelming.

Overwhelming and exciting at the same time.

But as we walked through the gothic colonnade where Mack and I had talked after overhearing Ben, Scarlett linked her arm through Mack's and laughed at something he said. And I couldn't help but wonder if maybe I'd just imagined all the flirtatious things he'd said to me tonight.

Then when he laughed at something Scarlett said and nudged her with his elbow, I wondered if it wasn't that I'd only imagined him flirting with me at all. But maybe this was just how he was with all our friends and that I had just been initiated into his friends-with-benefits circle.

I didn't realize that Hunter had stepped up beside me until he said, "It's hard staying friends with someone you have feelings for, isn't it?"

"What?" I asked, wondering how in the world he had just been reading my thoughts. "D-do you think I like Mack?"

Hunter shrugged. "It's easy to recognize the signs when it's something you're familiar with."

"As in, how things are with you and Scarlett?" I asked, hinting at how he and Scarlett had dated for a few weeks last year before deciding to go back to being best friends.

He nodded.

"But wasn't it your choice to cool things and just be friends?"

He pushed his hands into the pockets of his astronaut suit. "That's what we agreed to."

"But it's not what you wanted?" I guessed. "To just be friends?"

He nodded. "Sometimes I think it would be nice to go back to before I kissed her. To go back to before I knew what it was like to date her." He lifted a shoulder. "It's easier not to miss something that you've never had."

Interesting.

"So I'm guessing that Scarlett is the one who wants to just be friends?" I asked, gazing at his profile in the moonlight.

His green eyes flickered to mine briefly. "It's a little more complicated than that. But yeah, we wouldn't be like this if it was up to me."

We made it to the dorms, and he opened the door so I could walk in. I said, "For what it's worth, I hope things work out with you and Scarlett."

"Me too." He shrugged. "Someday."

Scarlett and Mack's laughter carried down the hall again, catching both Hunter's and my attention.

"Just so you know," Hunter said, meeting my gaze. "I don't think we have anything to worry about with them."

"You think I was worried?" I asked again, wondering how he could think I had feelings for Mack when I'd just barely started noticing things myself during the past twenty-four hours.

"I'm just saying." He held his hands up at his sides.

"Well, I never said I liked him," I said, probably feeling the need to reassure myself more than him. "I'm just getting over my crush on someone else, actually."

"Okay." He chuckled. "But as your friend, I just want you to know that even though Mack always teases Carter about taking you out because he liked getting a rise out of him, I've always wondered if there was something more to it."

My heart beat faster at his words. "W-what makes you say that?"

Had Mack said something to Hunter? Did Hunter know about our kiss?

"He hasn't said anything to me," Hunter hurried to say, as if worried he may have just led me on. "But I don't know. You used to like him back in the day, right? It wouldn't be the craziest thing, would it?"

I'd definitely heard of crazier things, I guess. And we did have the friendship thing down.

I'd never had a boyfriend before—never been on an actual date, really. But I was pretty sure friendship was a good foundation for a relationship to start on. Which we had.

Chemistry was also important—guessing from that kiss and the sparks I'd felt when we danced tonight, we probably had it, too.

The only other thing I could think of as essential for a relationship to work out was for the couple to actually want to be together. And I was starting to think that I wasn't too opposed to the idea—that there probably had always been a little part of me holding out for the possibility of something with the guy who had stolen my middle-school heart.

I just didn't know how Mack felt. But maybe if we did sit close as we watched the movie together, maybe I'd have a little more insight after that.

WHEN WE MADE it to the common room, I had to go to the bathroom first, and when I came back to find a seat, I was disappointed to find that Nash and Elyse were already seated on the couch beside Mack.

So much for his promise to keep me safe during the scary parts.

I grabbed a bowl of popcorn and decided to sit in the empty seat next to Ava while Scarlett turned down the lights and started the movie.

"Have you seen this one before?" Ava whispered to me as we watched a lady climb out of the shower with a towel wrapped around her body, suspenseful violin music playing in the background.

"No." I shook my head. "Have you?"

"It's one of my favorites." A slow smile lifted her lips. "It gave me nightmares for a month the first time I watched it."

Oh, yay...

The lady on the TV screen started brushing her teeth with one hand while she reached out the other to wipe the fog off the mirror. The music got more intense as her reflection became clearer, and just as a loud crescendo of violins screeched, a man wearing a dark hoodie suddenly appeared behind her in the mirror's reflection with a bloody knife in his hand.

I jumped in my seat and let out a tiny scream as the camera zoomed in on the guy's hooded face. And when the lady let out a screeching yell that made my blood curdle, I knew that there was no way I was going to make it through another two hours of this and still hope to get any sleep over the next month.

So when the lady turned around and the guy was no longer behind her—as if she'd simply imagined his reflection in the mirror, I took my popcorn bowl and slipped off the couch.

"You're leaving?" Ava asked with a frown on her face. "Already?"

I nodded. "I don't do well with scary movies." Then looking at Carter who she was cuddled up next to, I said, "I'll see you at home."

"Drive safe," he said.

And then hunching over so I wouldn't distract everyone sitting around me, I tiptoed around the back of the couch and toward the back of the room.

I shut the large double doors firmly behind me so I wouldn't be able to hear the movie. But when I turned around and looked down the hall that was dark and empty aside from the various paintings of the previous headmasters and headmistresses of our school, I knew I didn't want to be there, either.

Which was a problem, because I also didn't want to go outside and walk to my car in the dark parking lot by myself.

Why had I said yes to this?

Why hadn't I done what I usually did and gone home to sleep instead of staying up late to watch a scary movie?

Oh yeah, because Mack had said he'd keep me safe, and I was apparently really weak when it came to promises of sitting next to him.

Footsteps sounded down the tile floor, and I could have jumped out of my skin as I imagined the guy in a hoodie with a bloody knife coming toward me. But then I saw it was just Addison Michaels and her stepbrother Evan coming around the corner and told myself to stop freaking out.

Just turn on your phone's flashlight and run out of here. It'll be fine. There's no such thing as ghosts.

"Not enjoying the movie?" Addison asked, a knowing look on her face when she and Evan reached me.

"Nope," I said with a heavy sigh. "Definitely not a fan."

"I hate scary movies, too," Addison said. "That's why I'm just going to bed."

"I'm hoping to do that, too." *If I ever get up the nerve to walk outside to my car, that is.*

Evan opened the door for Addison and followed her into the common room. Once I was alone again, I drew in a few deep breaths, hoping that if I could just get my breathing under control I would be fine enough to get to my car. Because once I was in the safety of my Mercedes, I could lock the doors and drive home.

I leaned against the wall, letting my head fall back as I closed my eyes. I tried to visualize that it was daytime—that the sun was shining, birds were singing, and it wasn't officially the first half-hour of Halloween when the doors to the spirit world were opened and the spirits of the dead had just started roaming the earth.

I don't believe in ghosts. I pinched my eyes shut tighter beneath my glittery mask. *The history of Samhain that I read about in Mrs. Aarden's witchy book is not real.*

But even as I spoke the words in my mind, I knew that part of me did believe in spiritual beings—the part that still remembered my Grandma Hastings' stories of seeing her dead grandmother's ghost visiting her bedroom one Halloween night.

I shook my head.

"*Sunshine and rainbows. Sunshine and rainbows. Sunshine and rainbows.*"

I opened my eyes after chanting my mantra several times and saw that I wasn't alone in the hall like I'd thought.

Nope, just a few feet away was a tall guy wearing a suit and cravat.

At first I thought it might be the ghost of a headmaster from centuries past, until I saw the ghost's face.

"Mack!" I gasped, putting a hand to my chest. "What are you doing sneaking up on me like that? Are you trying to give me a heart attack?"

"Sorry." He stepped closer so I could see him better. "I wasn't trying to scare you."

"Well, you failed at that," I said, wondering if my heart was ever going to return to normal speed after ratcheting up higher and higher the past several minutes.

"I noticed you hadn't come back and wanted to make sure you were okay." He set his hands on my shoulders. "Why were you mumbling something about sunshine and rainbows?" he asked. "What was that about?"

"I was just trying to distract myself," I said, looking up into his eyes and daring him to make fun of me.

"And did it work?"

I sighed. "Not really."

"Didn't seem like it." His eyes crinkled at the corners.

"Well, you suddenly appearing in front of me didn't help much, either." I folded my arms across my chest. "How did you come out here without making a sound?"

"I'm part vampire."

I glared at him, not amused.

He chuckled. "You just couldn't hear me over your sunshine-and-rainbows chant." He smoothed his hands up and down my bare arms, warming my skin. "Sorry I didn't sit next to you in there like I promised. Nash stole the spot I was saving for you and there were no more empty couches."

So he had tried to sit next to me?

Why did that suddenly make me feel infinitely better?

"Wanna know what helps distract me when my mind starts spiraling?" he asked, looking at me in a way that made me feel warm.

"Sure," I said, slightly worried about what his answer might be since you never really knew what you were getting with Mack.

"Going snorkeling in Hawaii," he said with a wicked grin.

I resisted the urge to roll my eyes, not amused at how unhelpful he was choosing to be. "Well, next time I'm in Hawaii and watch a scary movie, I'll remember that snorkeling is the cure for a restless mind."

"It always helps me." He shrugged, like he'd actually been helpful.

"I'm sure it does. I'm sure just being in Hawaii is actually nice."

"It totally is. I highly recommend it." He smiled, and even though he was so far not helpful with his suggestions, I did like the way the smile lit up his face.

And my mind couldn't help but think that his smile was a nice distraction.

"Wanna know another thing that helps?" he asked.

Even though I was less sure that his suggestions would be helpful now than I'd been a moment ago, I said, "Sure."

He let his hands travel down my arms slowly, sending goosebumps prickling on my skin. Then taking my hands in his, he said, "Spending time with my friends is also something that helps me. You're with a friend now, don't you feel a little better?"

So he was saying that him being here with me should cure my anxiety?

I guess I did feel less scared than I'd been a moment ago.

"I do feel a little better," I admitted.

Though part of that could also be because he was now holding my hands and I liked the way my hands felt in his.

"Wanna know another proven activity for distracting you from unwanted thoughts and feelings?" He took a step closer so his body was only inches from mine, his head and shoulders hovering over me. I had to angle my head back to meet his gaze.

"Why not?" I asked, my voice coming out breathy from being slightly overwhelmed by his proximity. I cleared my throat and tried to make my voice sound more normal and less affected by the handsome boy just inches away from me. "So far you're at least one for two."

He let one of his hands slide up my arm, his touch a gentle caress on my bare skin. And then slipping his fingers into the hair at the nape of my neck, he whispered in a low voice, "It might be better to show you this one instead of simply telling you."

"Show me?" I breathed out, anticipation surging through my veins and making me feel my heart beating everywhere.

He licked his lips. "It might require a more hands-on technique." His gaze darted down to my mouth. "Something that involves my very specific teaching skillset."

He was going to kiss me.

Mack Aarden was going to kiss me again.

And I hadn't had to beg him to do it this time, either.

He leaned closer and reached up to remove the mask from my face, the gentle graze of his fingertips sending little tingles across my skin. "Do I have your permission to show you what I'm talking about?" He slipped the elastic from my mask around his wrist. And then, running his thumb gently across my cheekbones, he mumbled, "Can we continue our lesson from last night?"

His voice was so low and husky that my insides swirled with heat and butterflies flapped uncontrollably in my stomach.

I wanted to continue that lesson more than I wanted anything else in the world right now.

And so when I gasped out a "Yes," it was all I could do to draw in oxygen because I'd suddenly forgotten how to breathe.

Forgotten how to do everything besides stand there and wait for him to teach me everything he knew about kissing— which I hoped would take a *very* long time.

Multiple lessons, if I was lucky enough.

He dipped his head closer, and I could almost feel the sizzle of electricity sparking in the millimeters of space between our lips. But before he could close the distance between our lips completely and give me what I craved so badly, the door behind us creaked open and Nash stepped out.

Of course. Nash would be the one to make sure I missed this once-in-a-lifetime chance to kiss Mack.

"What's going on here?" Nash asked, his eyes wide with shock. "Were you—" He gripped Mack's shoulder and yanked him away from me. "Were you about to kiss my sister?"

"No, Mack was just..." My mind scrambled as I tried to come up with an excuse for why Mack was basically pressing me into the wall. "I was scared, and um, he was just teaching me some techniques for dealing with my fears."

"As in, he was kissing your fears away?" Nash shook his head, clearly not believing it. Then looking at Mack, he said, "Do you have a thing for my sister? Do you two actually have a secret fling going on?"

Did everyone at school believe those rumors Ben had talked about?

"We don't have a secret relationship." Mack shook his head and stepped away, holding his hands in front of him. "I was just, well..." He scratched his head. "I was just teaching her something. It's hard to explain."

"I bet." Nash folded his arms across his chest, looking more intimidating than usual with his white Phantom mask and black cape.

"Anyway," Mack said, looking as uncomfortable as I felt. "I was actually planning to head home since I've already seen the movie. So I'll see you two later."

My chest fell at the thought of him leaving without giving me that kiss. But I knew there was no hope of getting the moment back after Nash's interruption, so I said, "Drive safe, Mack. We'll see you later."

"Have a good night," Mack said. Then seeming to remember he still had my glittery masquerade mask, he pulled it from his wrist and handed it back to me, saying, "I'm glad you decided to stay for the dance after everything earlier. It was nice."

I wasn't sure if he was referring to the dance being nice as a whole, or if he was talking more specifically about the times we'd spent dancing and then the moments from just a minute ago. But since it probably didn't matter anyway with Nash standing right here and dissecting our every word and move, I said, "I'm glad I stayed, too."

"Yes, I'm glad you two enjoyed your time at the dance." Nash put a protective arm around my shoulder, as if to show some sort of macho territorial-ness. "Now if you'll excuse us, I'd like to talk to my sister for a moment alone."

21

CAMBRIELLE

"WHAT THE HECK was that all about?" I turned toward Nash once Mack had disappeared out the doors that would take him to the student parking lot.

"You're asking *me* what that was all about?" Nash put a white gloved hand to his chest. "I think I should be the one asking *you* that question." He took his white Phantom mask off his face. "Did you forget all about what Mack does with girls?"

"Of course I didn't forget," I said.

"Then why did it look like you were about to kiss him?" Nash asked. "You can't just kiss a guy like Mack and hope not to get hurt. You know his interest in girls never lasts very long."

"So?"

"So...you're the opposite of that," Nash said. "You aren't a weekend-fling type of girl. When you like a guy, you like him in a serious way. And..." He ran a hand through his blond hair that had been slicked back all night, and then shrugged. "Is it so wrong that I don't want to see you get hurt?"

"I appreciate that you don't want me to get hurt," I said. "That's really great of you. But what if I just want a fling?" I asked, playing the devil's advocate since he'd never cared to ask what I actually did want. He'd just jumped to conclusions. "Why can't I do that? I mean, you flip-flop between girls all the time. Why does there always have to be a double standard with you guys? I'm not this little girl who needs protection from my big brothers all the time. I can make my own choices."

"I'm just trying to watch out for you, Cambrielle," he said. "You may think that you're okay just being this weekend girl for Mack, but I know you and I know that it's not going to be like that."

I hated that he thought he knew what was best for me. Just because he was a guy and a year older than me, he thought that he knew better.

But he wasn't me. He wasn't in my head, and he hadn't had all the experiences with Mack that I'd had over the past several months.

Plus, look what being careful had gotten me earlier tonight. I'd bided my time; I'd waited for a guy I liked to notice me. I'd taken months to plan it out and not hurry and jump into something.

And it had all turned out to be a huge sham. Just a prank where my inexperience with relationships had gotten the better of me and made me look like a fool.

"How about you just let me make my own mistakes then?" I continued. "How about you let me make my own decisions when it comes to guys who may or may not be interested in me? And then if I get hurt, you can tell me 'I told you so.'"

"Because you already know you'll get hurt," Nash said. "Just listen to yourself. You already know you'll get hurt if you try something with Mack. And you still want to do this?"

I touched his arm. "I don't need my big brothers interfering with my love life—or lack of a love life," I said. "How am I supposed to ever have a normal high school relationship if you and Carter keep interfering every step of the way?"

"Are we stopping you from going on dates? Or having a boyfriend?"

"How is any of this not you doing exactly that?" I lifted my hands in the air.

"I'm not stopping you from going on dates." Nash lowered his voice. "I'm just trying to stop you from getting hurt by Mack and guys with short attention spans like Mack."

"Well, if that's the truth, then why didn't you stop me from getting hurt by Ben?" I asked. "Where were you then?"

"What?" His eyebrows knitted together. "What are you talking about?"

I sighed. "Ben was only pretending to like me because I was on some list he and his friends have of girls who are impossible to get close to."

"What?" he asked again, like he didn't understand what I was saying.

So I shrugged and said, "Ben's friends dared him to kiss me. That's why I ran out of the haunted house, because my lack of experience made that a huge fail."

"You kissed Ben?" Nash asked, shock filling his eyes. "Why would you do that?"

"Because I wanted to." I paused, realizing this probably wasn't really helping my case any. Then I said, "Anyway, if I'm still okay after that, I think I'll be okay if I kiss Mack one time and he decides he just wants to be friends afterwards." I looked up at him. "That is, if he even wants to kiss me. I didn't exactly get to find out if that's what he was about to do tonight."

"Oh, he wants it," Nash said, like it was obvious.

"You think so?" I asked, my heart doing a somersault in my chest at the thought of it being true.

"Of course he does," Nash said. "He's a guy and you're not exactly the ugly duckling."

"Well then, that's good, isn't it?" I said. "Shouldn't kissing happen between people who both want it?"

"Yeah, but an innocent peck is not all that Mack would want."

"It's a good thing that's not all I'd want, either," I said.

Nash stumbled backward. As if he couldn't believe that his innocent little sister had just said she'd want the same things that a hormonal seventeen-year-old guy would want.

"But you don't know what it's really like, Cambrielle," Nash said. "You're so inexperienced. It's different. Once you take things to a certain level, different emotions get involved and it's harder to stop. Harder to keep the logical part of your brain functioning at full capacity."

My brother really did think I was so naive that I didn't know how things worked. But since he really seemed super worried that I was planning to go from zero to one hundred in a single night, I said, "I'm not planning to hook up with Mack, okay?"

"Ew. Gross." He made a face like I'd just said the most disgusting thing in the world.

"Sorry, you're the one making it sound like you think that's what I'm trying to do here," I said.

"Of course I don't think you're going to do that," Nash said, still looking like he was having a hard time keeping his punch and popcorn down.

"Well, good," I said.

Nash sighed and leaned against the stone wall behind him, seeming to realize this conversation wasn't going to go the way he wanted. "It's just, why does it have to be Mack? Why can't you go after someone harmless like Harden Sykes?"

Harden Sykes being the guy in my math class who had skipped two grades and therefore still had some time before he fully hit puberty and had enough testosterone pumping through his body to make him interested in dating.

"Because I don't want to kiss Harden. I want to kiss Mack."

Nash lowered his head, giving it a little shake of defeat. "Well, just try not to get your heart broken, okay?"

"I'll do my best."

He glanced around the empty corridor, as if he wasn't sure what to do now that he hadn't talked me out of wanting to kiss one of his best friends.

I wanted to end things on a slightly better note than we'd started on, so I looked at my brother who probably only had the best of intentions in all of this and said, "Since you're already out here, would you mind walking me to my car so I don't get kidnapped by any of the ghosts entering the human realm tonight?"

"Sure." He chuckled and put an arm around my shoulder. "If I can't keep you from all the guys with flesh and bones and raging hormones at our school, at least I can keep you safe from the ghosts."

Nash made sure I made it to the safety of my Mercedes. After locking the doors and watching him walk back into the dormitory to finish the scary movie, I pulled my phone out of my pocket to text Mack before I lost my nerve.

Me: **You still interested in showing me that final technique for distracting myself from unpleasant thoughts?**

His text came through almost immediately.

Mack: **Yes.**

My heart fluttered.

Me: **Is your hot tub still hooked up?**

Him: **It is...**

My hands shook a little as I typed out my next text, knowing that I was setting myself up to possibly be hurt like Nash had said.

But since I was tired of playing the waiting game and waiting for the universe to just make things happen for me, I sent the next message.

Meet me there in fifteen minutes?

I held my breath as I waited for his response, my heart pounding so hard against my ribs.

If he says no, at least it's through a text and not to your face.

My phone vibrated in my hands a few seconds later. I was so anxious that I dropped it in the cup holder in the console beside me.

I quickly snatched it back up and read the words that would have made my middle-school self think she'd died and gone to heaven.

Mack: **Just use the gate to get to the backyard. I'll be waiting.**

22

MACK

I'D BEEN in the middle of getting ready for bed, thinking I might actually fall asleep soon, when Cambrielle's first text came through. But as soon as I saw that she was inviting me to spend time together in the hot tub, I was back to being wide awake.

So awake in fact that it felt like I'd just chugged down several energy drinks.

And as soon as I saw the words *hot tub*, I dug through my drawers, looking for the right pair of swim shorts for the moment.

It probably didn't matter which pair I wore, since they were all basically the same and they'd be under the water most of the time, but it just seemed like it should matter. This moment could be important enough to warrant extra care in what I wore.

Because it felt different than the other times I'd planned to meet up with a girl. More important.

Because I cared about Cambrielle and wanted whatever happened between us tonight to be the start of something special and not the end.

And the fact that I actually *cared* about how tonight went told me that this really might be different with Cambrielle.

Because I liked her.

Liked her a lot, actually.

I probably had feelings growing for her under the radar for longer than I knew—since the first time she'd let me stay in her room and had made me feel safe enough to open up to her about what I was going through.

Maybe longer.

I found a pair of black swim shorts with a white drawstring in the cut I liked best and quickly changed into them.

Then, since my parents were already asleep for the night, I slunk through the main part of the house in the dark and out the enclosed porch in the back. The sky was more overcast than it had been when I'd left the school, filtering more of the light the stars and the moon were giving off, so I switched on the string lights we had hanging from the open roof of the pergola above the patio.

I lifted the cover from the hot tub, checked the temperature of the water, and waited.

And waited.

And waited.

I checked the time on my watch. It had been at least twenty minutes since Cambrielle had texted me.

Had she changed her mind?

Had Nash dissuaded her after all?

I'll give her another ten minutes.

But since it was colder out here than was comfortable for just my swim trunks and T-shirt, I lit the gas fire pit table, grabbed my lucky Columbia hoodie from a hook inside the patio, and settled onto the patio couch, telling myself that if she didn't come in ten more minutes I'd go inside and try not to take her no-show too personally.

One minute ticked by. Followed by another. But then footsteps sounded on the gravel path on the side of the house, making my heart race. A moment later, Cambrielle's petite silhouette appeared in the foggy night.

"Sorry I'm late," she said, walking closer. "It took longer to get the contacts out than I thought."

"It's okay." I stood.

When she stepped under the soft glow of the string lights and I could see her better, I had to gulp down my attraction because she looked drop-dead gorgeous.

She'd removed the wig, the dress, and the faerie makeup and was wearing a white, semi-sheer swimsuit cover-up over a black two-piece bathing suit I'd never seen her wear to previous pool parties. As I took her in from the messy bun on the top of her head and down to her feet in sandals, I couldn't help but hope that tonight went the way I wanted.

Hoped she was wanting what I'd assumed from her texts earlier: to continue where we left off at the school.

"Should we get in?" she asked, gesturing to the hot tub beside us.

"Y-yeah." I cleared my throat, my froggy voice making it obvious how affected I was by her beauty. "Let's do this."

I pulled my hoodie and T-shirt over my head and tossed them to one of the patio chairs nearby.

She kicked off her sandals, and as she untied her cover-up and let it drop from her shoulders and arms, I couldn't keep my hungry eyes from raking in every inch of her that I could see.

She had told me she was self-conscious of not being the skinniest ballerina at the ballet academy, but as she dropped the cover-up on the chair where I'd tossed my shirt and hoodie, and approached the hot tub, I thought that everything about her was perfect.

Every person had certain traits that they were more attracted to than others, and it was very apparent to me in that moment that I was very attracted to everything that made up Cambrielle.

You also like her personality, too, I reminded myself as the physical attraction I had for her became more dominant in my mind the closer she stepped toward me. *It's not just because she's smoking hot.*

Although, yes, Cambrielle Hastings was smoking hot. So hot I was pretty sure I might get overheated before I actually immersed myself in the hot tub's water.

I climbed into the hot tub first. Before sitting down, I turned to watch her climb up the steps—a somewhat bashful expression on her face when her gaze flickered to mine.

"Help me get in?" she asked when she reached the part where she'd need to step down into the water.

"Of course." I offered her my hand to steady her as she put a foot down, and it was all I could do to keep from pulling her into my arms right then and there and kiss her.

But since she was the one who had initiated our little rendezvous, I helped her down like the gentleman I knew I should try to be and then took a seat in one of the corners.

Cambrielle sat next to me, and as the bubbles from the jets pulsed around us and steam rose from the water into the chilly night air, I told myself to just look at her face. Just look at her face instead of trying to check out every curve she had hiding in the water.

I could do that.

"So," she said, looking up at me through her long lashes.

"So," I replied like an idiot, completely stalling because I had no idea what I was doing.

Yes, I knew I was more experienced than her. Knew that a guy with the reputation I had should be completely smooth and in his element in a situation like this.

But I was so not in my element right now because this girl was so beautiful and amazing and made me so freaking nervous.

She scooted closer, her leg brushing against mine, and a live wire could have just been dropped into the hot tub for how electric my body's reaction was to it.

Calm down, Mack, I told myself as I checked her over. *Stop acting like you've never sat next to a girl before.*

She just looked at me, waiting for me to make a move. And with each heartbeat that galloped in my chest, I knew I was getting closer to completely blowing it with her.

"Is everything okay?" Cambrielle asked, a frown puckering her lips as she studied me. "Is something wrong?"

"No, of course not," I hurried to say. "I, um, I'm just..." I ran a hand over my hair. "You just make me a little nervous."

"*I* make you nervous?" She put a hand to her chest, like it was a foreign concept to her.

"Yes." I swallowed the lump in my throat. Then deciding that just being honest was probably the best choice, I added,

"You sitting close to me when you look like that makes me very nervous."

She looked down into the water where our legs were pressed against each other then back up to meet my eyes again. "Should I move away?"

When it looked like she might head toward the opposite end of the hot tub, I grabbed her arm and said, "No, don't."

"Then what exactly is going on?" She glanced down at my hand on her arm and then back up to my face, her brow furrowed in probably one of the most adorably confused expressions I'd ever seen. "D-did I read things wrong back at the school?" she asked. "Did I just make things really weird by inviting myself over?"

"No." I shook my head before she could get the wrong idea. "No, of course not. I just said I'm nervous. Not that I don't want to be exactly where I am right now." I slipped my hand down her arm and interlaced my fingers with hers. "I think part of me is still having a hard time reconciling this version of you." I let my eyes give her a good once-over to indicate how attracted I was to her. "With the girl I was throwing mud pies at a few years ago."

"So you still see me as a little girl then?" she asked, her big, blue eyes wary.

"No." I shook my head. "I most definitely don't see you as a little girl."

There was absolutely nothing about the way she looked tonight that would make anyone think she wasn't anything besides a nearly full-grown woman.

I sighed, wondering how I could explain this better since I was doing a terrible job of it so far.

I pressed my lips together, searching for better words,

then said, "I guess what's really going on is that I'm wondering how in the world I didn't notice everything I'm noticing about you sooner."

"So you're saying you aren't having second thoughts about us being here?" she asked quietly, a hint of hope in her voice that made my heart swell.

"No second thoughts." I slipped my hand to the nape of her neck. "Just lots of new thoughts that your brothers would probably kill me for having."

"But we're not going to think about my brothers right now, are we?" she whispered, her gaze dipping to my lips.

I shook my head slowly. "The only thing I want to think about right now is you and me..." I leaned closer. "And this thing that's happening between us."

So before I could let my anxious mind overthink anything else, I closed the distance between our lips and did what I'd been fantasizing of doing since last night.

She gasped when our lips connected, in the same cute way she'd gasped last night. But after the initial surprise seemed to hit, she sighed. And the way she sighed into my mouth was my new favorite thing because she sighed like she'd been holding her breath since coming over here. Like she'd been as nervous as I was about what might happen but had just been better about hiding her nerves than I was.

When she slid her hand up my arm and then my shoulder, touching me tentatively, like she wasn't sure she was allowed to, I knew I was the luckiest guy in the world to have this moment with her. Because unlike what I'd done in the past, she didn't do this with every guy willing to kiss her for a weekend. She'd saved it. Saved it until this very moment when she finally shared it with me.

The thought that she'd saved this kind of moment for someone like me made me feel both so unbelievably special and undeserving at the same time. Because how in the world could I dare hope to deserve a moment like this with someone as special as Cambrielle Hastings?

But as undeserving as I felt, when her lips joined mine in the give-and-take, I could also sense that despite everything that should have pushed her away from me, she wanted this to happen, too. She craved this kiss and this moment alone as badly as I did.

I wasn't sure exactly what I should do with my hands, since she was new to making out and I didn't know how receptive she'd be to my hands exploring her mostly bare back and sides while she was only wearing a bathing suit. But the more we kissed, and the more she touched me— letting her thumbs trace along my collarbone and slide across my shoulders and arms, making a path of fire blaze everywhere on my skin—I knew I had to touch her, too. Needed to feel more of her so I would know this was real and not just another fantasy that my mind had conjured up to torture me with tomorrow.

So, ignoring all the warning bells in my head that told me her brothers would kill me if they knew I'd touched their sister in the hot tub, I dared to reach my hands under the water and gently slid them across her ribcage and up and down her back.

"Yes, please," she mumbled against my mouth, the yearning in her voice causing my lower stomach muscles to clench. "Pull me closer, Mack."

I went still for a split second, caught off guard by the desire in her voice, but then I traced my hands down the

23

CAMBRIELLE

MACK and I had only kissed each other once before—just those few stolen moments in the gazebo in the park last night. But the instant our lips touched, it was like we'd never been apart because we picked right back up from where we'd left off.

Only this time, we were in the hot tub in his backyard, and instead of having our jackets and T-shirts between us, it was just our swimsuits and skin. So much more skin than I was used to feeling on a guy.

But as I let my hands trace their way across the corded muscles of his shoulders and arms, and when he pulled me onto his lap, I couldn't help but think that this was the perfect scenario for a second kiss with Mack.

His arms tightened around my waist, and he gently pulled me with him as he leaned back into the jetted back of the hot tub's wall.

"Is this okay?" he mumbled, breaking away for a second and sounding as out of breath as I was.

"Yes," I said, thinking it was sweet of him to care about how I was feeling. "This is exactly what I wanted to happen tonight."

His lips curled up into a contented smile. "Me too." And then his lips were pressing against mine again.

As I'd gotten dressed in my bathing suit earlier, part of me had worried that I wouldn't know what to do if I got the chance to kiss Mack again. Part of me worried I might make the same mistake that I made last night with he who shall not be named and never be able to face Mack after I left this hot tub. But as Mack pulled me even closer in the water and as he deepened the kiss, nothing embarrassing happened. I didn't do anything that sent me jumping out of the hot tub and running back to my house next door.

No, when Mack's tongue slowly grazed against my bottom lip, I welcomed the deepening of the kiss and just let myself get lost in the exchange.

And it felt so good. So unbelievably good to open myself up and experience Mack this way.

I'd never thought I'd be interested in French kissing someone before, but there was something about the way it felt with Mack that was addicting. And the only thoughts that I could make out as my mind clouded with the desire I had for him was that I wanted more.

More time alone with Mack. More of the warmth swirling through my veins as he kissed me. Just more time to get to know him this way.

He trailed kisses along my jaw and down my neck, making me gasp as a path of fire followed everywhere his lips touched. And as I let my head fall back while he kissed across my collarbone to my shoulder, my mind became mush. I wondered if I'd ever be able to draw in a decent breath again because it felt so good. So incredibly good.

"This must be what it feels like to be taken up to heaven," I whispered before I could stop myself.

"So you like that?" Mack mumbled against my neck as he made his way back up. "Do you like it when I kiss you like this, Cambrielle?"

"Yes." I sighed, pressing my fingers into his shoulders more tightly. "I. Don't." I breathed. "Ever want you to stop."

I never wanted him to stop because there had never been another moment in my life that had felt this good. I'd never felt this kind of euphoria before.

"Good," he said, his lips curving up into a smile on my skin as he chuckled. "I'm not planning to stop until you tell me to."

His hands slid down my back and smoothed across my hips, and when he pressed me impossibly closer, I had the first thrill of nerves hit me because I realized where this could lead if we weren't careful.

And even though I doubted Mack had plans to take things further than kissing tonight, I knew things sometimes got out of hand when hormones and hot tubs were involved.

"Did I do something wrong?" Mack pulled his head back, as if he'd been able to read my anxious thoughts the moment they slipped into my mind.

"No..." I said.

"No?" he asked.

I tucked some stray hair behind my ear. "I mean..." I looked at him bashfully. "I just got slightly nervous."

"Because of me? Is this too much?" he asked. "Because I

can slow this down. I know this is all new and I can be a lot sometimes. And—"

"It's not too much." I put a finger to his lips before he could suggest we stop and go back into our separate homes. "I guess I just want to make sure you're fine with just kissing and not expecting more. Because I know you're probably a lot more experienced than I am and—" I stopped, not sure how to finish my sentence without completely humiliating myself.

"And you want to make sure I'm not going to try to hook up with you tonight?" he asked.

I nodded, my whole body burning with embarrassment as I looked down at him.

But instead of laughing or looking like he was disappointed that this wasn't going to end in his bedroom, he cupped my cheek gently in his hand and said, "I'm only planning on kissing you, Cambrielle."

"You weren't hoping for more?" I asked, my voice shaking slightly with nerves.

He shook his head. "I know I don't exactly have the best reputation when it comes to things like this, but..." He pressed his lips together and really looked into my eyes when he said, "But despite any of the rumors you may have heard, I've never gone past second base."

"What?"

"I'm a virgin," he said.

"You mean you haven't...?" I asked before I could stop myself.

He shook his head again. "There hasn't been anyone I've wanted to do that with yet."

Mack Aarden, the king of kissing...was actually a virgin?

"Really?" I asked, still not believing it.

"Yes, really." He chuckled lightheartedly.

And I knew I should probably say something more, so I said, "I think that's sweet."

"Sweet?" He arched his eyebrows.

"Um...cool?" I tried again.

He laughed. "I'm fine with being considered sweet."

We just stared at each other, smiling.

Then after a moment, he said, "So now that we know we're on the same page—" He leaned his forehead against mine. "—is it okay if I kiss you again?"

My grin stretched wide across my cheeks as I said, "I think I would like that."

24

MACK

"YOU'RE REALLY good at this, you know," I told Cambrielle after we'd been kissing in my hot tub for an unknown amount of time. It could have been fifteen minutes, could have been an hour. I really didn't know since time passed so quickly with Cambrielle.

"I had a good teacher." She gently smoothed a hand across my chest, giving me a flirtatious look. "A *really* good teacher."

"I told you I was a good teacher." I grinned. "And now that you've said it, I guess we can put that on my resumé after all, can't we?"

But she shook her head and gave me a serious look before saying, "Sorry, but I'm slightly territorial, and so I'm not going to want to share my kissing tutor with any other students after this."

"Oh, you're not?" I arched my eyebrows, loving the playful exchange.

She shook her head again and wrapped her arms behind

my neck to pull herself closer. "Is that going to be a problem?"

"Well..." I said, pretending like I needed to think about it.

"Mack." She smacked my chest gently, making water droplets splash into the air.

I couldn't help but chuckle because I loved this. I loved being lighthearted and fun, and also super romantic with this girl at the same time. It was the perfect mix of a relationship that I'd never had before.

Not that we were in a relationship.

I mean, we'd barely kissed twice.

But if she was anywhere near the same wavelength that I was on, I already knew that I wanted this to be more than a one-night thing.

I wanted it to continue long after the sunrise in a few hours.

Possibly much longer than that.

So after glancing at her lips and feeling a thrill of excitement twist in my stomach because I still couldn't believe this was even happening, I said, "As long as you don't plan to steal all my techniques to open a private tutoring practice of your own, I'll keep you as my only student."

"Good plan," she said, leaning closer so her chest pressed against mine in a way that almost short-circuited my brain. "And maybe we can discover some new techniques together."

"I like the sound of that." I brushed my lips against hers, and then we were kissing again.

Usually, being in the hot tub for as long as we'd been here would have me overheated and waterlogged, but with the cooler fall weather and a storm brewing in the sky above, it was perfect. Perfect enough that I could probably stay here until the first rays of sunshine peeked across the trees.

We kissed until we were breathless, and I would have been happy to continue, but then a flash of lightning lit up the sky above, followed by a loud crack of thunder. I knew it was time to head inside.

"I guess we better call it a night, huh?" I asked as the first few droplets of rain landed on my face.

"I guess." She pushed some of her damp hair back against her hairline. "I mean, I don't think we got to the part of the lesson where you were supposed to teach me how to keep a guy wanting more, but I suppose we should stop."

"Oh, I definitely want more," I said, giving her a quick once over.

"Oh, you do?" She gave me a knowing smile, like she did have some insight into how much I wanted her.

"Yes." I smoothed my hand along her side, feeling the ridges of her ribcage against my palm. "But since I do sometimes try to be a gentleman, I'm forcing myself to walk you home instead and bid you goodnight."

"So you don't just dress like a gentlemanly duke from the eighteen hundreds, you even know how to act like one, too?" she asked.

"Tonight I do, at least." I leaned my forehead against hers. "But who knows, maybe next time you'll find yourself alone with a Rake."

Her eyes widened, a look of both alarm and intrigue filling her expression at once.

I chuckled and helped her off my lap. While she pulled the elastic from her hair to redo the messy bun on top of her head, I tilted my head back up to watch the rain falling from the sky. If we were ever going to make it out of this hot tub, I needed to keep my hungry eyes away from her as she arched her back to fix her hair.

When she was done, she held out a hand to me. "Ready to go?"

"I guess." I took her hand and stood beside her, even though I wasn't really ready to leave my backyard with her yet. "Let's get you back home before your brothers find out what I've been doing with their sister."

"HERE, YOU CAN WEAR THIS." I tossed Cambrielle my hoodie when I noticed how badly she was shivering after she'd toweled off.

"Thanks," she said. As she pulled the gray hoodie over her head, I grabbed an extra towel from the basket nearby and wrapped it around my shoulders for some warmth.

After covering the hot tub and turning out the gas fire pit, I took her hand and led her through the opening in the woods between our houses.

"Want me to help you climb up to your balcony?" I offered when we made it to the side of her house, looking up at the large tree I'd climbed those few nights she'd invited me to stay in her room the first week of school.

"And fall to my death when I slip on a branch in the rain?" Her eyes widened. "I don't think so."

"It's my favorite way to sneak into your house..." I lifted a shoulder. "But suit yourself."

"I think I'll take my chances with the back door." She gestured at the door next to one of their garages.

"Taking the easy way out as always," I said, a half-smile on my lips as she pulled me over there.

"That's just me, I guess. Lazy-bones Hastings."

She looked like she was going to punch in the code to unlock the door, but instead of doing that, she turned and leaned her back against the stone exterior of the house.

"Not quite ready to go inside?" I asked, leaning against the wall beside her so we were both protected from the rain.

"Not yet." She angled her beautiful heart-shaped face up at me, which I studied carefully in the dark night. I couldn't help but think she was the most beautiful person in the world.

And there was a huge part of me that didn't want to say goodnight either, fearing that we'd never get such a magical night back again.

I knew we'd joked about me only using my teaching skills on her for the foreseeable future—but was that because she actually wanted to pursue a relationship with me? That she actually saw this going somewhere?

Or was it just a way to have some fun before something better came along?

I didn't think Cambrielle would be the kind of girl to be fine having a weekend fling—she had always been a lot more intentional about things in the past.

But I really didn't know.

I still had a lot of things to learn about Cambrielle, despite knowing her for half my life.

Which reminded me of something I'd wondered about earlier.

"What did Nash say to you after I left you guys at the school?" I asked.

"He just wanted to make sure I was being smart," she said with a shrug.

"Yeah?" I asked, hoping she'd give me more than that.

"Yeah." She nodded.

"And that's all?" I prodded when she didn't continue.

"Not quite." She looked down at my chest instead of my face, and it made me worried.

I swallowed, my mouth suddenly dry. "I'm guessing he wanted you to be smart regarding your choices with me."

"He thought he needed to remind me that you have a certain reputation when it comes to girls." She let her fingers trace up the skin from my abs to my chest. "That you have a reputation for losing interest quickly—despite whatever promises you make in the moment."

I gulped, because all of that was true. I hadn't necessarily led girls on, on purpose. I'd meant what I'd said to them at the time. I just tended to change my mind quicker than I originally planned.

"Are you still worried about that then?" I asked, my stomach in a knot of nerves.

"Well, I'm here with you instead of sleeping in my room," she said with a shrug, like that should explain how she felt.

"Yes, you are."

She was staring at her fingers that were currently tracing some sort of pattern on my chest, looking like she still had more to say. So I waited.

Waited as patiently as I could even though it felt like my heart was going to pound out of my chest.

Finally, she looked up again, meeting my gaze in the stormy night. "But I would be lying if I didn't admit that part of me is scared about what's happening here." She sighed. "And if you're going to change your mind tomorrow."

And there it was.

The truth.

Which I couldn't really blame her for, could I? Since if I ever learned anything in my history class, it was that history usually repeated itself. And if you took a quick trip into my past, you'd find the same patterns repeated over and over again.

But how in the world could I convince Cambrielle that this *felt* different to me this time—more real and more solid—when I couldn't really explain it myself?

I didn't know.

But I had to at least try.

So leaning a shoulder against the wall, I said, "I know my past isn't exactly the best example of me being great at dating and relationships." I peered cautiously into her eyes. "I've been living day to day for so long, it seems that thinking too far into the future just brings more anxiety than I can deal with."

She nodded, looking like she understood but was also disappointed.

I reached for her hand. "But even though I'm not sure what my life will look like a year, or even a month from now, this thing we have—" I rubbed my thumb across her knuckles. "—whatever it is, it feels different than things I've had before, and I..." I sighed, thinking I was probably just messing this up even more the longer I spoke.

Because I was nervous.

So nervous because I'd never felt this way about a girl before.

Never wanted to consider trying to stick around for longer than a night or a weekend.

"And I don't know," I continued. "I think it would be nice to try something different for a change." I dared meet her gaze, feeling my cheeks flush. "Maybe try to see if those rumors we have swirling around about us secretly dating could actually have something to them. See if everyone else knew what I was too blind to see."

"Are you saying you aren't going to forget about me in the morning?" she asked cautiously. "That you might actually like me?"

And the hope that I heard in her voice made me even more sure of my answer than I'd been a moment ago.

"I do, Cambrielle," I whispered. "I think I might like you a lot."

I was just leaning closer to kiss her and show her how I felt in a way that words couldn't say, when headlights from a vehicle flashed from the front of the house.

"That must be Carter or Nash," Cambrielle said, alarm filling her expression.

I looked down the drive. The headlights seemed higher—like they were on Carter's truck. "It's probably Carter," I said, my heart-rate ramping up speed. Looking back to Cambrielle, I asked, "Ready for him to find out about our hot-tub rendezvous?"

"Oh no!" she yelped, putting her hands on her cheeks. "He can't find out about that." She shook her head as panic filled her expression. "He would..." She shook her head again. "Like, I don't think he'd kill you, but I definitely don't see that going over well."

"So I'm guessing that's my cue to slink off into the woods?" I asked.

"Yes, sorry." She grabbed my arm and all but shoved me away from her. "I mean, I don't regret what happened. Like at all." She looked up at me. "But, like, you need to go. Now."

The lights from Carter's truck flashed on the trees just before he turned the corner to get to his garage. In the few seconds of time I had before he would catch us, I bent down, pressed a quick kiss to Cambrielle's cheek, and said, "I'll talk to you later."

"Yes, tomorrow." She nodded, pushing on my chest again. "Now go."

Right before Carter's truck lights could become a spotlight on me, I darted across the driveway and hid behind a bush.

By the time I had turned around to watch Carter's garage door lifting, Cambrielle had disappeared inside.

Man, that was close, I thought, breathing hard.

Then once Carter's truck was in the garage and the door had closed behind it, I wandered back through the woods to my house, thinking that tonight might have been the most exhilarating night I'd ever had.

And sneaking behind my best friends' back to see their sister might be my new favorite activity.

25

CAMBRIELLE

I SLEPT IN SUNDAY MORNING, not getting out of bed until eleven-thirty since my body apparently needed the sleep after such a late night. But once I was awake enough to remember all the events of the evening before, I immediately rolled over to check my phone to see if Mack had texted me.

And sure enough, when my screen lit up, there was a text waiting.

Mack: **I hope you slept well. Also, in case you were wondering, I still didn't change my mind.**

A wide grin stretched across my cheeks, because I didn't realize until that moment just how much I needed that reassurance.

How much that even though he'd said he wanted things to be different this time, different with me, there was still a part of me that worried last night would just be another on the long list of Mack's weekend flings.

I knew the weekend still wasn't over, and only time

would tell what was in store for us, but I decided to be happy that the sun had come up and Mack was still thinking about me and wanting to continue whatever we had growing between us.

I sat up in bed and leaned against my pillows as I typed my response.

Me: **I slept great. Just woke up actually. And in case you were wondering, I didn't change my mind either.**

If I needed the reassurance, I figured he might need it, too.

I was in the middle of typing a second text to ask him if he'd have time to hang out today when there was a knock on my door.

"Cambrielle?" Nash's voice came from the other side of the door. "Are you awake yet?"

Had he been just sitting out there waiting for me to wake up and somehow heard me move or my mattress shifting?

"I just woke up," I called from my bed.

"Mind if I come in?" he asked.

"Um..." I looked around my room, suddenly paranoid that if he came in here, he would somehow sense what I'd done last night—somehow know that part of me had changed when I'd left my bedroom in search of beginning something with Mack.

"I just want to chat with my sister for a few minutes." He jiggled the doorknob. I couldn't remember if I'd locked my bedroom door last night or not, so I panicked and tossed my phone beneath the pillow beside me.

In as calm a voice as I could muster, I said, "Sure, you can come in."

He opened the door a second later, like he'd been about to open it anyway before I'd invited him in. After glancing around my room suspiciously, as if expecting to find something or someone in here with me, he stepped the rest of the way in. "Hey."

"Hi." I studied my brother who looked freshly showered and dressed in a sweater and jeans, like he'd already done his Sunday morning laps in the pool.

While I liked to sleep in on the morning after a late night, Nash could never seem to sleep in. No matter what time he'd gone to bed the night before, he was wide awake by seven A.M.

Nash shut the door behind him. After taking his usual seat on the chair in the corner, he said, "I just wanted to check in with you and see how you're doing this morning."

I bet he did. In our previous conversation, he'd all but told me that he knew better than I did about who I should or should not like.

"I'm doing good," I said, ignoring the elephant he was trying to bring into the room.

"Yeah?" he asked, the expectant look on his face telling me he thought that I should be saying more.

But since I *wasn't* going to be an open book when it came to my feelings for the opposite sex for the first time in my life, I just kept my mouth shut and pretended like there was nothing more to add.

He studied me for a moment, and when I didn't offer anything, he pressed his lips together and said, "You slept in later than usual. Did you do anything after you left the school?"

"Not really," I said with a shrug. "Just came home and got ready for bed."

Made out with Mack in his hot tub.

"Nothing else?" Nash narrowed his gaze.

I scratched the side of my head as if trying to remember any other interesting details about my night. "I had a hard time taking out my pink contacts, and it took a few minutes to wash off the makeup..."

Nash puckered his lips into a frown. "You didn't meet up with Mack?" he asked, his blue eyes probing. "You didn't meet up with Mack to have that fling you said you wanted?"

Until this point, I'd been doing what my mom and dad called "lying by omission." I'd told him about the other things I'd done last night and just left out the part he was wanting to know about.

But in that moment, to protect something that was new and special and something I didn't want interference from my brothers, I made the split-second decision to lie.

To outright lie to my brother about my love life.

Because for the first time in my life, I might actually have a love life worth protecting.

So with a shrug, I said, "I thought about what you said on my ride home and realized you were right and probably knew more about guys than I did. So I just went to bed."

Lie.

"Really?" he asked.

"Yeah," I said. "And now that it's morning and I've had some time to think about it, I'm glad I didn't let my emotions get the better of me because that would be so weird to kiss Mack."

Another big fat lie. Kissing Mack was pretty much the best feeling in the world.

"It could have definitely complicated things," Nash said, his gaze measuring me like he was still suspicious that I hadn't just gone to bed last night like I was pretending.

His lie-detecting radar was working just as it should because I was totally lying through my teeth.

But since I was now committed to this new narrative, I said, "Yeah, and we're becoming such good friends it would be dumb to possibly mess it up."

The jury was still out on whether that statement would end up being a truth or a lie. But I was telling myself that risking our friendship for the possibility of something more was worth it.

"How was the rest of the movie?" I asked, deciding to change the subject before he could ask me any more questions.

"It was good," he said, adjusting his position in the chair. "I'm pretty sure I'll have nightmares until I can forget about the guy climbing through the mirror, but that's the price you pay for a fully-lived Halloween."

"Eh, I'll let you be the one with the nightmares," I said. Then remembering back to the few times I'd seen him and Elyse dance, I asked, "Did you convince Elyse to cuddle up to you during the movie?"

"No." His expression fell.

"What?" I asked, genuinely surprised.

He shrugged. "I don't know what it is, but I'm like terrified of her."

"You're afraid of Elyse?" My eyebrows knitted together. "But she's literally the nicest person I've ever met."

"I know..." He leaned back and ran a hand through his tousled blond hair. "It's like, she's so perfect and amazing that I can't help but think that she's too out of my league to ever be interested in me."

Out of Nash's league?

Was he being serious right now?

I knew he sometimes felt like the "second choice" brother—comparing himself to Carter who had always been a little more popular with the girls since he'd hit puberty a year and a half before Nash. But Nash had filled out more in the past year and had even reached his goal of being six-foot just last month. So while Carter had his whole half-Latino, blue-eyed, charming vibe going for him that Ava couldn't get enough of, that didn't mean her twin had the same taste.

Even if Elyse did have the same taste as Ava—if there was some sort of genetic component to whom identical twins were attracted to—you really couldn't get much closer to that particular look than Nash, since my brothers still did look a lot alike. Only a few shades of skin tone and three inches in height kept people from confusing them as twins themselves.

Aside from looks, there was so much more to him than that. Even despite all his meddling and teasing ways, he was crazy talented and had such a fun-loving side to him that you couldn't help but love the guy.

And if last night with Mack was any testament to how amazing something could turn out if you just took the risk and put yourself out there, I figured my brother deserved to have something work out like that for him.

So I told him, "I think you're overthinking this too much.

I mean, Elyse is pretty great and one of my best friends, but you're pretty awesome, too. I don't see why she wouldn't like you. Or in the least, want to go on a date."

"You think so?" he asked, his gaze flickering to me like he didn't quite believe it.

"Of course," I said. "Remember that I, as your sister, can say that even after living with you during middle school when you were at the peak of your annoying streak. But you're in your senior year now, and you're on almost every girl's list of the top-ten most dateable guys at our school. Why wouldn't a girl like Elyse fall for your special charm?"

"My special charm?" He cocked an eyebrow, like he wasn't sure the description was something to be proud of or worried about.

"Just take it as a compliment." I shrugged. "I mean, I'm your sister, so that's as good as it's going to get from me."

"Fair enough." He sat up straighter, and it did seem like my pep talk had boosted his confidence a little.

Which made me feel slightly less guilty about lying to him about Mack.

He stood. "Well, I'm probably going to go practice *The Music of the Night* for my audition."

"Don't you already know the whole musical by heart?" I asked.

"You never can be too prepared," he said. "I don't want to give Miss Crawley any reason not to cast me as the lead this time."

He'd gone into a slight depression when he hadn't been cast as Jean Valjean in last winter's production of *Les Miserables*. But as soon as Miss Crawley had announced what they'd be doing this winter, he'd immediately downloaded the music and started practicing. He'd even passed on the opportunity to play in this fall's production of *The Music Man* because he didn't want his role in that to possibly keep him from getting the lead in this one.

So yeah, saying my brother was invested in becoming the Phantom would be an understatement.

But I was sure he would get the part. He'd been trained by the best vocal teacher in New Haven and had taken acting classes over the summer to prepare for an epic senior year. No one was more prepared than Nash was to rule the stage this winter.

"Maybe I'll come down later and practice my dance audition," I said. "I can't look like the lazy Hastings sibling when it comes to auditions in a few weeks."

"Maybe you should," he said.

He left my room then, and as soon as he'd shut the door behind him, I grabbed my phone from beneath the pillow beside me to see if Mack had texted me back.

He had.

Mack: **I'm glad to hear you haven't changed your mind because if you did, I'd just have to change it right back.**

I smiled as a thrill of anticipation filled me. This was actually happening.

Me: **I mean, if you convincing me includes more of what we did last night, maybe I do need my memory refreshed.**

Because I was pretty sure I could kiss him forever and never want to stop.

Mack: **If we weren't having lunch with my**

grandma in a few minutes I'd sneak up your balcony right now and show you exactly why you don't want to step away from this.

My stomach fluttered at the thought of him doing just that—fluttered over the fact that Mack Aarden, the boy whom I'd always thought was infinitely out of my reach, was even saying these things to me.

Like, was this even real life? Because I was pretty sure it felt like I'd stepped into a fairytale.

Me: **If only you didn't already have plans. Because that would have been fun.**

Mack: **It would. I'd love to say that I could come over after lunch, but if my mom is feeling up to it, I'm planning to spend the rest of the day with her.**

Me: **I totally get that.**

As much as I wanted to spend all my free time with Mack, I was not about to come between him and his mom. Because while none of us really knew how long we had here on earth, they did know her time would be coming to an end soon and Mack would never be able to get these precious moments with his mom back.

Mack: **But I'll be in our foods class tomorrow, so you better be there too.**

Me: **Pretty sure it will be my favorite class tomorrow.**

I felt bad that Elyse was stuck with Ben now because of our partner swap, but I couldn't be any happier with the arrangement we had.

I knew I should probably change into my dance clothes

so I could practice my audition piece, but since I needed to make sure Mack and I were on the same page regarding my brothers, I sent him another text

Me: **In the meantime, if you hear from Nash or Carter and they ask what you did last night, whatever you do, do not mention me.**

Mack: **You don't want me to tell your brothers that I did you?**

Me: **Ah! That is not what I meant.**

Mack: **Too bad…**

Me: **Har har. Also, it sounds so much more scandalous when you word it like that.**

Mack: **Being scandalous is fun.**

Me: **This is serious.**

Mack: **Okay.**

Me: **So what are you going to do if my brothers ask you about me?**

Mack: **Deny. Deny. Deny.**

Me: **Good.**

I tossed my phone to the side, needing to breathe for a moment.

I could do this.

I could totally sneak around behind my brothers' backs with their best friend.

Piece of cake.

"WHEN WILL COACH James announce who made the team?" Cambrielle asked me after school Monday afternoon as we walked down the sidewalk from the gym toward the student parking lot.

I'd had basketball tryouts right after school and she'd finished her study session with Scarlett, Ava, and Elyse just before tryouts had ended, so it gave us a few minutes to see each other. It was the first time we'd been alone since I'd left her at the side of her house early Sunday morning, and I'd be lying if I didn't admit that I was slightly nervous to be with her again after all the things that had happened.

Nervous because I hadn't exactly made it to Monday morning with a girl before, so I wasn't quite sure how this was supposed to work.

Like, were we just two people who liked each other and sometimes kissed?

Or were we secretly boyfriend and girlfriend now?

Something else?

"I think Coach said he'd have the roster posted by tomorrow after school." I adjusted the strap of my gym bag on my shoulder. "But I'm pretty sure Carter, Hunter, and I will all make it."

Tryouts had snuck up on me with everything that was going on, but I had played enough during the off season at the Hastings' basketball court that I'd been able to keep up on most of my skills.

"It would be crazy if you didn't make it," Cambrielle said, her usual encouraging self. "Crazy if you all weren't the starting line-up."

"I guess we'll see." I shrugged. And then, since potential boyfriends were supposed to be interested in their potential girlfriends and not just talk about themselves, I asked, "What about you? Are you ready for your audition in a couple weeks?"

"I think so." She let out a long breath, a hint of anxiety in her eyes. "I mean, I'm pretty sure I'll make it since most people are auditioning for speaking roles, but you never know."

"Are you nervous about going on stage again?" I asked.

"A little." Her gaze flickered up to mine. "It's been a while since I've performed in front of anyone."

"Aside from those couple of minutes I spied on you on Saturday." I gave her a half-smile.

"Yes. Aside from that." Her cheeks flushed. "But since the last time I was on stage was when I passed out from starving myself, it's a little scary to face that again."

"Well, for what it's worth," I said, daring to rest my hand on the small of her back. "I'm excited for everyone to see what I saw in your ballroom on Saturday."

"Yeah?" she asked, looking up at me with the most adorably bashful expression.

"Yes." Then leaning closer, I whispered, "Just don't let any other guys fall for you while you're on stage. Because I want that to be *our* thing."

It felt risky to say that—to touch her back in a way that would tell anyone watching us that she was *mine*—since we were still in the testing-things-out part of our relationship. But when her cheeks flushed and a shy smile lifted her lips, it was worth it.

Worth it because it reassured me that she probably felt the same butterflies I felt whenever we were together.

"So you're saying that my dancing skills are what did it for you?" She adjusted the weight of her backpack on her shoulder.

"That and your kissing skills," I said. "I mean, all it took was one practice kiss and I was basically a goner."

She glanced around the deserted parking lot, like she was afraid someone would see and overhear us and be onto our little secret. But finding no one around, just a few dozen cars from the students who lived in the dorms, she looked back up to me and said, "I'd like to say that's all it took for me, but we both know that would be a lie. It was probably game over for me when you invited me to play night games in seventh grade when my brothers tried to say I was too young."

"It was the night games that got you?" I asked. I'd known she'd liked me back when I was in eighth grade and she was in seventh, her crush had been obvious and cute, but I'd always assumed it was because I was the only guy she spent much time around who wasn't related to her.

"You were nice." She shrugged.

"So it had nothing to do with the sexy mustache I had back then?" I wiggled my eyebrows flirtatiously.

"No." She scrunched up her face. "Let's just say I liked you *despite* that mustache and was so thankful when you learned how to shave."

I chuckled. "I guess it's a good thing my mom pulled me aside one day and told me to get rid of the ugly caterpillar on my upper lip."

"Your mom is basically a saint," Cambrielle said. "You probably owe all your success in Spin the Bottle to her for encouraging you to shave."

"Too bad the bottle never landed on you when I spun it though." I smirked. "We totally could have had that first kiss years ago."

"Pretty sure my brothers would have made you spin again."

"You're probably right."

We made it to my gray Toyota Land Cruiser a moment later, and I opened the back door to toss my gym bag onto the seat.

After looking around the parking lot to make sure we were away from prying eyes, I leaned against the side of my vehicle and pulled her against me.

"This is kind of nice, isn't it?" I asked, smoothing my fingers through the ends of her soft hair when she pressed herself against me. "Just spending time alone without everyone else."

"It is nice." She turned her face upward, her chin on my chest. And I loved how tiny she felt against me. I was six-five and she was barely over five feet. I was basically a giant compared to her.

But I kind of loved that about us.

Us.

I smiled as I thought about that word and what it meant.

I'd never been an "us" with anyone before.

"I'm guessing you'll be going home after this?" Cambrielle asked, slipping her hands inside the jacket of my school uniform. I still wore my workout clothes from basketball practice but had put my blue blazer on to fend off the autumn chill.

"It's almost dinner, so I probably should."

"No time for another one of your lessons?" She arched an eyebrow, a flirtatious smile on her lips.

I studied her raspberry-colored mouth, the image of us kissing flitting through my mind. "You want a lesson right here in the school's parking lot?" I licked my lips as anticipation swelled in my veins.

"You do have tinted windows." She glanced at my vehicle behind me, her lips parted in a seductive way. "It could be a short lesson."

Okay, who was this girl? And what had she done with the innocent little sister of my best friends?

I swallowed. "Dinner isn't for another thirty minutes. I think I could make time for a brief lesson."

I took her backpack from her and set it on the far end of the second row of seats, pushing my gym bag over with it. I was just about to climb in myself, planning to pull her onto my lap, when voices sounded from behind us.

I craned my neck to see who the voices belonged to, and that was when I saw Carter and Ava walking toward Carter's truck a few parking spots away.

Crap!

They could not see us.

"What do we do?" Cambrielle asked, her eyes wide with panic as she looked at her brother. "My car is on the other end of the parking lot."

I glanced at our surroundings, trying to find a place for her to hide. But there were no cars or trees in the immediate vicinity that she could hide behind.

Carter and Ava were presently looking at each other, so they hadn't seen us yet, but any big movements would bring their attention to us.

"Just hide in here," I said, gently shoving her into my car.

I'd pushed her in there just in time, because as I was shutting the door, Carter and Ava finished laughing about something and looked my way.

"Oh, hey Mack," Ava said, waving to me with a big smile on her face.

"Hey." I shut the door the rest of the way and hoped the window tint was dark enough to hide Cambrielle. I cleared my throat. "This weather is great, isn't it?"

Why did I just randomly bring up the weather?

If that wasn't a way to make someone suspicious, I didn't know what was.

"Um, yeah." Ava frowned, looking around at the trees that had their last leaves clinging to their branches. "It's, uh, it's beautiful if you're into chilly, overcast days, I guess."

"My favorite kind of day," I said, plastering a smile to my lips. I actually preferred sunshine and cloudless skies, but I'd started this conversation so I needed to stick with it. "Anyway, I better get going. See you guys tomorrow."

"See ya," Carter called, a confused frown on his lips as he opened the passenger door of his black Ford Raptor for

Ava, like he knew I was acting weird but didn't understand why.

But if thinking I was weird distracted him from seeing his sister in my SUV, I was fine with it.

I walked behind my vehicle to climb into the driver's seat. As I pulled my seatbelt around me to buckle in, I glanced at the second row where I expected to find Cambrielle.

Only, instead of finding Cambrielle sitting where I'd set her, she was now crouched down on the floor in a contortion I could never get into, especially in a school uniform.

"What are you doing down there?" I asked.

"Hiding from Carter and Ava, of course," she said.

"But I don't think they can see into the back," I said. "You don't need to sit down there."

"It's fine," she said, barely lifting her head. "I'm small and can fit."

"I guess that's true," I said. Tiny people could fit in tiny places, I supposed. "We'll just wait for Carter to drive away, and then you can sneak out."

I looked through my driver's window to see if Carter was pulling out yet. But when our gazes met, he made a waving motion with his hand.

"Dang it," I said to Cambrielle. "Carter's waiting for me to head out first."

"What?" She made a rustling sound like she was poking her head up to see what I was seeing.

"I think he's planning to follow me out." I waved to Carter and smiled, hoping he hadn't noticed I was talking to someone in a vehicle I was supposed to be alone in.

"But my car is here. I can't go home without my car," Cambrielle said. "Someone will notice."

"It's fine." I put my Land Cruiser in reverse and started pulling out of my parking spot. "I'll just pull off to get gas or something, and then I'll bring you back."

So I headed out of the parking lot and down the tree-shrouded drive that led to the school's gates. Once out, I turned onto the road and headed toward the opposite end of town where we lived, with Carter's truck following close behind.

"This must be what it feels like to be a criminal," Cambrielle said.

I chuckled. "If you get this excited about being a stow-away, I can't wait to see how excited you get when we actually do something illegal."

"You're planning to have a life of crime then?" Cambrielle asked.

"I don't know. Maybe." I glanced over my shoulder. "I've already snuck into the home of a billionaire multiple times to sleep in his daughter's room. And I'm currently kidnapping said daughter. Maybe a life of crime should be my extra backup plan if the NBA or the kissing tutor thing don't work out."

"I've always wanted to secretly date a bad boy," Cambrielle's voice drifted over the seats, a hint of a smile in her voice.

"And here I thought you were this innocent little creature." I chuckled. "If I'd known about your dark side, I totally would have tried corrupting you sooner."

"I'm sure it would have been fun."

A minute later, the "Welcome to Eden Falls" sign came

into view through the trees, and soon we were driving past the various businesses and shops on Main Street. I spotted the gas station I usually went to, turned into the parking lot, and pulled up to a pump.

I planned to idle there for a few seconds, just to wait for Carter's truck to pass on his way to his house. But instead of continuing down Main Street like I expected, he turned into the gas station parking lot behind us.

"Is he actually following us?" I wondered aloud.

"What?" Cambrielle popped her head up again to see what I was talking about, only to immediately duck back down.

"Don't you guys have someone who fills all your vehicles up with gas when he details them?" I looked back to Cambrielle with a confused expression.

"Yeah. Vaughn tops them off every few days." She frowned as she peeked her head up again to look through the window at Carter's truck that was passing the gas pumps and pulling into a parking spot. "Maybe he's getting something from inside? I think Ava has an addiction to the mixed sodas they started serving here, and so they stop here a lot."

"Looks like I'll be filling up with gas then." I looked at my gas gauge. "With, like, half a gallon of gas since I just filled up on my way to school this morning."

I climbed out, opened my gas tank, and started filling it up. It stopped itself after about ten seconds since I really didn't need any gas. But I needed to make it look like I actually needed this stop on my way home, so I just leaned against my Land Cruiser and scrolled through my phone to pass the time like I normally did when I filled up.

After a minute or so, I put the gas nozzle back where it

belonged, hit the button saying I didn't need a receipt, and then headed inside the gas station.

Carter and Ava came out of the doors right before I reached them, a big Styrofoam soda cup in Ava's hand and a bag of Starbursts under Carter's arm.

"Hey." I nodded to them when we met.

"Hey." Carter nodded back and Ava just smiled and waved.

I continued into the building and texted Cambrielle.

Want anything while I'm in here? I'm going to wait until Carter and Ava are actually gone this time so they can't follow us anymore.

Her text came through a few seconds later.

Cambrielle: **I'd love a diet Dr Pepper with raspberry puree and coconut creamer.**

Me: **So you're a fan of the drinks too?**

Cambrielle: **Ava got me hooked.**

I chuckled and went to order her drink from the soda counter in the back.

Carter's truck was nowhere to be seen by the time I made it outside with Cambrielle's drink and a bag of sunflower seeds.

"You can probably climb into the passenger seat and ride like a normal person," I told Cambrielle, setting her drink in the console beside me.

"Finally." She sighed. "My legs were starting to cramp up."

It took her a moment to get off the floor, but eventually, she slipped out the back door and climbed into the passenger seat beside me.

"Whew," she said, leaning against the seat and pushing some of her hair out of her face. "That was close."

I chuckled. "Apparently, this secret relationship thing is going to be more exciting than we expected."

She grabbed her seatbelt from behind her. "Apparently."

"Your drink." I offered her the soda cup once she was buckled in.

"Thanks." She took it from me and took a long sip from it. "Ah, this is so good. Thank you."

"Anything for my partner in crime."

We drove back to the school, and despite it being an overcast day, the clouds had parted enough that we could see the sun setting behind the trees on our way.

"Where are you parked?" I asked when we pulled into the student parking lot again.

"That way." Cambrielle pointed to where her red Mercedes was parked next to a tall, mostly naked tree.

I pulled into the spot next to her car and put my SUV in park. "We made it back."

"Finally," she said with a little laugh.

"How's your drink?" I asked, eyeing the Styrofoam cup that she'd been sipping on the whole drive back.

"Delicious." She held the cup out to me. "Wanna taste?"

"Sure." But instead of taking her cup and putting the straw in my mouth, I set it in one of the cupholders and pulled her in for a kiss.

Her lips curved up into a smile as I kissed her. She whispered, "I was hoping you'd do that."

I chuckled and kissed her again. After tasting her mouth for a few seconds, I pulled away and said, "Yes, that coco-raspberry Dr Pepper is delicious."

She laughed. "Maybe you'll have to get yourself one next time."

"Nah." I shook my head. "I think I prefer experiencing it this way."

I pushed the button to unbuckle her seatbelt and slid my hand behind her waist to pull her onto my lap.

She squealed on her way over the console and her butt bumped against the car horn, making us both laugh, but then she settled in on my lap and we were kissing again.

"You're not worried about anyone seeing us?" Cambrielle asked between kisses. "Because the front windows aren't tinted, you know."

I reclined my seat to a forty-five-degree angle. "Better?" I asked, nodding at the tinted window that was hiding our faces. "Does that give you enough privacy?"

"That's much better." When she leaned forward and brushed her lips against mine, my stomach filled with butterflies.

I slid one hand into her hair, the other hand going to her hip and squeezing. I loved the little bit of softness she had there. Loved it not just because I was a butt guy and had always been more attracted to girls with a little junk in their trunk, but because it told me she was taking better care of herself than she used to—allowing her body to just be normal and healthy and not starving herself to fit an impossible ideal the media and dancing world had her buying into.

"Are you hot?" she asked after a second, pulling away. "It's so hot in here."

"It's a little toasty," I said, not actually caring about the temperature because I was too into the kiss to be bothered by it.

"Can you help me out of this?" She leaned back and started tugging on the sleeves of her navy-blue blazer.

"Of course."

I slid my hands under the shoulders of her polyester blazer and helped her roll it down her arms. She pulled her arms free and then tossed it onto the passenger seat beside us.

"Better?" I asked.

"So much better." She pushed her long hair to the side of her neck and rested it over her shoulder. "Do you want help out of yours?"

"Sure."

I sat up eagerly and allowed her to slide her hands up my chest and along my shoulders as she helped guide my own blazer down. She pulled on the sleeves to free my arms, and after tossing my jacket on top of hers, she lowered herself back down to kiss me again.

When her warm hands spread along my chest and sides, squeezing as she explored, I was right back to being in heaven.

"I have to leave in a few minutes, okay?" I said breathlessly a few minutes later as I trailed my hands up and down the side of her legs.

"I know," she said. "I've just been dying to do this for two days."

"You have?" I asked.

"Of course," she said. "I think you've turned me into an addict."

We kissed for another minute, but then her phone started ringing.

"It's my mom." She groaned after looking at the caller ID

on her watch. "She's probably calling to see if I'll be home for dinner."

"Which means they've probably already delivered dinner to my house, too."

"I guess we'll have to try this again another day then." She sighed and lifted herself off my chest.

I nodded. "Pencil me into your calendar for a few minutes after school tomorrow?"

She gave me a heart-melting smile. "Of course."

We stared at each other for another long moment. But knowing that I actually did need to leave if I wanted to spend any time with my mom before she went to bed for the night, I patted her legs and said, "Time to climb off."

She pouted and sighed, looking disappointed. But then she said, "Okay."

I opened the door and helped her out. Then I grabbed her blazer and handed it to her. While she put her jacket back on, I climbed out and grabbed her soda and backpack from the second row.

"Text me later?" I asked as I handed her her things.

She nodded and took them from me. "Of course."

27

CAMBRIELLE

"WHO ARE you texting with a big smile on your face?" Elyse asked me Thursday afternoon. We'd just finished our homework in the school's library and were waiting for all our basketball-playing friends—Mack, Carter, Hunter, Scarlett, and Ava—to come back from their practices.

"No one," I said, pressing the button to lock the screen of my phone and hide the text Mack had just sent, saying he'd be up to steal me away after he showered off.

"No one?" Elyse arched an eyebrow. "You sure? Because that doesn't look like a 'no one' smile."

"Um..." I cleared my throat that was suddenly thick with guilt "No one important?"

"You sure you weren't texting Ben?" she asked, wiggling her eyebrows playfully.

"What? No."

"No? But I thought...?"

"I can't believe I forgot to tell you." I shook my head,

realizing that with everything that had happened with Mack this week, I'd completely forgotten to warn Elyse about Ben.

"Tell me what?" Elyse furrowed her brow.

"That he's a total fraud."

"A fraud?"

"Yes," I said. Then I told her everything. I told her about what I'd overheard during the Halloween dance. About his stupid plan to kiss all the girls on his stupid list. About how he'd done it all just because of a dare. And then how he'd tricked me so badly that I'd kissed him.

Elyse put a hand to her chest when I finished my story. "I had no idea he was like that. He's always been so nice to me."

"Yeah. That's part of his method, I guess," I said. "I can't believe I forgot to tell you about it sooner because from what I overheard, it sounds like he was planning to go after you and Addison next."

"What?" Her light-brown eyes widened. "Why me?"

"I don't know," I said. "But I'd probably stay away from him if I were you."

"Yikes." She leaned back in her chair. "Thanks for the warning."

"No problem."

When I started packing my books into my backpack, my phone buzzed again. I glanced at it, itching to pick it up since it was probably Mack telling me where to meet him. But when Elyse eyed my phone suspiciously, I decided to ignore it. I could totally wait until I had all my things in my backpack before I looked at my phone, right?

I was just slipping my tablet into my backpack when my phone buzzed again.

"You gonna check that?" Elyse asked with a half-smile on her lips, almost daring me to resist.

"It's probably just my mom asking me if I'll be home for dinner," I said with a shrug, hoping to come off as uninterested even though I was slightly dying inside.

"Here." She set her own phone on the tabletop. "Your hands are busy, I can check it for you."

"No, don't!" I nearly shouted when she reached for my phone.

Her eyes lifted to mine, really intrigued now. "I was just joking," she said. "But with a reaction like that, I have to know what's going on."

"It's nothing," I lied, feeling my cheeks flush.

"Come on, Cambrielle," she said. "Do you really think I'm that dumb? You're obviously on edge about who is texting you."

"I know." I sighed and slumped back into my chair.

"So, have you been texting a guy?" She smirked.

And since I knew it was pointless to lie when the truth was obvious, I said, "Yes."

"Who is it?" She leaned closer. "Someone I know?"

"I can't tell you who it is," I said. "No one can know."

"How come?" She narrowed her eyes. "Is it someone you shouldn't like? Is it Ben? Were you just making up that stuff earlier to confuse me?"

"No, of course not," I hurried to say. "It's definitely not Ben. It's just..." I trailed off, trying to figure out what to say.

"I'm really good at keeping secrets." She smiled. "You know you want to tell me."

"Ahhh," I said, feeling torn. It would be so nice to have someone to gush over my relationship with. Crushes were always more fun when you had someone to talk with about them.

I looked at my friend, debating on whether I dared leak the secret to her or not. Could I trust her?

Would Mack be fine with me telling Elyse? I knew I was the one who came up with the whole plan to keep it secret in the first place. But if Mack was keeping it a secret from his best friends, shouldn't I have to keep it a secret from mine?

"I could just *accidentally* peek at your phone if you're not allowed to tell me..." she said, walking her fingers across the table toward my phone. But before she could lift it up, I swiped it away from her.

"Sorry," I said. "I want to tell you, but me and this guy promised each other we wouldn't tell anyone."

She frowned, her face falling with disappointment.

"It's just so new. I don't want to jinx it," I added, hoping it would help. "But for what it's worth, if I was going to tell someone, I'd tell you first."

"You know I can just follow you wherever you go and find out that way," Elyse said.

"But you're a good friend, so you won't," I said.

"Promise it's not some jerk I wouldn't approve of?" She raised an eyebrow.

"He's definitely not a jerk," I said, unable to keep a smile from my lips as I thought about Mack and how amazing he made me feel when we were together. "He's special."

She studied me for a moment, like she wasn't sure she could trust my judgement when I was being so secretive. But then she shrugged and said, "Then I hope you enjoy texting this mystery guy."

"Thank you," I said, meaning it.

She nodded. "And if something does go wrong, I'm sure your brothers, Hunter, and Mack will be happy to take care of him for you."

I laughed somewhat hysterically because she had no idea she was suggesting Mack take care of himself. But since I couldn't explain that, I just said, "I have no doubt that my brothers wouldn't have a problem seeking revenge if I did get hurt."

"Speaking of brothers..." Elyse said, nodding toward the open library doors. "Looks like my brother and your brother are done with basketball practice for the day."

Sure enough, when I looked behind me, I saw Mack, Carter, and Hunter standing with their gym bags in a huddle with a few other guys from the team.

Mack glanced in my direction, and when our eyes locked, I felt breathless for a second. Because instead of looking at all the other girls milling around the library and the hall—the girls who were popular and skinny and perfect —he was looking at me.

It was too good to be true.

And yet, it *was* true.

I looked away not too long after, since continuing to stare at the gorgeous boy who lived next door would make my feelings super obvious. But when I turned back to Elyse, I worried she may have sensed too much from the few seconds of eye contact Mack and I had shared because she studied me with a curious expression on her face.

"My half-brother is quite the catch, isn't he?" She raised a knowing eyebrow, watching me for my reaction.

And I knew I was caught.

"Um, sure." I cleared my throat, trying to hold onto what

little thread of mystery I had. "I mean, if you're into the tall, dark, and handsome sort of thing."

Which, obviously I was.

She had been into it, too.

Which made me wonder if she was going to be bothered by the fact that I was with Mack when she'd liked him just a few weeks ago.

But instead of looking upset, she simply smiled with a sparkle in her eyes, leaned closer and whispered, "Your secret is safe with me."

Well...so much for Elyse not figuring it out.

But if anyone could be trusted to keep a secret, it would be her. So when she pulled away again, I said, "Whatever you do, don't tell my brothers. They won't understand."

She made a gesture of zipping her lips, and then said, "Secret boyfriend who?"

I smiled gratefully. "Thank you."

As soon as she left, I looked at my phone and saw Mack's text: **Meet me behind the big oak tree after practice.**

I texted him back, glancing at him across the way as I did so.

Me: **Yes**

And then, since I really couldn't have anyone else looking at my phone and discovering our secret, I hurried and changed his name in my contact info.

"SO, I think Elyse knows about us," I told Mack after pulling away from the kiss he gave me when I met him at the oak tree.

"What makes you think that?" he asked, wrapping some of my hair around his finger as he played with it. It was a little thing, I knew. Him touching my hair. But I loved that he did it because it was a signal that he was mine. "Did she ask you?"

"Not outright," I hurried to say. "But she saw me texting you, and I guess I looked a little happier than usual, so it made her think it was a guy. And then, when she saw you look my way in the library earlier, she put two and two together."

"I looked at you for, like, three seconds." He shook his head.

"I know." I shrugged. "But apparently, that was all it took."

"She must be a mind reader or something." He chuckled lightheartedly.

"Probably."

"Well, we almost made it five days with our little secret." He sighed, combing his fingers through my hair and making chills race across my spine.

"It's better than four, I suppose."

"That's definitely true." And I loved the little half-smile he got on his lips. "Is she going to tell Ava? Because we all know that if Ava finds out, it's only a matter of time before Carter finds out and tries to beat me up."

"She said she'd keep it a secret, and out of all our friends, I trust her the most." I shrugged. "But I did change your name in my phone. Just in case someone decided to go snooping."

"You gave me a new name?" He arched a dark eyebrow. "What is it?"

"Alfred," I said.

"Alfred?" He scrunched up his nose at the thought of being renamed Alfred. "Are you serious?"

"It was the least exciting name I could think of."

"Well, if you're going for the boring route—" He slipped his hands around my waist and pulled me closer. "—I'm going to go for the exciting route and change your name to Mistress."

"Mistress?" My jaw dropped open. "You can't do that. Like, you really can't. It makes our relationship sound illicit. *Illegal.*" I shook my head.

"Oh, I have to use it now." His smile broadened, like he was loving how worked up I was getting over this. "In fact..."

He pushed himself away from the tree and fished his phone out from his back pocket.

"What are you doing?" I asked when he unlocked his screen and started typing something into his phone.

"I'm changing your name to Mistress."

"But you can't do that," I said. "What will people say when they see 'Mistress' written across your phone?"

"They'll know that I'm having a lot of fun sneaking around with a very pretty girl," he said flirtatiously. And I appreciated the compliment. Loved that he thought I was pretty.

But he really couldn't change my name to *that.*

"Just put me in as something like Portia, or Roxy if you want something exotic-sounding." I started jumping, trying to steal his phone from him. But that was the hard thing about being over a foot shorter than my secret boyfriend. All he had to do was hold his arm up straight above his head and I had no chance of getting ahold of anything he didn't want me to grab.

"If I was looking for an exotic-sounding name, I'd stick with Cambrielle," he said with a wink, continuing to tap on his phone screen with his thumb.

"But what if someone sees me texting you now?" I asked, breathless from my jumping. "Like, you don't think having the word 'Mistress' at the top of your screen will raise some questions?"

He finished changing my contact info and returned his phone to his back pocket with a smile. "If I have to be Alfred, then you get to be my Mistress."

"I could have changed your name," I said. "I would have changed it to something different, if you asked."

But he just shook his head with a wicked smile on his lips and said, "Sorry, it's already done. It's set in stone now."

I crossed my arms. "You're the worst sometimes, don't you know?"

"The worst and the best." He kissed me on the top of the head.

After glancing around the area to make sure my little jumping scene hadn't drawn any curious eyes, I looked back at him and said, "Well, if I'm your mistress, you better give me a better goodbye kiss than that."

He laughed like I'd hoped, and proving that he was never one to back down from a challenge, he pulled me close again and gave me exactly the kind of kiss I'd asked for.

28

MACK

I PULLED into my garage around five-thirty, after spending a half-hour behind the oak tree with Cambrielle.

I expected the kitchen to be empty when I stepped inside, since my mom spent most of her time in her room, her nurse or my grandma Jackson nearby during the day, and my dad was usually at work until dinner. But as soon as I stepped inside, I found my dad sitting at the kitchen table. And in front of him was one of my mom's recipe binders.

Were the Hastings not providing dinner today then?

"Hey Mack." My dad looked up from what he was doing, his tie loose around his neck and his brown hair tousled like he'd been running his fingers through it.

"Hey," I said, dropping my gym bag on the chair beside him. "Planning to cook something tonight?"

But when I took a closer look, I saw that he was actually leafing through the binder dedicated to my mom's dessert recipes.

Yes, my mom had such a big sweet tooth back before she

got sick that she had a huge binder full of cake, cookie, and pastry recipes that she'd printed off through the years.

"No, the Hastings are still having Marie cook extra for us." Dad ran a hand through his hair. "I'm just looking for the pumpkin pie recipe your mom always makes for Thanksgiving."

"But Thanksgiving isn't for three weeks."

"I know," he said. "Dawn was here earlier, though, and asked if we were still planning on coming to their house for Thanksgiving this year—something I guess she and your mom arranged a couple of weeks ago."

"And she asked you to bring something?" I frowned, surprised that Mrs. Hastings would have my dad make something when they'd been bringing us dinner lately.

"I assumed it would be easy enough to make so I offered." He shook his head like he was regretting it. "I temporarily forgot that your mom was the one who did most of the cooking and that I have no idea what I'm doing."

"I'm sure you could always just tell her never mind. I don't think she'd care if we showed up without it."

"I know." He rubbed his hand across his face. "I just..." He sighed. "I just wanted to feel like I could do something. Ava, Elyse, and their mom are going to be there, too, so I didn't want our family to be too big of a burden."

Our family.

As in, all of us were considered a family now. The twins, my dad, mom, and me.

"Did you say that the twins' mom will be there, too?" I asked, realizing belatedly that he'd slipped her in there.

Had he invited her himself?

I mean, I liked Ava and Elyse and was slowly adjusting

to them being my half-sisters now, but it was just kind of weird to include their mom in what had always been a family tradition.

We didn't know her.

At least, *I* didn't know her.

Dad obviously knew her well enough to have a fling at their high school reunion back in the day.

"It wasn't my idea." Dad held up his hands, like he understood exactly where my mind was going. "Miriam will be in town that week to visit the girls, and so your mom said we should include her as well."

"How would Mom even know that?" I frowned. She wasn't exactly queen of the social scene like she used to be. She barely knew what day it was, let alone had the energy to keep up with the comings and goings of random people.

"I guess your mom and Miriam have been in contact ever since things came out, and I think she just wants her to feel welcome here with us. Thinks it will help the twins feel better about spending more time with us and possibly moving in for the second semester."

"What?" My body stiffened with the shock of this news. "The twins are going to move in?"

What the heck?

"It's just something we've talked about," Dad hurried to say. "I was planning to tell you about it."

He had? Because it seemed like a lot of things were happening these days that I didn't know about.

My dad had always been more of a practical thinker. Didn't get too emotional over things, so I'd guess the logic was there. Lose one female in the household and add two more to fill the hole.

Not that I really believed he was thinking like that. I knew he loved my mom, that he was just as devastated as I was at the thought of losing her, but the idea of him moving on with the twins and also having their mom as part of the picture just rubbed me the wrong way.

Like, couldn't we have one last Thanksgiving with just us? Just my mom, my dad, and me like it had always been?

Couldn't one thing in my life just stay the same for once?

Did we really have to make all these changes so quickly? Couldn't we just take a minute to breathe?

I shook my head. "Well, I guess I should be grateful that I found out *before* all their things were moved in." I laughed humorlessly. "Maybe I should move out when Mom dies so you can just start over with your new family."

The hurt was instant in Dad's expression. As if I'd just slapped him in the face.

"I'm sorry all of this is really inconvenient to you, Mack," my dad said in a low voice, like he was barely restraining the emotion threatening to spill out. "But Ava and Elyse are my daughters. They're my family, too. And I know the timing sucks for everything. But..." He shrugged. "I'm not trying to replace you and your mom with them. I just know that I missed out on the first seventeen years of their life and there's only so much time when they'll be living in Eden Falls, and I want them to feel like they have a family here."

I knew deep down that this was as hard for him as it was for me, but in this moment, it felt like he was already moving on.

"It's fine," I said, even though my tone didn't match my words.

Dad rubbed a hand across his face, looking exhausted. I

was about to head to my room when he spoke in a soft voice. "I'm sorry we weren't able to find a cure, Mack."

I looked at him again, a chill racing down my spine.

He scooted his chair back and held his hands out at his sides helplessly. "I'm sorry I couldn't save your mom." When our gazes caught, his golden-brown eyes were hollowed out. "I thought we had a chance at keeping her here for longer. At least until you graduated. I mean, I went to school for this." He looked blankly at the kitchen island behind me. "I save people's moms and dads and kids every week when I go to work. I save people who are decades older than your mom." He swore and pressed the heel of his hand into his eye. "But I can't save my own wife." His voice wobbled, and when he looked at me again, there were tears in his eyes. "I can't save her like we all wanted."

I could feel the helplessness that he was feeling, because even though I wasn't a renowned neurosurgeon like he was, I was just as powerless as him to save the person we loved more than anyone else in the world.

After just forty-one years on this earth, my mom's time was up.

She really was dying.

And the decades I'd have to live without her were starting faster than I'd planned on.

"So it's really the end?" I asked, even though I didn't want the answer.

But my dad nodded solemnly. "She's declining faster than we expected." He pinched his eyes shut and sighed. "I tried everything I could to buy us more time, but..." He let out a long, tired breath. "We might only have a week before she loses consciousness."

One week.

One week to be with the person I loved most in the world.

"Do you think Mom knows how close it is?" I asked.

"I think so," he said. "I think she feels it."

"So she wasn't planning to be at this Thanksgiving dinner with us, was she?" I asked, my mouth suddenly super dry.

My dad shook his head. "I think this was her way of making sure we have somewhere to go after she's gone."

AFTER MY CONVERSATION with my dad, I ate my dinner without really tasting it, read through a chapter for my AP English class without really taking in anything I was reading, and then sat in my mom's room for another hour without really talking.

I wanted to talk—knew that there was only a short amount of time left to have a lifetime of conversations with my mom—but I couldn't seem to find any of the right words to say.

What was I supposed to say when the only thing I wanted to do was scream and curse the universe for doing this to my mom? For doing this to me and my dad?

She didn't seem up to much talking tonight though, anyway, since the muscles in her throat were becoming more and more paralyzed. So instead of having a conversation with words, I pulled up the music app on my phone and played different songs for us to listen to together.

She'd always loved music—always kept up with the

current songs playing on the radio unlike some of my other friends' parents who were stuck in the decade they'd gone to college in, so music had always been a way for my mom and me to connect.

Only, instead of smiling and telling me with her words which songs she liked best, she now used her good hand to squeeze mine harder to signal which songs were her favorites. When she squeezed my hand for a particular song, I added it to a playlist I'd been compiling over the past several weeks titled "Mom's Favorites" for me to come back to later.

Justin Bieber was singing the last verse of his song *Believe*, which I'd dedicated to my mom last Mother's Day, when my dad came in and said it was time for the nurse to do her nightly routine and get my mom ready for bed.

So after the song ended, I kissed my mom on the forehead and whispered, "Goodnight, Mom. I love you."

She squeezed my hand three times with a faint smile on her lips, and then after looking at her once more to commit everything about her to my memory, I left the room.

My dad usually helped the nurse with the nightly routine, so I went to the kitchen to fix myself a cup of tea. My mom had always made her own loose-leaf teas when she was healthier—telling me all about the various healing properties the herbs had as she made them.

Then she'd brew a pot before bed and we'd sip it on the enclosed porch and look at the stars, with just candles for light. It had been one of my favorite parts of the day when I was little. A time to just relax and end the day on a peaceful note.

We didn't have any more of her loose-leaf tea in the

pantry since she hadn't felt well enough to make some for a while, but we did have some backup chamomile tea bags in the pantry. So I used the kettle to fill my mug with hot water, lit a few candles on the porch, and then sat on the couch as my tea brewed.

I stirred my tea bag around with its attached string, debating on whether to follow through with something I realized I needed to do tonight, or if I should wait until tomorrow at school.

Time was slipping by a lot faster than I wanted, and with my mom only having another week where she was conscious, I needed to make the most of that time.

Which meant I'd need to cut down as many distractions as I could.

My dad said he'd already arranged with the school for me to stay home for the next couple of weeks if I wanted. I could complete my schoolwork remotely. And Coach James had already said that with it being the pre-season and us not having games until after Thanksgiving, I could skip out on practices here and there and not be penalized.

So all of that was taken care of.

There was just one other person I needed to contact. One person who had proven a very good distraction over the past few weeks.

Someone who made time seem to disappear when we were together.

I knew she wouldn't be expecting it. And that it might ruin everything we'd built recently. But when time was running out way too fast and all I wanted was for time to slow down, I knew I needed to take a step away from the person who made time fly.

So after removing my tea bag from my mug and adding a splash of the creamer Mom had introduced me to, I pulled out my phone and texted Cambrielle.

Me: **Are you still awake?**

Mistress: **yes**

Me: **Is it okay if I come over for a minute? We need to talk.**

29

CAMBRIELLE

MACK WANTED TO TALK?

I stared at the last text he'd sent me, feeling my stomach twist with nerves as thoughts of impending doom hovered like a storm cloud over my mind.

He hadn't asked to meet up. Or if I could sneak out and meet him in the garage for a few minutes.

Instead, he'd asked if he could come over because we needed to talk.

Talk. Not flirt nor kiss, or make each other laugh in the way I loved.

While I didn't have a lot of experience with boyfriends, or having difficult conversations with guys, I wasn't too inexperienced to know that the phrase "we need to talk" never had a happy ending.

And since I really didn't want to have the conversation I thought he was trying to have, I texted him: **It's kind of late. Could we talk tomorrow at school instead?**

If he was having second thoughts right now, surely he might change his mind back by morning. Things always looked better in the morning.

His text came through a second later.

Alfred: **I won't be at school tomorrow.**

I frowned at the text.

Me: **You won't?**

Alfred: **I'm going online for a couple weeks.**

Something must be happening with his mom then. He wouldn't miss school and basketball practice unless something had changed.

So, maybe his wanting to talk with me had nothing to do with us?

Maybe he was just having a hard time and needed me to distract him?

So I texted: **Let me say goodnight to my parents first and then you can come over.**

MACK SHOWED up on my balcony fifteen minutes later, wearing a plain white T-shirt, gray sweatpants, and a black zip-up jacket. He usually wore his favorite gray Columbia hoodie this time of year as a good-luck charm for basketball season since he dreamed of being scouted by the Columbia basketball scouts. But I hadn't given it back to him after our hot tub kiss, so he'd started wearing the black jacket to our secret meet-ups instead.

"Hey," I said, stepping back from my balcony door to let him into my room, my heart pounding at the sight of him.

"Hey," he said. And when his face was lit by the string lights I had hanging across my ceiling, I couldn't help but notice that he wasn't smiling like he usually did when we met up.

Something was definitely wrong.

"What's going on?" I asked, not sure I really wanted the answer. Because if it was something with his mom, then my heart would break for him.

But if it was something to do with us, and he was planning to break up with me, I would be devastated.

Devastated because even though we'd been together for less than a week, I'd never been so happy.

He took a seat in the cream chair I'd been reading *Wuthering Heights* from when he'd first texted me.

"Thanks for letting me come over," he said, leaning back in the chair, his expression distant. Cold. "I, um..." He scratched the back of his head. "I just had something I needed to get off my chest before I went to bed."

The sick feeling twisted my insides again. "Yeah?"

He nodded, the muscles in his jaw clenching.

I held my breath as I waited.

He was going to break up with me.

Why else would he say he needed to *do* something before he went to bed?

"I was talking to my dad earlier this evening and he had some bad news."

"Bad news regarding your mom?" I guessed, wondering how the bad news would lead him to breaking up with me.

"Yeah." He sighed and looked at the painting of the beach that I had on my wall. "I, um, well..." He let out a long breath. "There's not exactly a nice way to put it, but he basically told me that we only have a week before she slips into a coma."

"Only a week?" I asked, putting a hand to my chest. "But I thought she had another month or more."

"So did I," he said, his gaze flickering to mine. "And I just..." He looked at the beach painting again, seeming like he wanted to say more, like he was trying to explain how the timeline could have moved up so suddenly. But after struggling for a moment with his bottom lip trembling, he just shrugged and wiped his eye.

And the sight of him like this, so helpless and broken, shredded my heart.

"I'm so sorry, Mack." I went to his side and touched his arm. "I'm so sorry."

He sniffled, and when he looked at me, he had tears streaming down his beautiful, bronze cheeks.

He wiped his nose. "I just thought I'd have a little more time, you know?" He shrugged, scrubbing his palm across his cheek to wipe away the tears. "Like, it's just happening so fast and even though I knew we only had a few weeks left, I guess I just thought there was a little more time than this."

"I think we were all hoping for a lot more time," I said.

"Anyway," he said, seeming to remember something. "That wasn't the only thing I needed to talk to you about."

"It wasn't?" I asked, a foreboding feeling hollowing out my chest.

"No." He sat up straighter and cleared his throat. "I, um, after my dad told me the news, I got to thinking about everything and how precious time is right now, and how I've been spending it lately and well..." He let the words drift off, as if unsure how to say what he wanted to say.

And when I saw the look of regret in his brown eyes, I knew what was coming. Knew the fairytale I'd been living in this week was coming to an end.

I braced myself for his next words, telling myself that whatever he said next I could get through.

So I waited for him to continue. After another long pause, he said, "And since time is such a limited resource right now, and I only have a finite amount of it left to focus on my mom, I need to remove all of the distractions right now."

"And I'm a distraction?" I asked, the words hurting me probably more than they should, given that I knew the circumstances he was saying them under.

"Yes," he said. "I mean, no." He gave his head a shake. "I mean, I just...I just think it's best that we be friends right now."

"Friends?" I asked, suddenly not liking the word very much.

He must have sensed how I was feeling because he quickly said, "I'm not breaking up with you right now. I just need some distance."

He said he wasn't breaking up with me "right now," but did that mean he was planning on doing it someday?

I pushed those thoughts away. But then he was looking at me like he was worried I was going to take this badly and he'd have to deal with an emotional ex-girlfriend on top of everything else already overfilling his plate. So even though my heart was breaking inside because I was pretty sure this was just the beginning of the end, I put on a brave face and said, "I understand."

"Y-you do?" He narrowed his eyes, like he wasn't sure he believed me.

I plastered on what I hoped was a reassuring and not at all heartbroken smile onto my lips. "Don't worry about me. I'll be okay."

He studied me again, and I almost thought I saw a hint of regret in his expression. Like he wasn't as sure about this "break" as he'd been when he first came here.

And for the tiniest moment, I thought he was going to take it back and tell me never mind, and that he didn't want any distance and instead wanted me by his side through this upcoming week.

But then the look disappeared, and he said, "Thank you for understanding."

He stood and put his hand on my door handle to leave. When I took in his black jacket, I realized that if we were going on a break, there was probably something I should return. So I opened the bottom drawer of my nightstand and pulled out his lucky Columbia hoodie.

"Here, I guess I should probably give this back to you," I said, offering it to him.

He glanced at the gray hoodie in my hands then met my gaze and said, "You can keep it."

"Are you sure?" I asked, not feeling like I should have it with our new situation.

But when I held it out to him again, he shook his head and said, "Just keep it safe for me, okay?"

"Okay." I hugged it to my chest.

He hesitated by the door for another moment. And then, as if on impulse, he walked the few steps across the carpet to me and pulled me into an embrace. He seemed to breathe in my shampoo, and after kissing me on top of my head, he said, "It's just a little break, okay?" He pulled away and searched my gaze. "Just until..." He let the words taper off, like he didn't want to finish his sentence. Didn't want to think about what had to take place before he could focus on anything besides his mom.

And even though I still wasn't confident he'd come back to me like he said he would, I nodded. "Okay."

He hugged me once more and then left.

I watched him climb down the tree outside my window and run toward the gate between our houses.

After he disappeared, I pulled his hoodie over my head, turned out the lights, and climbed into my bed. And as I lay there cuddled up in Mack's hoodie, I prayed that he would have the strength he needed to make it through the next few weeks because I had a feeling he would need all the strength he could get.

30

MACK

MY GRANDMA and my mom's siblings came to visit over the next few days, filling my house with chatter and laughter that had been missing recently. When my dad told me my mom's family was coming to town, I had expected everyone to be crying and sad. But instead of focusing on what was coming, we all sat with my mom and talked about all the old memories that we each had with her.

And even though I hated the reason why everyone was talking about all the mischief my mom used to get into when she was younger, it was fun to learn more about the part of her that I didn't get to know about since I hadn't known her as anything other than a mom.

My friends visited a couple of times, which was nice. Ava and Elyse seemed slightly uncomfortable at first, like they didn't know where they fit in since they were the daughters of the *other woman* my dad had been involved with in the past. They seemed unsure about how to talk to Grandma Jackson when she asked them questions about themselves. But once they saw that my mom's family was just as understanding as my mom had been when we'd first discovered the news that my dad was their father, they seemed to settle in.

Hunter and Carter kept me updated on what was going on with basketball practice. Scarlett and Nash told me all about the school drama that I'd missed out on. One of the highlights being that Ben Barnett was now on every girl's blacklist after Elyse had talked to a few other girls at school about their interactions with him and finding out that she and Cambrielle hadn't been his only victims.

It was good to see my friends, and their visits helped keep some of the gloom away.

Cambrielle came over with everyone else, too, but I noticed that while everyone else was their usual chatty selves, Cambrielle was a lot quieter than usual.

Our gazes would catch every so often as everyone else chatted, but then she'd look away with a sad expression on her face, and it made me wonder if I'd completely messed everything up by cooling things off with her.

I thought I'd made it clear that it was just a short break, just so that I could focus on my mom and make this time last so I could imprint it in my memory forever.

But maybe I hadn't made it clear enough.

Or maybe she was having second thoughts of her own.

ON TUESDAY MORNING, my mom suddenly seemed to feel a lot better. In the days immediately before, she had stopped talking. Had become unable to eat or drink since swallowing was impossible. But it was almost like the tumor had shifted or maybe even miraculously shrunk because when I went in her room to sit with her, she smiled at me and said, "Hello, my darling," in the familiar tone I'd worried I may never hear her use again.

My heart caught in my throat for a moment, and I wondered if I'd just imagined her speaking to me. But then she smiled again and in her usual candor, she said, "You look like you've just seen a ghost."

I blinked my eyes a few times, looking at her wasted form on the hospital bed my dad had brought in last week, trying to make it fit with the lively note she had in her voice. And for a second, I wondered if I somehow *was* seeing a ghost.

"Sorry, I just..." I said, scooting closer and taking her hand in mine. "You're talking."

"You've never known me to keep my mouth shut for too long, have you?" Her dark-brown eyes shone bright.

"H-how are you feeling?" I asked once I could speak again. "Better? You look better."

I couldn't look away from her, because even though she was barely more than skin and bones, she looked radiant.

"Better now that you're smiling," she said.

How was this possible?

I'd heard of miracles before. My dad had spoken about unexplainable things happening to his patients before. About them coming in with a huge tumor that would somehow disappear on its own. Or about a patient only having a prognosis of weeks to live and miraculously surviving for several years.

The instances were few and far between, but even though we weren't a religious family and didn't claim to know the workings of the universe, my dad freely admitted that there were things that couldn't be explained by science and could only be described as a miracle.

So was it possible that we'd received one?

Had all the time we'd spent preparing for the worst been only something to help us appreciate each other even more?

I hoped so. Because if my mom was going to get better and if we'd just received the miracle we'd been hoping for, I knew I would never take a single moment of my mom's life for granted.

Never.

Before I could even pull together everything I still wanted to talk to my mom about, I realized I had tears leaking out the sides of my eyes. Tears of joy and thankfulness that she was talking and smiling and happy.

"Something wrong, Mack?" Mom looked at me with concern etched in her eyes, noticing the emotion streaming down my cheeks.

"No." I shook my head and wiped at my eyes. "I'm..." I drew in a deep breath to calm my emotions. "I'm good. I'm just so happy to talk to you again."

"I'm happy to talk to you, too." She squeezed my hand. "In fact, I've been wondering about something the past few days."

"You have?"

"Yes," she said. "I never got the chance to ask you if you ever did anything about that girl you liked."

"That girl?" I asked, trying to remember exactly who she might be talking about since I'd never told her about my brief relationship with Cambrielle.

"The girl named 'Nothing,'" she said. "Who liked another guy."

Oh.

So she remembered the conversation we'd had before the Halloween Dance.

"So, did you ever do anything about it? Or did you let her go off and date that other guy?"

Here we were, after a full week where my mom could barely string more than a few words together, and the first thing she wanted to talk about was a girl who I may or may not like.

But I guess it made sense. My mom had always been a hopeless romantic and had gobbled up any information I was willing to share about my love life.

And so I said, "I actually danced with that girl at the Halloween dance and even convinced her to date me for a little while."

"You did?" she asked. "And you didn't think to tell your dear old mother about it?"

I shrugged. "It was a secret."

"Ooooh," she said. Her eyes sparked with excitement. "A secret relationship."

I chuckled, loving that my mom was so animated and just lapping this all up.

"It was very forbidden." I winked.

"It *was*?" she asked.

"I cooled things off with her last week," I said, feeling a hint of sadness roll over me at the thought that it could be over between Cambrielle and me if she didn't take me back when I was ready.

"Why did you do that?" she asked. "Was something wrong with the girl?"

"No," I hurried to say before she could think anything was wrong with Cambrielle. "I just..." I shrugged. "I just needed some space with everything going on right now."

"So it's my fault?" she asked. Not acting like she felt guilty or defensive that her illness had taken priority over everything, just stating a fact.

I met her gaze. "I just didn't want any distractions right now."

"I guess I can understand that."

She gave me a sad look. But then she said, "What's the girl's name?"

"You want to know the name of the girl I dated for five days?" I asked, surprised she would care when it hadn't worked out.

"I know you said it's a secret, but could you make an allowance for your mother if she promises to take it with her to the grave?"

My eyes widened, and I literally couldn't believe she'd just said that.

"Oh, I know it was a bad joke." She patted my hand. "But if I can't joke about it, what's the use in having this stupid brain tumor?"

My mom.

I was pretty sure if my dad would allow it, she'd arrange for him to have a comedian speak at her funeral just to keep everyone from crying.

And since I couldn't deny my mom anything, I said, "It's Cambrielle."

It took a moment for things to register, but then her eyes widened and she said, "*My* Cambrielle?"

Yes, even though Cambrielle was the daughter of my parents' best friends, my mom had always claimed Cambrielle as hers, too.

I nodded.

And my mom, knowing a little of my past history with girls, said, "You treated her well, didn't you? Because I know I'm your mom and should side with you, but if you break my girl's heart, I'll have to spank your butt."

It was of course an empty threat, but it just went to show how deep her affection was for Cambrielle.

"If you're asking if it was the same as it was with all those other girls, I can tell you that no, it wasn't," I said. "It was different." I sighed, remembering back to the past few weeks and how I'd felt when I was with Cambrielle. How she'd brought out a different side to me that I'd never had before and made me want to be better for her.

"Well, if I know Cambrielle like I think I do, then I know that she's probably pretty torn up that my perfect son could let her slip through his fingers."

"Maybe," I said, picturing the way Cambrielle had looked at me when she'd come over yesterday and how she could barely meet my eyes as everyone had talked.

"But if you're not invested," Mom said, breaking into my thoughts. "Then it's good you broke things off quickly. Because if I know anything about teenage girls, I know that when met with an opportunity to be with someone as amazing as my son, it would be impossible not to fall hard and fast."

"You're just saying that because you're my mom," I said.

MACK   297

"No, I'm saying it because it's true." She squeezed my hand. "I'm so proud of the man you're turning into, Mack," she said, moisture pooling in her eyes, suddenly emotional. "So proud." She smiled through her tears. "If I did anything right, it was having you. You were my miracle baby who came here and gave me a reason to keep going when things felt impossible."

Tears pricked at my eyes, because even though she wasn't saying the exact words, it felt like she was saying goodbye.

But why would she be saying goodbye now when she seemed to be doing so much better?

She held her arms out for me, and I moved from my chair to sit on the side of her bed. I pulled her frail body against me.

"I love you so much, Mack," she said into my chest. "So much that if they let me haunt you after this life, I will. I'll haunt you just so I can watch you do all the amazing things I know you'll do."

I gulped, looking down at her. "I love you too, Mom."

I'd never thought of being haunted by a ghost in a positive way before, but if such a thing was possible, I'd do anything to have her stick around. Or in the very least, visit every once in a while.

I smoothed my hands across her bony back, resting my head against hers as I tried not to say the words I'd had bouncing around my brain for months. Tried not to say them because I knew they were selfish and would only bring her more pain.

Don't say it. Don't say it. Don't say it.

But I couldn't not say it. Because even though she was

more herself than she'd been in weeks, something told me this really might be the end.

"I don't want you to say goodbye, Mom," I whispered into her hair. "What am I supposed to do without you?"

She lifted her head from my chest to meet my gaze with her dark-brown eyes. "You'll live, my darling boy." She brushed my cheek and gave me a smile that I'd try to recreate in my mind forever. "That's all I wish for you. That you'll live each moment that you're given—the ones you want to run away from and the ones so good you want time to stand still for. Feel them all. Because that's really all we're here for anyway. To live."

31

MACK

DAD CAME into the room a little while later and requested some time alone with Mom. They chatted for about an hour, and while he was in with her, I researched miracle healings from glioblastoma multiforme brain tumors online.

Even though my dad had said that we were at the end, I couldn't believe that Mom would be so vibrant and coherent if she was going to die in a matter of days.

But as I was scouring the Internet, I came across an article that triggered something my dad had mentioned several months ago when I'd asked him what to expect. And as I read more, I realized my mom might actually be experiencing what some people referred to as terminal lucidity—a period where patients with neurological disorders can have a sudden and unusual improvement in cognitive function days or hours before death.

I held my breath over the next day, feeling like I had a huge anvil hovering over my head as it waited for just the right moment to drop on me. But when one day turned into two, I started to wonder if maybe my initial thoughts of my mom being miraculously cured had actually been on point.

I asked my dad when we were alone Wednesday night if he thought it was possible, but he just shook his head and said, "I don't think so, son."

It rained all day on Thursday and Friday, and even though I didn't usually mind stormy weather, I couldn't get over the feeling of gloom and impending doom weighing on my heart.

My mom's family came to visit again, and I overheard them discussing some funeral plans with my dad Friday afternoon, telling him some of the extended family in other states were wanting to have an idea of when to book their flights. And I had to lock myself in my mom's room when they started talking about those things because I didn't want to think about who might be speaking at her funeral, what songs they should play, or what clothes they would dress her in when she hadn't even died yet. Why talk about that stuff when she was still alive?

"Will you open the curtains for me?" Mom asked an hour later, after we'd listened to a few of her favorite songs on her playlist. "I want to watch the rain."

"Of course," I said.

I opened the light-blue curtains wide and watched the late autumn storm through the huge windows that overlooked our backyard and the flower gardens I'd planted for her last spring and summer.

"I love the rain," Mom said with a faint smile on her lips.

"I know you do," I said, remembering how she had danced in the rain more times than I could count growing up.

"Whenever it rains, I want you to think of me, okay?" Mom said, her gaze sliding away from the window and over to me.

"I will." I swallowed. "You know I will."

The rain let up a little while later and my mom asked me if I could get her some ice to suck on since her mouth was feeling dry.

So I padded into the kitchen, the tile floor cool against my bare feet. I grabbed a plastic, child-size cup from the cupboard and a spoon to feed the ice to her with, and then filled the cup with pebble ice.

"Here's your ice," I said when I walked back into my parents' room, shutting the door behind me to block out the noise coming from the living room. But when I turned to look at my mom, I found her slumped in her bed with her eyes closed.

I walked closer and set the cup on the table beside her. "Mom?"

But she didn't respond.

"Are you asleep?" I asked quietly, not wanting to wake her if she was. But when I looked at her, something seemed different. The energy in the room had shifted.

I touched her shoulder, gently nudging her as a sense of dread gripped my heart. "Mom?" My voice cracked.

She still didn't respond. Her eyelids didn't even flutter.

"Mom." I shook her arm harder. "Mom, Mom. Are you asleep?"

Still no reaction.

"No, no, no, Mom." My hands shook as I tried to get a response aside from her shuddering breaths. "No, please no."

I touched her face, her arms, her sides. I shook her harder.

She had to wake up.

Just wake up.

I was only gone for a minute. Two minutes max. She couldn't have slipped away in that short amount of time.

But when she still didn't open her eyes after another few seconds, I knew she was gone.

And she wasn't going to wake up this time.

32

CAMBRIELLE

I WAS SITTING by the fireplace in my family's library with my dad and Ian on Friday night, halfway listening to them talk business as I read from *Wuthering Heights*.

Ian was just bringing up the value of merging one of my dad's companies with a newer tech company when my dad's personal phone started ringing.

He checked the caller ID and said, "It's Brendon. I better answer this."

I watched as he walked to the other end of the room, wondering why Mack's dad might be calling.

"Hello, Brendon," Dad spoke into his phone with his back turned to Ian and me. And as he said, "Uh huh" and "Oh no" and "I'm so sorry," I tried to piece together what they were talking about.

Had Mrs. Aarden died then? Was that what had happened?

I sat still, my heart pounding hard as I listened some

more and watched the way my dad was running his hand through his blond hair.

"Let me grab Dawn and we can take care of all that, okay?" Dad said. "We'll be there in a minute."

He hung up, and when he turned back around, his expression was grim.

"Is Mrs. Aarden gone?" I asked, not really wanting to hear the answer.

"She went into a coma about thirty minutes ago," Dad said. He looked at Ian. "Will you tell Nash and Carter? I'm not sure if Mack is up for the company, but I figure they should know."

Of course he'd want my brothers to know, because as far as everyone at my house knew, Carter and Nash were the ones who were closest to him. Not me. Not the girl who had been his secret girlfriend for all of five days.

Five glorious days before Mack's world fell apart.

"I'll go find them." Ian stood from the black leather armchair he'd been sitting in and left the room behind my dad.

Once I was alone, I grabbed my phone from the end table beside me and scrolled through my messages to find the message thread I had going with my contact named Alfred.

Yes, I hadn't had the heart to change his name back to Mack after he'd broken things off with me. Part of me hoped that if I kept his name as Alfred, it meant that we actually had shared something special enough to come back to when Mack was ready.

I typed out my text.

Just heard about your mom. I'm SO sorry. I

want to be there for you. Please let me know if you want me to come over or do anything. I know I acted weird when I was over this week, but I promise I'll be normal. I'll be whatever you need me to be.

I pressed the send button and held my breath, hoping he would let me at least act like his friend during this. I knew he tried to put up a strong front sometimes, but I didn't want him to feel like he needed to go through the next days and weeks alone.

My message went to *read*, and I held my breath as the conversation dots showed at the bottom of the screen, telling me he was responding.

His text came through a moment later.

Alfred: **OK**

OK?

What was that supposed to mean?

I stared at my phone for several more minutes, wondering if he was going to say anything else.

When nothing else came through, I went in search of Carter and Nash to see if they'd been in contact with Mack yet. But the only person I found was Ian drinking a glass of orange juice in the kitchen.

"Do you know where Carter and Nash are?" I asked my oldest brother who looked the most like my mom with brown hair and brown eyes.

He finished draining his glass and set it on the counter, wiping his mouth with the back of his hand. "They just went over to see Mack."

"Did Mack ask them to go over? Or did they just go on

their own?" I asked, wanting to know if Mack had preferred my brothers' company over mine, or if they were just more comfortable with inviting themselves over.

"I think they offered to hang out with him, and Mack told them to come over," Ian said with a shrug.

So while I'd received an "OK" text, my brothers got the "please come help me" text.

So maybe the thing between Mack and me really was done. I'd helped him get through the lead up to him losing his mom and my more capable brothers would take it from here.

33

CAMBRIELLE

I HEARD Carter and Nash get home around eleven, just as I was getting ready to go to bed. I opened the door to my room and found them in the little sitting room by Nash and Ian's bedrooms.

"Hey," I said, leaning against the wall.

"Hey." Nash looked up from his phone, looking exhausted.

"How's Mack?" I asked. "You guys were just over there with him, right?"

"Not good," Nash said, leaning back against the couch. "He was pretty emotional when we went over there."

"Crying?" I asked, unsure what Nash meant by emotional.

"Yeah, crying and angry," Carter said.

"Throwing his dad's medical books at the wall and screaming," Nash added.

"So pretty bad then," I said, even though I should have

assumed as much. If my mom had just slipped into a coma and I knew I was never going to be able to talk to her again, I'd be a complete disaster. "Did he calm down at all while you were there?" I asked. "Or is he still throwing things?"

"His dad got him to stop breaking stuff," Carter said, glancing at Nash for backup. "But I don't know if he's going to be okay. I've never seen him like this."

"Yeah, I've never seen him like this, either," Nash agreed with Carter.

I sighed, wishing I didn't feel so helpless right now. "Did anyone say how long until she dies? Will it happen tonight?"

"It didn't sound like it would be that soon." Carter shrugged. "But it could be Sunday or Monday."

"I hope Mack will be okay," I said, feeling heavy.

"I'm sure he will," Carter said, his blue eyes drifting up to mine. "It will just take time."

I WENT to bed crying tears of my own that night. Crying for Mack and how hard this was for him. Crying for Mr. Aarden who was losing his soulmate. And crying for myself and all the other friends and family of Brianna Aarden who would miss her warm presence and megawatt smile.

I hadn't spent a ton of time with her recently since I hadn't wanted to intrude on the family's last few weeks with her, but she'd always been my favorite out of all my mom's friends. She'd been into gardening and nature—sometimes calling herself a green witch with a chuckle and a twinkle in her eye.

I didn't think she believed she was a witch with actual

magical powers or anything like that. She mostly made teas from the ingredients in her garden—sometimes using a small cauldron for added flair. But all her witchy books, candles, and pagan holiday celebrations were something that had made her unique and fun and interesting to me.

It took me a long time to fall asleep, and when I did eventually drift off, I dreamed I was riding Starlight through the woods under the light of the full moon and we were chasing after Mack as he raced his four-wheeler down a trail that led toward the Richardson's mansion.

It didn't make sense, of course, since the Richardson's mansion was on the other end of town, but it not being real didn't keep me from screaming out in my dream when I saw Mrs. Aarden's ghost in the windows of the Richardson's mansion, beckoning for Mack and me to join her for a cup of tea inside.

I startled awake, feeling damp with sweat, my blankets twisted around me. My heart was pounding so hard from the dream. I had to pee, so I switched on the string lights above me and hurried to my bathroom, telling myself as I emptied my bladder that while Mrs. Aarden did love her daily tea rituals, she was not going to be coming back as a ghost and inviting me to teatime after she was gone.

I flushed and washed my hands, and just as I was tiptoeing across the carpet to climb into my bed, I heard a sound outside my balcony and had to hold in a shriek.

There was a loud thud right after that, like someone had just climbed over the rail and dropped down on the balcony landing.

I looked at the door handle and deadbolt to make sure

they were locked, and then I scooted closer to one of my windows to see who was out there.

When I peeked out the curtains, I saw a dark, hulking shape in the form of Mack.

What was he doing here? It was after two-thirty in the morning.

I opened the door and came face to face with Mack.

He looked terrible. His eyes were bloodshot, his white T-shirt was on backwards and inside out beneath his jacket, and he looked like he might collapse on the ground at any moment.

I thought he might be sleepwalking again, since that was something he did. But then he stumbled into the room like his climb up the tree outside had taken all of his energy and said, "You told me to let you know if I needed something, right?"

"Yes." I pressed a hand to his chest to steady him. When he looked like he wasn't going to collapse on me, I quickly shut the balcony door and locked it. Then I stood before him again and asked, "What do you need? How can I help you?"

"I need you to help me forget what's going on." He put his hands on my hips and pulled me closer to him. "Can you just help me forget for a few minutes that my life is falling apart and that I'm never going to have another conversation with my mom? And that I have to live in a future that she's not a part of?"

"H-how?" I asked, not sure how I could do any of that when I was just a regular sixteen-year-old girl. "How can I do that?"

"Let me be with you," he said, nudging my forehead with his nose. "Distract me." He moved his lips to my temple and pressed a slow kiss there that made my lower belly swirl with heat. "Just kiss me until I can forget and escape."

Even though I wasn't sure that kissing me was the best way to deal with everything he was feeling right now, I couldn't deny him this. Not right now when he was drowning and just looking for a life jacket.

He'd told me once before that snorkeling in Hawaii and kissing were two of his favorite ways to distract himself from unpleasant thoughts and feelings. And since he was too far from Hawaii to go snorkeling in this moment, I decided to be that distraction for him right now.

So when he tilted my chin up and whispered, "Please," while looking at me with pleading eyes, I nodded my permission. And when his lips brushed against mine, I kissed him back.

The kiss was slow at first. Slow and sad, and I could almost feel his heart breaking as his lips moved in a steady rhythm with mine. It was like he was unraveling. All his defenses, all the walls he'd built around himself to make it through the tragedy that he'd known was coming for his family the past few months crumbled, leaving just this boy whose heart had been broken open to feel everything.

He kissed me deep and long, and I welcomed it. Because even though I was so sad for him and hated that he was a wreck right now, part of me was relieved. Relieved that he hadn't forgotten about me and that it was me he was turning to right now in his darkest hour.

With his hands gripping my waist, he walked me backward until my back was pressed against one of the solid wood posts of my four-poster bed. And when he lifted me into the air with a light grunt, I wrapped my legs around his waist to keep him close.

"I missed you," I sighed against his lips.

"I missed you, too," he said, pressing himself closer and making me gasp for air.

His hands slid up my back, tangling in my hair and fisting in the loose fabric at the back of my pajama shirt.

I slipped my own hand behind his head and ran my fingertips in his curly hair. He must have liked it because he let out a low groan that made my heart skip a beat. He pressed his fingers into my back, hard enough that it almost hurt. Almost hurt, and yet felt so good at the same time.

"Mack—" I whispered when he lifted me again, wondering what he was doing.

"I just want to lie down with you," he mumbled against my lips. "Is that okay?"

For a brief second, I wondered what he planned to do if we lay down together, but I trusted him and figured he was just asking since his body was tired after everything, so I said, "Yes."

I held tight onto his shoulders as he carried me to the head of my bed and laid me down with my head on my pillow. I was already barefooted, but he wasn't, so he kicked off his shoes and knelt on my bed.

I watched him remove his jacket, swallowing hard as I took in the toned strength of his arms and the triangle of skin at his waist where his shirt rode up above the waistband of his sweats. He had always been beautiful to me. His eyes, his lips, his face, but I'd never realized how attracted I was to the rest of him until now that he was hovering so close to me in the privacy of my room.

I reached out to touch his chest after he tossed his jacket to the ground, and when he lowered himself down beside me, I slipped my hand up to caress his light-brown cheekbone with my thumb. He was perfection. From the top of his head and down to his toes—all six-foot-five of this broken boy was perfect.

He watched me with hesitant eyes, breathing hard as I slid my hand down his neck, across his shoulders, along his sides, memorizing the parts of him I hadn't touched in a week. And when I reached beneath his shirt to run my fingers along the muscled planes of his hips and abdomen, he closed his eyes and sighed like he needed this touch as much as I did. I pushed my hands farther up to feel the skin along his side, and he twitched with surprise and mumbled, "That feels good."

"I like it too." His warm skin under my fingertips felt incredible.

He opened his eyes again, and when I took in how huge his pupils were and recognized a desire I hadn't seen before, I had to remind myself that he was a virgin. That we both were. And that while we had insane chemistry and this could easily turn into something more with him beside me on my bed, I didn't want tonight to go that way.

Not yet.

Not right now.

Tonight was about distracting Mack. Not about making life-altering decisions that we might regret when we were thinking more clearly.

He slipped his fingers behind my neck to cradle my head and whispered, "I'm going to kiss you again, okay?"

And then we were kissing again. He was crushing his

lips to mine, and I tasted the salt from the tears he must have cried earlier. It broke my heart to think about how he must be feeling right now. Desperate and lost and so overwhelmed with feelings of loss that he needed this escape from reality.

His arm slipped behind my waist, his hand flattening against the small of my back as he pulled me somehow closer, pressing me against him. And with no space between us, our kisses grew deeper and longer. It was as if we didn't need air, and this kiss was the only thing that mattered. My body ached for him—a deep, longing that made me lose sense of everything besides Mack and me and this moment.

He slid his tongue across my bottom lip, asking for permission to enter, and I opened my mouth to his. Our tongues fluttered and danced together, my lower belly flipping and stirring.

I arched closer, wrapping my arm behind his waist as the kiss deepened further, pulling him closer as my whole body pulsed with heat. And then I was rolling onto my back, and he was covering my body with his.

He felt heavy. Heavier than I was expecting. Not because he was overweight. But because he was solid and six-foot-five.

But it felt so good. So good to have the weight of him on me.

"Is that okay?" he asked breathlessly.

"Yes," I gasped.

Because it was. Better than I thought it would feel to have his body covering mine.

He ran his hand down my side, along my pajama shorts and behind my thigh and I shivered under his caress because I loved the way the heat of his hand felt on my skin.

He trailed frantic kisses along my neck and across my collarbone, leaving little blooms of heat everywhere his lips touched. And just when I didn't think I was ever going to draw in a full breath again, he slid off of me and rolled me back to my side with him so I could fill my lungs with oxygen again.

"You sounded like you couldn't breathe," he said, meeting my gaze. "Is this better?"

"Yes," I gasped once more. "I mean, I liked being like that. I just..." I trailed off, not knowing what to say.

"I'm just a lot bigger than you," he finished for me.

I nodded. "But I like how tall you are," I said. "It's nice."

"You feel nice, too," he said. As if to prove his point, he slipped his hand across my back where my shirt had ridden up, pressed his forehead against mine and said, "I love the way you feel next to me."

He moved his hand across my side and squeezed the small layer of insulation I had over my ribs, and for a moment, the self-conscious part of me worried he wouldn't like the way I felt. But then he whispered, "I think I love everything about you, Cambrielle."

And even though he hadn't said he loved *me*, my heart soared because he wouldn't have said that and wouldn't have touched me and looked at me the way he was if his feelings had disappeared the night he'd broken things off with me.

His hand spread a little higher along the sides of my ribcage, and that was when I realized I wasn't wearing a bra under my pajama shirt.

A thrill of anxiety flooded my body because if his hand traveled much higher, he would discover that for himself.

His hand moved up another inch and the alarm bells

went off in my head. I quickly covered his hand with my own to stop him.

He frowned, as if worried he'd done something wrong, and so I said, "Sorry. I'm not ready for that."

He stopped and froze, like he hadn't realized what he'd been doing. "Sorry." He leaned his forehead against mine, breathing hard as he pinched his eyes shut. "Sorry I wasn't thinking."

"It's okay," I said, sliding his hand down with mine until it rested on my hip. "Just, you know...not yet."

He swallowed and nodded, and we just stared at each other for a while, studying each other as we let the frenzy of the past few minutes calm. And I appreciated that he wasn't pushing me to do more. And that he wasn't running away, either.

He rested his head on my pillow, looking deeply into my eyes. "Sorry I didn't ask you to come over earlier," he said.

"It's okay." I met his gaze, so he'd know that I understood. "Carter and Nash are your friends, too. I get it."

"I know," he said, looking past me to the other pillows on the bed. "I just..." He sighed, meeting my gaze again. "I just didn't want you to see me that way. I wasn't exactly my best self earlier tonight."

"I wouldn't expect you to be your best self right now."

"I know," he said, his Adam's apple bobbing. "I just wish I could be."

We were quiet for another long moment, and I could tell he was thinking about his mom again because his eyes suddenly filled with tears. He wiped them away with the back of his hand.

I scooted closer, slipping my arms around him to hug

him. "I'm sorry about your mom," I whispered. "Sorry all of this is happening."

"Me too," he said, kissing the top of my head before brushing some hair away from my face. "I'm really going to miss her."

34

MACK

WHEN I WOKE on Saturday morning, I was surprised that I actually felt somewhat rested. It had been weeks since I'd slept through the night, and with what happened yesterday, I'd thought it would be a long time before I slept through the night again. But when I opened my eyes and saw where I was, I realized why I'd slept so soundly.

It was because of Cambrielle. Because of the girl who was currently cuddled up beside me, sleeping in my arms.

I bent my head close to breathe in the smell of her shampoo. She always smelled so good, and there was something about the scent and feel of her back pressed against my chest that was comforting.

I'd thought before that it was her room that had the magical sleeping powers. But now that I'd been around Cambrielle a little more and had gotten to know her better, I figured that it was just her and not her bedroom.

I gently combed some hair back that had fallen across her face and watched her sleep. I'd always made fun of girls for thinking it was so romantic when Edward Cullen told Bella that he liked to watch her sleep, but I kind of understood it now. It was peaceful and an intimate moment that not many people got to see.

Her eyelids fluttered and she breathed deeply in a way that told me she was waking up. Since I didn't want to look like I'd been creepily staring at her for hours, I laid my head back down on the pillow and pretended like I was just waking up, too.

She stretched her legs out and arched her back a little, her butt bumping against me, and after gasping like she hadn't remembered I was here, she twisted around to face me.

"Hi," I said, looking down, unable to keep a small smile from my lips when I looked at her.

"Hi," she said back, a pink flush coloring her cheeks. She studied me for a moment like she wasn't sure I was really here, and then she asked, "How did you sleep?"

"Better than I expected."

After I'd come to her room like a hormone-crazed madman, I'd cried for a long time while Cambrielle just held me. I thought I'd never be able to stop crying and that I'd never feel happiness again, but sometime around four in the morning I'd eventually passed out. And while the ache was still hovering around my heart this morning with the knowledge of what was happening at home, I wanted to focus on this quiet moment with Cambrielle and make the most of the good things I still had in my life.

So I'd focus on the fact that I'd slept through the night and that Cambrielle was still with me when she could have turned me away.

"That's good."

"And you?" I asked.

A slow smile slipped on her lips. "Really good."

"That's good." I moved my hand up her back and twisted some of her hair around my finger. "So, um, I'm not sure if it was obvious after last night," I said. "But if you're okay with it, I'd kind of like to take back what I said about us being on a break."

"You would?" A hopeful smile lifted her lips.

I nodded. "I can't promise that I'm going to be the best version of myself all the time—and I know it might be a little much for you with all the baggage that I have, but—"

"I want to be with you," she cut me off, putting a hand to my chest. "I know things will probably be hard for a while, but I want to be there for you."

"Yeah?" I asked, not sure she understood what she was getting into. I mean, I didn't think I'd go crazy like I did last night and need to be restrained by my dad so I would stop throwing books at the wall. But I didn't think I'd be able to pretend like I was happy all the time, either. I'd tried that already and it hadn't exactly worked out so well. Cambrielle always saw through my act, anyway.

"And I want to tell everyone about us this time," she said. "No more Alfred and Mistress."

I grinned at our nicknames.

"You didn't like putting on a facade for everyone?" I raised an eyebrow. "Because I actually thought it was fun."

She smiled. "It was fun. But if this is going to work, I need to be able to talk about you with my friends and family. I want to be able to brag about how amazing and sexy my boyfriend is."

Her boyfriend.

I was surprised at how much I liked the sound of that.

I'd never been introduced as anyone's boyfriend before.

There was just one complication.

Okay, two.

Maybe three.

"But what about your brothers?" I asked. "I have a pretty fresh memory of Carter talking about dismembering me in the night if he ever heard that I touched you."

She rolled her eyes. "You know that's just talk, right?"

"He seemed pretty serious when he said it."

"Well…" She slid her hand across my chest and then to my bicep, giving it a gentle squeeze. "He may be strong for someone who's six-foot-three, but you've got two inches on him and put in just as many hours in the gym as he has lately. So I'm pretty sure you could take him."

"So you think he'll challenge me to a duel?"

She shrugged. "It would kind of help fulfill that one particular *Bridgerton* fantasy I had about you."

"A fantasy?" I arched an eyebrow, suddenly very interested in watching this show she was obsessed with. "I think you might need to describe this fantasy of yours."

"It's not like that." She smacked my chest. "It's more that —" she started but then stopped when someone knocked loudly on her door.

"Cambrielle?" Nash's voice called, an agitated note to it. "You need to wake up. Mack disappeared sometime last night, and Mr. Aarden is worried he may be in danger. We need to help look for him."

Oh crap, oh crap, oh crap.

I glanced to the doorknob.

We forgot to lock it.

I started to sit up so I could jump out of Cambrielle's bed and escape before Nash could discover me in bed with his sister, but in the next moment, the door swung wide open and Nash stepped inside.

"Mack?" he asked, putting a hand to his chest.

And his first reaction seemed to be relief. Like he was relieved to see that I was still alive and well. But then he took in my position beside Cambrielle, and probably sensing that I'd slept over, his relief turned immediately to something like rage. He walked to the side of Cambrielle's bed, yanked on my arm, and said, "What the heck are you doing in here?"

35

CAMBRIELLE

"IT'S NOT what it looks like." I jumped out of my bed and put myself between Nash and Mack before Nash could do something stupid like punch Mack in the face.

"Really?" Nash asked, fire in his blue eyes when he looked down at me. "Because it looks like one of my best friends just had a sleepover with my sister."

Okay...so maybe it was what it looked like.

"How long has this been going on?" He glared at me. "Since Halloween? Were you just lying to me about not going after him?"

"No, it's just—" I started.

But he didn't wait for me to explain. Instead, he looked at Mack and said, "How could you do this to my sister? She's sixteen, Mack. She's not old enough to be sleeping with guys. Especially not guys with a reputation like yours."

Okay, hold up. He was assuming an *awful* lot here.

I was about to explain what was really happening when Carter came running into the room.

"What's going on in here?" he asked, his gaze traveling from Nash to me and then to Mack. When his eyes caught on Mack, he seemed temporarily relieved like Nash had been when he'd seen that Mack was alive and well and not off doing whatever dangerous thing they thought he had gone to do in the middle of the night.

But then he looked back at me and my bed, and then at Mack's jacket and shoes that were still on the floor. And putting everything together quickly, his expression mirrored Nash's.

"What did you do to my sister?" Carter charged toward Mack. "I told you not to touch her!"

"I didn't." Mack stepped back until his back was against the wall. Holding his hands up, he added, "At least, we didn't do what you're thinking. We just slept."

"You really expect me to believe that?" Carter asked. "When you've bragged to me about how many girls you've taken to the falls?"

"Yes." Mack stood to his full, intimidating height, not looking as scared of my two brothers as I thought he should be. "I actually do expect you to believe it."

"And why would we believe that?" Nash asked, crossing his arms over his chest.

"Because it's true," Mack said.

Nash turned his steely blue gaze on me. "Did Mack use his mom's coma to take advantage of you last night?"

"Oh my gosh! No!" I said, hardly believing he had just said that.

Like, how in the world could he even think that about his best friend?

Or me, for that matter?

And because he was being an idiot and I was so sick of my brothers thinking they had any say in who I dated and what I may or may not want to do with them, I found myself saying, "But you know what? Even if he had, that would be *my* decision." I poked him hard in the chest. "And none of your business."

Nash took a step back, as if shocked that I dared suggest I be the one making decisions like that for myself without my older brothers' consent.

I wanted to go off on Nash and Carter about a few other things now that I'd gotten started, but my mom appeared in the doorway then, probably hearing the commotion from wherever she'd been in the house, and I decided to leave my grievances with my brothers for another time.

"Mack," my mom said. "Your father's worried sick about you. I think it's time for you to go home."

"Yeah, okay." Mack glanced at everyone apologetically. Then, looking like he couldn't escape the charged room fast enough, he grabbed his jacket and shoes from the floor and rushed past my mom and out of the room.

"Did you hear that, Mom?" Nash said once Mack was gone. "Mack was—"

But my mom held a hand up to cut my brother off. "Thank you for your concern, Nash. But I heard the whole thing." To me, she said, "I'd like to see you in my room now, Cambrielle. It sounds like we have some things to talk about."

36

CAMBRIELLE

MY STOMACH ROILED with dread as I followed my mom into her and my dad's bedroom. Their bedroom was on the opposite landing from the kids' hall. Inside, it was mostly white—white walls, white bedding, white curtains, white furniture—with little pops of navy blue and gold.

I didn't come in here as often as I had when I was younger, since I'd graduated from putting on my toy makeup at her vanity while I watched her get ready for work in the mornings. But each time I stepped inside, it reminded me of simpler days when life was slower and the only thing I had to worry about was whether I'd have a friend to sit with at lunch, or if my ballet teacher would give me a solo during the next recital.

Mom sat on the edge of her bed beside Duchess who had been sleeping there, the fluffy white comforter bunching around her legs as she did. And when she patted the spot next to her, inviting me to join her, I obeyed.

"So I know I said that I heard a little of your conversation with your brothers just barely," she said. "But would you mind filling me in on how exactly a seventeen-year-old boy came to be sleeping in my sixteen-year-old daughter's bedroom last night?"

"It's kind of a long story." I swallowed.

"I don't have anywhere I need to be." Mom crossed her arms. "So I have time."

"Okay," I said, trying to figure out where to start. Then, deciding that it was probably best to just start at the beginning when I found Mack sleepwalking in the woods, I started talking.

I told her about how the sleepwalking episodes happened a few nights in a row and how I'd let him stay on the trundle bed in my room after that. Then I told her about how he'd stayed in my room those two nights he was supposed to be in Ian's room, her eyes growing wider with surprise with each admission like she couldn't believe all this had happened right under their noses.

I told her about how Mack and I had grown closer during that time and bonded more and more as we spent time together. I told her how he'd helped me with Ben—leaving out the details of the practice kiss. And then, how I'd realized that my crush had never really gone away.

"Right around Halloween, we realized that we both liked each other and we started secretly dating."

"That long ago?" Mom asked, her brown eyes blinking.

"It only lasted for a few days," I said. "He broke things off when his mom got worse."

"But the boy was sleeping in your room last night. And had done that several times before? Don't you see how that would make me just a little worried?"

"But we didn't do what you're thinking," I hurried to say. "Yes, I like him a lot and I hope that when things calm down that we can date without it being a secret this time. But I promise I'm not like *sleeping*, sleeping with him."

"Why didn't you tell me what was going on?" Mom asked.

"I don't know." I lifted a shoulder. "I figured I had it covered and..." I sighed. "I guess it was nice having Mack trust me with something he didn't want anyone else to know about."

"I get that." Mom patted my leg. "But you're only sixteen, Cambrielle. And I know how things can get when you're spending so much time alone with a boy you like— especially when it's fun and secret and seems forbidden."

Was she going to forbid me from seeing him then?

"I wasn't planning to do anything stupid," I said.

"I know you're more mature than I was at your age," Mom said. "But I just don't want you to grow up too fast. I just..." She drifted off. "When I was your age, I was really insecure, and I thought my boyfriends would break up with me if I didn't have sex with them when they asked. And it led me to doing things that I wasn't ready for. I got sucked into an unhealthy relationship with Ian's father at a young age and ended up getting married and having a baby before I was really emotionally and financially prepared to, and it was just kind of difficult for a while there."

I knew all this. She'd told me all of this before.

"So you think that if I date Mack that I'm going to get pregnant at nineteen like you did?"

"No." Mom shook her head. "I just want you to make better decisions than I did. And if you're sneaking your boyfriend into your bedroom on a regular basis, I worry that you'll start doing other things and I just don't want you to grow up too fast."

Okay, so she was basically saying she was worried I was planning to have sex—like tomorrow—she just wasn't saying the actual words.

And even though it was completely awkward to talk about this with my mom, I said, "If it makes you feel better, I don't want to have sex for a long time."

"Really?" My mom put a hand to her chest, like she'd actually been worried I was planning to run to Mack's house right after our conversation and do the deed.

"Yes," I said. "I know I told Carter and Nash that I could make those decisions on my own, but I'm not ready for that."

"Well, that makes my protective Mama Bear heart feel slightly better," Mom said, her shoulders relaxing.

"I figured it would," I said, my face still burning over talking about this.

"Do you know if Mack is on the same page?" Mom asked. "Because I've known that boy since he was eight years old and know exactly how charming he can be. And I also know that his reputation isn't much better than Ian's when it comes to girls."

"I think he is. But even if he didn't have the same plans for that kind of thing, he wouldn't pressure me to do anything I didn't want to do," I said, remembering how he'd stopped when I'd asked him to last night. "He's a good guy."

"I know he is," Mom said. "I'm just too young to become a grandma, okay?"

"*Mom!*" I said, having had enough awkward moments to last me a while.

She chuckled. "Well, I'm glad you're being thoughtful about this."

"Can I go now?" I asked, ready to hide in my room for a long time so my cheeks could stop burning from embarrassment.

"I guess," she said. "But no more secrets and sneaking around, okay?"

"Okay," I said.

I got to her door and was just about to open it and leave when she said, "And Cambrielle?"

"Yes?" I turned around, worried she'd changed her mind and that she was going to forbid me from dating Mack.

"I'm going to have to tell your father about all of this."

"You are?" I asked, imagining how that would go and not liking the images that came to mind. "You're going to tell him everything?"

"He's your parent, too, and deserves to know."

Ugh.

This was going to be so embarrassing.

She continued, "I figured I'd better warn you so you won't be too surprised when he arranges for security cameras to be installed on your balcony to keep uninvited teenage boys from sneaking over from now on."

"Don't you think that's a bit much?" I asked.

Mom shrugged. "You're his only daughter. You know how protective he is of the ones he loves."

"I know." Which was apparently something my brothers had inherited from him, too, given the little show they'd put on in my room a few minutes ago.

But since I really couldn't do anything about it and I should actually feel pretty lucky this conversation had gone as well as it had, I shrugged and said, "I guess security cameras sound fair enough." I put my hand on the door handle. "Just tell him to put them on Carter and Nash's balcony, too. I heard the twins might be moving in with the Aardens next semester, and it's only fair that Carter and Ava get caught if they try sneaking over to each other's houses during the night."

My mom chuckled. "That's probably a good idea."

37

MACK

ME: **So on a scale of one to ten, how prepared do I need to be for Carter, Nash, and your dad to come after me with pitchforks?**

I texted Cambrielle when I'd been home for an hour and still hadn't heard from her.

Had her parents forbidden her from seeing me again?

Had they told the staff to keep me from stepping foot on their property from now on?

Or had she just not texted me yet because she assumed I was too busy getting a tongue-lashing from my dad for sneaking out in the middle of the night and nearly giving him a heart attack?

Yeah, my dad might have yelled a little when I snuck in the back door. Telling me this was *not* the time to pull any stunts.

I was pretty sure I would have been grounded any other

time, but given the circumstances, he'd let me get by with a warning.

My phone made a dinging sound, and I immediately looked at my screen to see what Cambrielle had said about the likelihood of me dying at the hands of her brothers and dad.

Mistress: **Probably an 11.**

I scrubbed my palm over my face. Yeah, this was not good. I'd tested Fate one too many times and now I was going to pay for it.

In a pretty painful way, most likely. Nash had gone through that scratching phase when we were kids.

Mistress: **Are you freaking out now?**

Me: **How'd you know?**

Mistress: **Because my dad and brothers are very scary. You should hear about the plans Ian has for you.**

Me: **I forgot about him. He does seem like he'd play dirty.**

Mistress: **Very dirty.**

Mistress: **Like, I think he's making mud pies to throw at your window right now.**

I laughed, appreciating this lighthearted conversation more than she probably knew right now.

Me: **So Ian isn't really a threat.**

Mistress: **He caught an early flight to Paris to spend time with one of his supermodel flings, so he doesn't know about the excitement from this morning yet.**

That sounded about right, I guess.

Carter had compared me to Ian a few times before, since he thought my weekend trips to the falls were comparable to Ian's jaunts around the world with a different woman each weekend. But yeah, Ian was working in a completely different stratosphere from me.

A stratosphere I had no interest in anymore now that I'd found out that the perfect girl for me had always been next door.

Me: **Any hint at what Nash and Carter have planned though?**

Mistress: **Probably look at us funny when they see us together and wonder why you'd secretly date their dorky sister.**

Me: **First off: You're not dorky. You're hot and fun and cool and amazing and wonderful and smart and a good kisser and did I mention hot. And second: That's all?**

I mean, I had considered using the whole "I went crazy last night and went back to my old coping mechanisms card" to help get me off their blacklist. But maybe it wouldn't be as bad as I thought.

Mistress: **Aw thanks! And yeah, my mom basically told them to back off and that them being so overprotective was just causing the sneaking around in the first place. So...I think they'll actually be okay. You know, after they get used to the idea.**

A second text came through.

Mistress: **But in all seriousness, I think they felt like crap when they realized how badly they**

freaked out on you considering everything you're going through. So don't be surprised if they come groveling at your door soon.

I didn't necessarily love the idea of them treating me differently because of everything happening right now, but it would be nice to have things smoothed over with my best friends. I needed them on my side right now.

Me: **And your dad? You haven't mentioned him yet.**

Mr. Hastings *was* a billionaire. If he didn't want me dating his only daughter, he definitely had the means to hire someone to take care of me.

Not that I really thought he would, since he was a decent guy and wouldn't kill his best friend's son the same weekend we were losing my mom.

But you could never be too careful.

Mistress: **My dad will be a tough sell. He definitely didn't like hearing that you slept over...multiple times. Looked like he was going to pop a vein when my mom told him. (I was watching them through a crack in his office door.) But my mom got him to calm down and reminded him how much he likes you.**

Me: **So basically, I'm a dead man.**

Mistress: **I don't think he's called the Mob quite yet.**

Me: **Well it was nice knowing you.**

Maybe my mom and I could haunt my dad together.

Mistress: **So dramatic.**

Me: **Your dad is a billionaire. He knows people.**

Mistress: **Just let him beat you in basketball a few times and I'm sure he'll warm up to the idea of us together.**

Us together. Despite the crap-hole that was my life right now, I liked how that sounded.

Me: **Done**

Mistress: **Also in case you haven't done it yet, you should probably change my name back to Cambrielle in your phone. Might make things less suspicious.**

Right.

Me: **Changing it back now.**

38

MACK

THE NEXT TWO days dragged on as I sat next to my mom and listened to her rattled breathing, watching her body slowly die. And then on Monday, November fifteenth at 5:45 A.M., my mom, Brianna Jackson Aarden, slipped from this existence to the next. Leaving her broken body behind with my dad sitting by her side.

I'd known the day was coming for a little over a year. Ever since they found the tumor, I had done my best to plan for the time when I couldn't just walk into the house or her bedroom and tell her about my day.

But when my dad came into my bedroom that morning to tell me the news, no amount of preparation could have steeled me for the intensity of the loss. A feeling so strong that it felt like I was being clawed apart from the inside and that the world would always be empty without her.

And even though I knew why my dad was there in my room so early in the morning when he knew I wasn't going to school that day, all I wanted to do was hide. To crawl under the covers or somehow sink through the floor, so I wouldn't have to hear him say the words, "Your mother is gone, son."

But I rolled over and faced him anyway, with his exhausted posture and hollowed out face, and listened to him say those very words.

Then, since I didn't want my dad to have to be alone when he'd just lost the woman he'd been in love with since he was seventeen, I dragged myself out of my bed, put on a T-shirt and slippers, and went downstairs with him.

When I walked into my parents' bedroom, it was silent. The sounds of my mom's rattled breathing no longer permeated the air. I walked to the side of my mom's hospital bed, and after taking in her body and her face that already looked different than it had yesterday, I touched her forehead briefly.

It was cold and clammy.

She really wasn't here anymore.

39

MACK

MY FATHER and I cried a lot over the next few days. I didn't sob like I had the first night that Mom was in a coma. I didn't wail or scream or throw anything at the wall. But the tears were there. A steady stream that went on so endlessly that I wondered if they would ever stop.

Cambrielle came over after school and listened when I needed someone to talk to. Talked about all the things happening at school when I needed it. We watched movies and listened to music, and even though I was sure she had a ton of her own things to do and an audition she was nervous about coming up next week, I appreciated having her there with me.

Ava and Elyse came over on Wednesday night to help my dad sort through some photos and mementos to display at the funeral since I couldn't bear to look at photos of my mom right now. We were all still getting used to the idea of becoming a family, but it was nice to see them make an effort to be there for my dad during this time. They listened to his stories about him and my mom and their life together, and I believed it was therapeutic for him in a way.

Carter and Nash invited me over to play video games on Thursday night, to get me out of the house, and it was exactly what I needed. They didn't ask me about how I'd fallen for their sister right under their noses, but they also didn't act like they were going to come for me in my sleep either, so I figured they were adjusting to the idea of Cambrielle and me dating. And it was just nice having some time that gave me some semblance of normality. Like not everything in my life had gone to complete crap when my mom passed.

My mom's funeral was beautiful. She'd always said she didn't want it to be held in a dingy funeral home, or a church since she hated how claustrophobic they made her feel. So we held the service in her favorite place in the world: our backyard, with her favorite pine trees as the backdrop.

And even though my mom loved the rain, and it would have been fitting for it to have rained on the day of her funeral, the sun was shining all day instead.

My dad and I opted not to speak, since we knew we wouldn't be able to make it ten seconds into our speeches without bawling like babies. But my mom's siblings and Mrs. Hastings did a beautiful job of telling stories about my mom and even had us laughing through our tears here and there.

I went back to school the next Monday, deciding that it was best for me to try to get back into regular life again. It was a short school week since Thanksgiving break would start after school on Tuesday. But it was nice to be around my friends and schoolmates again. And with our basketball games starting the next week, I really did need to practice with the team in order to play my best for the scouts that Coach said would be coming to watch me later in the season.

The house felt empty without my mom there when I got home from basketball practice in the evening. She must have been too busy cracking jokes and becoming everyone's best friend in the next life to come and haunt me. But it was probably for the best.

"WHAT DO you think Miss Crawley wants to talk to you about?" I asked Cambrielle on Tuesday morning just outside of her U.S. History class.

Cambrielle's audition for the play had been the day before, and Miss Crawley had told everyone that she'd be posting the cast list sometime later today so everyone could start memorizing their lines over Thanksgiving break.

"I have no idea," Cambrielle said, a hint of anxiety in her bright blue eyes. "I thought my audition went pretty well. I wobbled a few times, but I don't think it was too big of a deal." She hugged her books to her chest. "Do you think she wants to tell me I didn't make the cut before she posts the list?"

"No, I doubt that's it. I've seen you practice. There's no way she wouldn't cast you."

Cambrielle was an amazing dancer. And while I hadn't been able to watch her audition since I'd been in basketball practice yesterday, a little wobble here and there couldn't have messed things up that much.

"When do you meet with her?" I asked.

"During lunch."

"Want me to wait outside her office when you go in? Or just save you a spot at the table?"

"Probably just save me a spot. I have no idea how long she'll want to talk."

"Okay."

The warning bell rang, so I bent close and gently kissed her on the head.

"I'll see you later," I said.

"See you," she replied, and then went into her classroom.

When I turned around, I saw that while we'd said goodbye, several classmates had stopped to watch us. At first I'd assumed they were just awkwardly watching the guy whose mom had died the week before, because I'd been getting a lot of awkward looks since yesterday. But when I saw shock instead of pity, I realized they were reacting to the way I'd just kissed Cambrielle's head instead.

Which I guess meant that Cambrielle probably hadn't told anyone aside from our immediate friend group that we were dating.

I just smiled at their curious expressions and planned to head to my English class without saying anything. But then I noticed Ben standing among the crowd of onlookers and couldn't resist patting him on the shoulder and saying, "Thanks for messing things up with her, man. Because of you, she finally decided to give me the time of day." Then leaning a little closer I whispered, "Also, before you try bamboozling any other girls, you might want to work on your kissing skills. Cambrielle was *not* impressed."

His mouth hung open, like he couldn't believe what I'd just said. But instead of sticking around to hear whatever excuses he had for treating Cambrielle the way he had, I just kept on walking.

CAMBRIELLE ARRIVED at our lunch table with her tray only a few minutes after the lunch period had started.

"Did you already meet with Miss Crawley?" I asked when she scooted into the seat beside me.

"Yes," she said, her eyes bright and her cheeks somewhat flushed like she'd rushed here to tell me the news.

"And?" I asked.

A huge smile slipped onto her lips. "And she asked if I wouldn't mind playing the part of Meg Giry."

"Which I'm guessing is a good thing?" I wasn't familiar enough with *The Phantom of the Opera* musical to know who Meg Giry was, but I assumed from the look on her face that it was.

"Yes." She nodded excitedly. "At least I think so."

"So you won't be dancing then?" I tilted my head to the side, still not knowing much about this role that she was excited about.

"Oh, I will be," she said. "Meg is one of the dancers. But she also has a few lines. She's the one Christine confides in about her lessons from the Angel of Music. It's not a huge role, but I think I can do it."

"Well, that's awesome." I smiled and put my arm around her, pulling her against me in a side hug. "I'm excited to watch you on stage."

"Thanks." Her face had a healthy glow to it, and it was fun to see her so excited about this after hiding her talent from the world for a year and a half. "And if Elyse gets the part of Christine, then we'll have some scenes together, which will be fun."

I glanced across the table to where Elyse was. She met my gaze briefly before turning back to the conversation everyone was having about their plans for Thanksgiving break. I was happy that while things had been pretty awkward between us when we found out we were related, we were getting more comfortable as brother and sister now. And even though I hadn't been too thrilled about the idea of her and Ava moving in after winter break, the idea was starting to grow on me the more I saw how much my dad liked having their company.

Scarlett started telling everyone about her plans to volunteer at a soup kitchen on Thanksgiving. As she talked about it, I couldn't help but think about how much had changed since the time everyone was discussing their plans for the last holiday celebration we all had—the Halloween dance. And when I looked at the beautiful girl sitting beside me, I couldn't keep a slight smile from my lips as I remembered the way I'd teased her that October day. How I'd sat in this very spot as everyone else talked about their costume plans, and how I'd teased the girl next door about hoping that her room was ready for me to sneak into that night.

What a wild ride this past month had been.

Some terrible things had happened, of course. I'd lost my mom and I was forced to get used to a life without her in it.

But some pretty great things had happened during that time as well. I'd fallen in love at the same time my life was falling apart, and having Cambrielle by my side through everything just solidified how awesome she was.

I'd learned a few things about life as well. I'd learned that unlike what my more naive self had thought, life was more like a game of Tetris instead of a game of chess. I'd thought that like the game of chess, I had control over things. That I could make a move to one square and predict what would happen next. And based on that, I could know and plan for what the future would hold.

But life wasn't like that at all. You could make plans and do your best with the pieces that you had at any given moment. But even though you could make some predictions about your life in the future, you never really knew what piece was going to come next. Sometimes you were given an L-shaped piece instead of the T-shaped piece you'd saved the perfect spot for. And you suddenly had to pivot.

And just like in life, the longer you waited to accept the pieces you were given, the less powerful your next move could be.

Staying mad at the game for giving you the piece you hadn't been expecting didn't do you any good.

I knew I would probably have a lot more anger-filled days to come, since I was still only a human and not a perfectly programmed computer game. But it was comforting to know that I didn't need to figure out my whole life right now. Or figure out what I was going to do when my mom's birthday came, and she wasn't here for me to sing to.

Instead of focusing on the what-ifs, I could just focus on what was in this exact moment. I could take a deep breath and trust that I'd be able to figure things out as I went.

I think that's what my mom meant when she told me her greatest wish was that I'd just live. That she would want me to just stay present in the here and now and experience all the things that life had to offer. Because the goal in life wasn't necessarily to always be happy. It was to *live*.

I looked at Cambrielle and studied her for a minute as she laughed at something Ava said. And as I watched her and soaked in the lightness and comforting energy she had about her, I knew that things would be okay. As long as I didn't give up, I could experience moments of true joy again and that better days were ahead of me.

"What?" she asked, looking at me self-consciously when she noticed my stare. "Why are you looking at me like that?"

I just smiled, and leaning closer, I whispered, "I'm just thinking about how lucky I am that Ben was such a bad kisser."

Her eyes widened, and I loved that she always seemed so surprised by some of the things I said. "Why would you be thinking about that?"

I shrugged. "Because without that special kissing lesson, you probably never would have known how perfect we were for each other."

She laughed lightly, giving her head a shake. "You know it was the other way around, right? If I hadn't begged you to kiss me, you never would have stopped teasing me about taking me to the falls while never planning to follow through."

"You don't think I was going to take you one day?"

"No," she said. "It was always just a game to you until that kiss changed things."

"Then you probably would be surprised to know that I actually thought about kissing you under the waterfall several days before that."

"No, you didn't."

"I totally did."

Her cheeks glowed pink, and I loved that even after everything I could still make her blush with the slightest remark.

"I guess we'll have to agree to disagree on that," she said.

"I guess so." I shrugged. "Though—" I picked up a fry and dipped it in my ranch. "—now that you mention it, it's about time I take you to my favorite spot."

"You want to take me to the falls?" She arched an eyebrow.

"It's only right that I take you after dangling the carrot over your head all this time."

"It's a little cold for that right now though, don't you think?" she asked.

"I'll keep you warm." I winked and plopped the French fry into my mouth.

Her cheeks flushed darker, and I was tempted to whisk her away to the falls right then. But then she said, "I kind of think I'd prefer we go there in the spring or summer. The weather will be better then."

"You think we'll still be together this summer?" I asked, just to test her.

"I know we will," she said, not a shred of doubt in her expression.

"And why's that?"

"Because my brothers will beat you up if you break my heart," she said with a shrug.

I chuckled. After glancing across the table at Carter and Nash who were paying us no attention, I bent close and whispered in her ear, "Well, it's a good thing I don't plan to ever do that."

EPILOGUE
ELYSE

"It's weird seeing them together like that, isn't it?" Nash nodded toward Mack and Cambrielle who were standing a few feet away from us in the hall after school.

It was the day I'd been anticipating ever since hearing that the drama department at my new school was putting on a production of *The Phantom of the Opera*. The day I would find out if I'd be playing the role I'd dreamed of playing ever since watching the 2004 movie version of the musical in my family's tiny living room in Ridgewater, New York.

Miss Crawley, the drama teacher, said she'd have the cast list posted by the time school let out. But the last bell had rang five minutes ago, and there was still no sign of her or the list.

"You think it's weird for Mack and Cambrielle to be together?" I asked Nash, deciding to engage in the conversation topic he was offering as a distraction from my nerves. My nails could certainly use the reprieve from all the chewing I'd been doing to them right about now.

"Yeah, don't you?"

I looked to where his sister and my brother were standing. And while their height difference certainly made them stand out, I actually thought they were cute together.

When I'd first found out that they were secretly dating, I'd been a little shocked. I'd thought Cambrielle still had a crush on Ben at the time. But after seeing them together and thinking back to the way they always bantered back and forth with each other when I first moved here, it made total sense that it had happened.

So with a shrug, I turned back to Cambrielle's skeptical, blond-haired, blue-eyed brother who was way too cute for his own good and said, "I actually think they're perfect for each other."

"Perfect?" His eyes widened, like he couldn't believe I was telling the truth. "More like weird."

I smiled and nudged him with my shoulder. "I think that's just the protective-older-brother side of you coming out."

He shrugged. "Maybe."

I glanced back to the bulletin board where the cast list was supposed to be pinned. *Where was Miss Crawley? And why was she making us wait for so long?*

"Are you as nervous as I am to see if your name is on the list?" Nash asked, following my gaze.

"Yeah," I said. "I mean, there's probably no way to measure your nervousness compared to mine. That would take a much more scientific approach than I'm qualified to do right now. But if your hands are sweating, or if you're feeling a little nauseous, then we're probably at the same level of nerves."

And there I was. Rambling like an idiot.

Because that was what I did when I was nervous and talking to a cute boy.

He didn't seem to mind, though. He just chuckled light-heartedly and said, "Are you having heart palpitations, too?"

I nodded.

"Then yeah, we're probably tied." He shot me a wink and my heart skipped for a reason that had nothing to do with the cast list.

It had been doing that a lot around him lately.

Was he ever going to ask me out?

Miss Crawley's classroom door opened down the hall, and a second later, she appeared with a white sheet of paper in her hand.

This was it.

The moment of truth.

Her heels clicked on the tile floor as she approached the group of drama club students. The crowd parted like the red sea when she got closer, and everyone was silent as she went to the bulletin board and pinned the paper right smack in the center.

Then, with a flourish of her arm, the petite teacher who held my future in her hands said, "There you go."

And even though I was dying to see what fate had been decided for me, I hung back against the stone wall and let everyone else crowd around the paper. Because as anxious as I was for the role, I didn't need everyone to see the disappointment on my face if I wasn't cast as Christine.

Nash waited back, too. After watching a handful of students cheer while a few walked away with drooping shoulders, Nash looked at me and said, "You want me to look for you?"

"Sure," I said. "If you don't mind."

He walked across the hall to the other side, and after leaning closer and squinting at the list, he turned back to me with a huge smile on his lips. "You're Christine."

"I am?" I asked, rushing to his side, needing to see it for myself. And sure enough, on the second line down was my name next to the name Christine Daaé.

My chest felt light. This was actually happening!

I looked back at the list, and after reading what Miss Crawley had written on the first line, I turned to Nash with a big smile and said, "And you're the Phantom."

"I know." His grin stretched wide across his face. "*Finally*."

He put a hand to his chest, and I could almost feel the relief coming off him.

He really had wanted the part so badly.

I checked the list again to see who would be playing Raoul who was Christine's love interest in the show but frowned when I read a name I didn't recognize from auditions. Asher Park.

I tried to think if there was anyone named Asher in any of my classes, but no faces came to mind that matched the name.

"Do you know who Asher Park is?" I asked Nash. Maybe Asher was a freshman or sophomore? As a senior, I didn't have many of the younger students in my classes.

"Yeah, I know Asher." Nash frowned and looked at the list. "But he hasn't been coming to school this year."

Miss Crawley walked up to us then. "Is everything all

right?" she asked, seeming to notice our frowns. "You're happy with your parts, right?"

"Yes, of course," I said. "I'm thrilled."

"Me too," Nash said. Then he pointed at Asher's name and asked, "But how did Asher get the part of Raoul? I haven't seen him at all this year."

"Oh, yes. Mr. Park," Miss Crawley said. "He *has* been away the past few months. Going online after everything that happened last spring."

Nash nodded, waiting for Miss Crawley to continue.

"But he's returning after Thanksgiving break," she said with a shrug. "He heard about auditions from Mr. Park, the biology teacher, who is his older brother as you know. And requested to audition remotely."

"So he auditioned online?" I asked, slightly confused.

Was that kind of thing even allowed? Wasn't there something about seeing someone in person and feeling their energy that helped with that sort of thing?

I mean, she'd had me sing *All I Ask of You* with a few different guys yesterday to make sure the chemistry was there between me and a potential Raoul.

How would she know if this Asher guy and I would even work well together?

But not seeming to have any of the same concerns that I had, Miss Crawley patted my arm and said, "Asher is going to do amazing. I know you're new, and so you weren't here last year to watch him play Jean Valjean in our production of *Les Miserables*, but he is one of those rare talents that a teacher sees only once or twice in her career."

A rare talent? That was pretty big praise.

"So he's really good?" I asked.

"He'll be great," she said. "You have nothing to worry about."

I noticed, though, that despite Miss Crawley's high praise of this Asher guy, Nash seemed to be having an entirely different reaction to this news that Asher would be returning to the stage at Eden Falls Academy.

Miss Crawley stepped away to speak with a few other students who would be participating in the play. I looked at Nash, who was still glaring at Asher's name, and asked, "Is there something wrong with Asher that Miss Crawley isn't telling me?"

Nash pulled his gaze from the cast list and sighed. "He's —" He shook his head. "Let's just say that Asher and I have never really been friends."

So was it a competitive thing?

Nash glanced around at the students around us, and in a lower voice, he said, "I would just be careful working with him. Sure, he's *talented*." He said the word *talented* like it caused him physical pain to admit it. "But Asher doesn't exactly have a reputation for being a good guy."

BONUS EPILOGUE
CAMBRIELLE

FOUR YEARS LATER

"Someone smells good," Mack whispered in my ear after stepping up behind me in the kitchen. It was late February, and I was standing in the kitchen of our New York City condo, pouring a splash of creamer into my morning coffee. "Is that a new body wash?"

"New shampoo," I said, turning around in his arms to look at him. He was already dressed in his suit and tie—the uniform his basketball coach at Columbia University had him and his teammates wear for their game days. "So you like it?"

"I do." He nodded and sniffed my hair again. "In fact, I wouldn't be surprised if I start using it, too."

"You always do end up liking my shampoo more than yours." I laughed and carried my mug over to the little breakfast nook by the windows.

"What can I say?" He shrugged one of his broad shoulders before switching on the stove to cook his eggs. "You're my hero, and I want to be just like you." He shot me a wink.

"As much as I love being your hero, somehow I think it's better that you keep on being yourself." I winked back, knowing he was joking. "You stick with basketball, and I'll stick with dance."

"Okay, fine."

He grabbed the carton of eggs from the fridge and cracked six eggs in a bowl—yes, this six-foot-five fiancé of mine would have eaten us out of house and home a long time ago if his full-ride scholarship didn't help with expenses.

Okay, and yeah, if my parents hadn't been so awesome to let us live in their New York City condo for a fraction of what they could have charged, we would be in trouble.

But such was the life of a Juilliard student and a Columbia student, making their way in the big city.

When I'd quit ballet after my freshman year of high school, I thought for sure that I'd never fulfill my childhood dream of working for a dance company, or even having a shot at going to Juilliard.

But everything changed after I played Meg Giry in *The Phantom of the Opera*. A part of me that I'd let languish as I worked on my body image came back to life, and after that small success on the stage, I started lessons again so I could be ready to audition for the elite performing arts school.

I couldn't be happier with how things turned out. I didn't have a full-ride scholarship like Mack had for basketball at Columbia, but I had gotten in. I got to spend my days in the dance studio with professional ballet instructors who I looked up to, and I got to perform for audiences on a regular basis.

Once I was finished with my classes for the day, I got to come home to this little corner of the world I now called *home* and spend my free time with the guy I'd been in love with for half of my life.

I looked down at the diamond ring on my left hand, admiring the way it sparkled in the sunlight that was hitting it just right. It was so beautiful, and I couldn't help but smile at it every time I looked at it because of what it symbolized— a commitment to a lifelong bond with the man I loved more than anyone or anything else in the world.

Mack joined me at the table with his eggs and green smoothie.

"I did a good job, didn't I?" he asked, glancing at the ring he'd given me when he asked me this past fall to marry him.

"You totally did," I said. Then giving him a playful smirk, I added, "You did a very good job at following the advice your sisters gave you."

"Well..." He picked up his fork. "When the girl you want to marry is best friends with your sisters, it would be stupid not to ask them to go on an undercover mission to find out exactly what kind of ring she would want."

"Hey, I'm not complaining," I said, remembering the time when Ava and Elyse had not so sneakily started sending me photos of engagement rings and asking me which style I liked best. "If I'm going to be wearing this thing for the rest of my life, it makes sense that I should like it."

"That's exactly what I thought when I asked them to do it." He poked a chunk of eggs with his fork. "Because you know I'm never letting you take that thing off."

I laughed. "I wouldn't give it back to you even if you begged me to."

I finished my coffee and went into our bedroom to finish getting ready for school. And then, since I wouldn't have time to come home between my last class and Mack's game tonight, I packed an extra outfit for me to change into after school.

As the fiancée of Columbia's starting shooting guard, I always needed to look my best for when the cameras panned over for my reaction to the various plays he made. We'd become a bit of an interest in the media lately—Columbia's top NBA hopeful and the dancing heiress, as the entertainment news articles had described us. It had been strange at first to see photos of us walking hand in hand down the streets of Manhattan showing up in the news section of my social media feed. I'd been shocked anyone cared about our comings and goings enough to even take photos.

But it was fun having so many people rooting for our love story and asking us when the wedding would be—next summer in Eden Falls— or if I'd decided which famous designer would be designing my wedding dress—the fabulous Miriam Cohen, of course. Better known to Mack and me as Ava and Elyse's mom.

But even though all the extra attention could go to my head and confuse me into thinking that my life was supposed to follow the path of a fairytale, I knew better than to put stock into any of the press clippings.

Yes, the media couldn't get enough of Mack, his magnetic personality, and his unbelievable talent. But when it was just us at home and we were away from the various stages we played on, we were just two kids who had fallen in love behind my brothers' backs, who put in the work every day to keep our romance and friendship alive.

I zipped up my dance bag and wheeled it behind me as I walked back into the living area.

"Well, I'm headed off to school," I said to Mack who was wiping off the counter with a dish rag—yes, my fiancé knew how to keep a kitchen clean.

Thank you, Mama Aarden, for raising him right.

Mack rinsed off his hands and pulled me into his arms. Before I could leave, he said, "Have an amazing day at school, okay?"

"I will." I stood on my tiptoes to wrap my arms behind his neck. "You have a good day, too."

I kissed his neck and rested my face there for a moment, just breathing in the faint scent of his cologne.

He leaned back against the counter, pulling me with him, and nuzzled his face into my hair.

And even though most people would see this as an insignificant moment—just a regular goodbye before we headed off to our different schools and went about our day—it was everything to me.

Because it was the quiet moments that no one else saw that really showed what was important to us.

While we both had our own goals and dreams to chase, at the end of the day, we were a team. And no matter what came our way, I knew we would face it together.

Because that was what true love did.

Don't Miss Elyse's book.

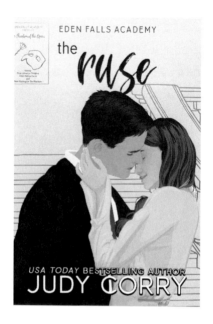

Grab it here: mybook.to/TheRuse

Dear Reader,

We made it!

Haha! I don't think I've ever put that at the end of a book before, but finishing this book was kind of difficult for me and I figured that with what Mack's story put us through, it might have been an emotional roller coaster for some readers too. Don't get me wrong. I loved writing this book. I love Mack and Cambrielle and their fun and sweet dynamic made me excited to hang out with them each day I was writing.

But there were some parts that I definitely procrastinated writing and at a couple points, even considered changing the outcome completely because I didn't want Mack's mom to die.

But this was the story I was supposed to tell, so I put on my big girl pants and wrote it.

Now why would I want to add such a sad storyline into a book about falling in love with your brothers' best friend? Probably because I'm a weirdo. But also, the story just kind of created itself as I was writing The Charade and getting to know Mack. And as I got to know him better I knew I had to write it.

My dad's mom actually died from the same kind of brain tumor that Mack's mom had. I never knew my grandma Florence, since she died at age forty-three when my dad was only five years old, but I've felt a pull to learn more about her and her life the past few years. So diving into this story gave me a reason and an opportunity to learn more about my grandma and from what I've been able to read, she sounded like a pretty awesome lady—even cracking jokes until the very end.

The dynamic between Cambrielle and her brothers was also really fun for me to write. I have three older brothers and while we were never in high school together since they were all several years older than me, I did end up hanging out with them and their friends my senior year of high school and freshman year of college.

They weren't as overprotective as Carter and Nash, they mostly just teased me about the boys I liked back then. But I did totally have crushes on their friends and roommates, so I can totally understand how Cambrielle felt about Mack for all those years. (There's just something about those brother's best friends, right??)

While I'd never go back to that time since I love my husband and kids and where I am right now, it was a super fun time in my life. And I love that I can kind of revisit it with my characters and their stories. I started dating my husband (the first time) when I was seventeen and I think it made me an eternal seventeen-year-old.

Anyway, thank you for taking a chance on Mack and Cambrielle's story. I really loved hanging out out with them during the past few months and I'm excited for them to pop up here and there in the upcoming books in the series.

If you want to stay in the know about my upcoming releases (Elyse's book *cough cough*) and other special behind-the-scenes news, sign up for my newsletter, join Judy Corry's Crew on Facebook or follow me on Instagram!

Also, if you enjoyed The Facade, please consider leaving a review and telling a friend!

Always grateful,

Judy

STAY CONNECTED

Join my Newsletter: https://subscribepage.com/judycorry

Join the Corry Crew on Facebook: https://www.facebook.com/groups/judycorrycrew/

Follow me on Instagram: @judycorry

Also By Judy Corry

Ridgewater High Series:

When We Began (Cassie and Liam)

Meet Me There (Ashlyn and Luke)

Don't Forget Me (Eliana and Jess)

It Was Always You (Lexi and Noah)

My Second Chance (Juliette and Easton)

My Mistletoe Mix-Up (Raven and Logan)

Forever Yours (Alyssa and Jace)

Protect My Heart (Emma and Arie)

Kissing The Boy Next Door (Lauren and Wes)

Eden Falls Academy Series:

The Charade (Ava and Carter)

The Facade (Cambrielle and Mack)

The Ruse — Coming 2022!

Rich and Famous Series:

Assisting My Brother's Best Friend (Kate and Drew)

Hollywood and Ivy (Ivy and Justin)

Her Football Star Ex (Emerson and Vincent)

Friend Zone to End Zone (Arianna and Cole)

Stolen Kisses from a Rock Star (Maya and Landon)

ABOUT THE AUTHOR

Judy Corry is the USA Today Bestselling Author of YA and Contemporary Romance. She writes romance because she can't get enough of the feeling of falling in love. She's known for writing heart-pounding kisses, endearing characters, and hard-won happily ever afters.

She lives in Southern Utah with the boy who took her to Prom, their four rambunctious children and a dog. She's addicted to love stories, dark chocolate and notebooks.

Made in United States
North Haven, CT
10 June 2022